Faerie Truths

...Tales to Disturb Us Awake

by Rose Guildenstern

Where the wave of moonlight glosses
The dim gray sands with light,
Far off by furthest Rosses
We foot it all the night,
Weaving olden dances
Mingling hands and mingling glances
Till the moon has taken flight;
To and fro we leap
And chase the frothy bubbles,
While the world is full of troubles
And anxious in its sleep.

Come away, O human child!
To the waters and the wild
With a faery, hand in hand,
For the world's more full of weeping than you
can understand.

—from **The Stolen Child**
by William Butler Yeats

Table of Contents

An Introduction
(with a heartfelt apology)

W e've lost ourselves, and you hold a book that just might be a key to finding our way back.

Does that sound absurd? Perhaps—but then again, truth often does. Consider this: humanity stands on a precipice, peering into a future shaped by its own hubris, foolishness, and collective forgetfulness. Our fate depends not on technology or politics or grand gestures of progress, but on something far older and simpler: the stories we choose to live.

A wise man once told me there are three paths to truth, depending on how you're managing your life: Holy Scriptures for when you're at your sturdiest, Shakespeare for when you're muddling through, and fairy tales for when you're down to your last thread and could really do with a magical potion or two.

After pondering this for decades, only now have I begun to grasp its merit. Holy Scriptures speak to the soul directly, yet most of us have grown deaf to them in our mind-FULL-ness, too clever by half to waste our valuable time on such drivel by "old, dead men." Shakespeare, that brilliant Bard, digs equally poetically into society and divinity alike, but who among us really reads him now except academics and actors? And then there are those fairy tales, echoing the ancient choruses of being, where rhythms of wonder and dread, notes of joy and sorrow, and the melodies of truth weave through all things, calling us to remember the Great Song that encompasses us all.

Yes, it just may be fairy tales that save us.

Fairy tales hold a peculiar power. They speak of fantastical princes and witches, talking wolves and even the occasional godchild, but beneath the surface, they speak of *us*—who we are, who we might become, and what it is we fear.

They are the oldest mirrors, and their reflections are not always kind. They do not flatter; they reveal.

Fairy tales were never meant to be safe. They were not written to pacify us, to shield us from the world's fatal edges. They were written to disturb us awake, to prepare us for the darkness that inevitably falls—and for the light that we must follow.

But somewhere along the way, we lost them. We forgot how to read them. We reduced them to pale reflections of their former selves, stripped of their fangs and claws, recast in the mold of modern-day sensibilities. In doing so, we made them comfortable, but we also altered them powerless. For in the end, it is not the wolves we should most fear, but the forgetting of them. For in forgetting, we lose not just the story, but ourselves and our ability to see the wolves for what they are.

You hold in your hands an answer to that forgetting. Not entertainment, really—an *intervention*.

This book is a collection of thirty mirrors, retold for a modern audience. Each tale has been reshaped, not to make it easier to swallow, but to make it impossible to ignore. Some are jagged, some humorous, and some so dark they'll curl around your spine and attack. Great liberties have been taken with each one, but I've sought to stay true to the spirit of the law as opposed to the letter of it. Each is told quite differently, quite deliberately, and was placed in this particular order to explore the broader Story—to pick at our flawed and echo-chambered social imaginary—like a novel written about our civilization. All are here to wake you up, shake the cobwebs from your mind, and remind you that the world is far stranger, darker, and more wondrous than you've been told (or allowed yourself) to believe.

Fairy tales have always been much more than they seem. Dismissed by some as childish entertainment, they are, in truth, profound and multifaceted, holding wisdom that deepens with age. In addition to the familiar fairy tale characters you know of old, you will also meet some prominent thinkers about fairy stories between

2

the covers of this book. Like J.R.R. Tolkien, a lord of fairy rings himself, who insisted, *"If fairy-story as a kind is worth reading at all it is worthy to be written for and read by adults. They will, of course, put more in and get more out than children can."* And indeed, as we grow older, these stories reveal layers we could not grasp in our youth—layers that challenge, provoke, and inspire us.

But fairy tales do not simply entertain; they prepare us. As G.K. Chesterton observed, *"Fairy tales, then, are not responsible for producing in children fear, or any of the shapes of fear... What fairy tales give the child is his first clear idea of the possible defeat of bogey. The baby has known the dragon intimately ever since he had an imagination. What the fairy tale provides for him is a St. George to kill the dragon."* These tales are not about fear; they are about courage. They remind us that monsters are real, but it is up to us to become the heroes to face them.

Even Albert Einstein, whose genius lay in unraveling the universe's secrets, understood the power of fairy tales: *"If you want your children to be intelligent, read them fairy tales. If you want them to be more intelligent, read them more fairy tales."* For fairy tales spark the imagination, the engine of human progress and creativity. They teach us to appraise, to wish, yet never stop refining our vision.

Faerie Truths includes retellings of many tales by Hans Christian Andersen, the master storyteller who said, *"Life itself is the most wonderful fairy tale."* This sentiment strikes at the core of their power: fairy tales don't just mirror life—they reveal the truths that lie at its very heart. They're a letter from our past about our present and ever-more-possible future.

Fairy tales eventually come back to (haunt?) all of us, as C.S. Lewis suggested, *"Someday you will be old enough to start reading fairy tales again."* In childhood, we read them for their adventures. In adulthood, we return to them for their truths.

Yet we live in an age that shuns the rawness of these tales, as Madeleine L'Engle lamented: *"Why we shudder at the violence in fairy tales rather than the violence of everyday life at the end of this century is beyond me."* Today, we sanitize the stories, smooth their edges, remake them in the image of our contemporary ideologies, and in doing so, strip them of their spirit. But as author Lois Lowry reminded us, even as the world changes, fairy tales endure: *"The whole world had changed. Only the fairy tales remained the same. And they lived happily ever after."*

The fairy tale isn't there to tuck you in and kiss you goodnight, however; it's there to yank off the blankets and point out the monsters lurking under the bed—and, crucially, to hand you the stick to deal with them. Because the dragon, you see, isn't the villain of the story; it's the test. It's the thing that makes you sharpen your sword, polish your armor, and realize you were the knight all along. It's the fire that burns away the dross and leaves you as you were always meant to be—if you're brave enough to face it.

Fairy tales have long warned us that the arrogance of our present-day narratives—our so-called science, gutted of any faith in the ineffable—will be our undoing if we persist down this track scrubbed clean of wonder. We still have a social imaginary, still shape our world through myths and stories, yet we stumble blindly as we pretend we see more than our ancestors, convinced that our beliefs are hard fact rather than fleeting constructs. The small cannot explain the All. But if we remember that the greatest truths have always worn the cloak of stories, then perhaps—just perhaps—there is still hope.

But what have we done with this hope? We've smothered it in pastel hues and stripped it of its teeth. We've forgotten that fairy tales were never just for children; they were meant to challenge us all, young and old, with the hard truths we'd rather not face. This book is not an escape from those truths. It is a confrontation. It is an invitation to step into the dark woods, face our greatest fears, and emerge on the other side with something new—something truer.

To face what we cannot bear to face any other way.

So, welcome to *Faerie Truths: Tales to Disturb Us Awake*. What's a *faerie truth* you ask? A *faerie truth* is the kind that looks like nonsense to the clever and folly to the powerful, yet, when all else crumbles, proves to be the only thing left standing. Take them, make them yours—but tread carefully. These are not bedtime tales meant to lull you into sleep. They are meant to rouse you, to unsettle you, to remind you of the many unnerving aspects of this world—and of the wonder that lies beyond the conquering of them.

It's high time for us to see beyond what we've decided is so.

Last of all, please accept my heartfelt apology in advance for all the times you want to throw this book across the room and curse its creator as you read. I did not know when I set out to write it just how entirely upsetting it would end up—for it turns out, I also needed to be provoked by its truths.

So step carefully, dear reader. *Faerie Truths* are not just paths through the forest—they uncover the forest in each of us. They are tangled, dark, and full of marvels. But if you listen closely, you might just hear the faint, distant howl of a wolf—or perhaps the steady beat of your own heart rediscovering the rhythm of the spheres.

If you've come this far, you've already taken the first step. Hold tight. The journey begins now, and the stakes could not be higher.

Let me tell you a story…

The Sleeper Must Awaken

Once upon a time, people did not sleep. Long before we divided ourselves into the neat little boxes of "us" and "them," there was a kingdom where humankind lived alongside the Fey. Humanity, so curious and yet so fragile, watched the Fey with both awe and unease, for the Fair Folk were terrible in their beauty and dangerous in their power. They lived outside the bounds of our understanding, their world a mirror warped and gleaming with truths too razor-edged for mortal minds.

The Fey saw us humans, too, and what they saw puzzled them. Homo sapiens, with our brief flicker of life, fretted over things the Fey found trivial. Birth, death, fear of the unknown—these were foreign concepts to creatures who never aged, who rarely died. And though the Fey were enchanted by the transience of our lives, they were also disturbed by it. We, in turn, found the very "otherness" of the Fey to be unsettling. For all their power and grace, the Fair Folk were creatures of illusion, of deception, and we have always feared most what we do not grasp—cannot possess.

But the truth is darker than that. We do not just fear the unknown—we destroy it. We shun it, push it away, box it up, and call it dangerous, evil, *other*. And so it was that we began to turn our backs on the Fey, pretending not to see them in the silhouettes of our forests, or in the glint of starlight reflected on the still surface of a pond. We turned away from their terrible beauty and pretended that our world was whole without them. But the Fey are not so easily forgotten. They have long memories, and they do not forgive.

It was on the day of a great celebration that the curse began. A child was born to a king and queen—a daughter so fair and full of promise that her parents believed she was blessed by the gods themselves. The kingdom rejoiced, and the queen, filled with joy, ordered a feast that would last for days. She sent invitations to every corner of the land, including even the Fey. There were thirteen of them, but the queen, in her mortal foolishness, invited only twelve.

The thirteenth Faerie, known only as the Dark Queen, came anyway.

The feast was splendid, with golden plates and fine foods. One by one, the Faeries offered their gifts—beauty, elegance, wisdom, kindness. But as the twelfth Faerie stepped forward, a bitter wind swept through the hall. The great doors flew open, and the thirteenth Faerie entered. The Dark Faerie Queen arrived not with a crash or thunderclap but with a slow, creeping silence that swallowed all sound. She appeared in the doorway like a shade pulling itself free from the walls, her form unfurling as if the night itself had taken shape. She was tall—taller than any mortal—and dreadfully slender, her limbs long and nimble, but there was something unsettling in the way she moved, like a marionette cut from invisible strings. Every step seemed both too slow and too fast, her body bending and shifting in ways that made the very air shiver around her.

Her skin, if you could call it that, was not the smooth pallor of other Faeries, but a disturbing, shifting darkness, as if her flesh was woven from the death of stars. There was no light in it, only void, and when she turned, you could swear you saw galaxies whirl for a heartbeat before being devoured by blackness.

Her gown was a thing of nightmares and wonders, crafted from shadows so deep they seemed to pull the light from the candles, guzzling it whole. The fabric draped her form like smoke, swirling and twisting with each breath she took. It clung to her as though afraid to let her go, and yet, it never quite seemed to touch her, as if her body rejected the world of the living even as it moved through it.

"You have forgotten me," she whispered, though her voice was like thunder in the hearts of those who heard it. "And for that, you will pay. Be prepared to forget so, so much more."

The king stood, quivering. "Please, forgive us, we did not mean—"

But the Dark Queen would not be placated. She turned to the infant princess, lying innocent in her cradle. "This child, so loved, so blessed—she will prick her finger on a spindle on her fifteenth birthday, and she will fall into a sleep from which she will never awaken. She will sleep the sleep of death, and through her, all of humanity shall suffer the same fate. From that day forward, you will all sleep, half of your lives lost to the deathlike embrace of night. In your sleep, you will dream, but your dreams will carry the weight of your fears, your divisions, your hatred of what you do not understand. You will wake each morning, unable to see clearly, forever bound by the curse of blindness and separation. You will never again truly see one another—not for what you are—except for what you fear."

And then, with a bitter smile, she departed, her cloak swirling behind her like a cyclone.

The hall was silent. The curse had been cast, and no one dared speak. But then the twelfth Faerie, the youngest and friendliest of the Fair Folk, stepped forward, like the first breath of dawn after the longest night.

Her form was softer, less defined than the barbed, extreme angles of the Dark Queen before her. She was not tall or imposing, but delicate, as though she had been spun from the finest threads of a dream. Her skin, pallid as moonlight filtered through a misty forest, glistened with a transparent, opalescent glow that made her seem not entirely there. The light in her hair was not harsh, but gentle, like the light you see behind closed eyelids when a dream begins to form. It was the light of hope, of things that have not yet come but are perchance within reach.

Her face was lovely, kind, and impossibly radiant—not with the characteristic cold beauty of the Fey, but with something far more genuine, something that continues. Her eyes, large and luminous, were not bound to any color but shifting from the deepest blue to the warmest gold, the way the sky changes at twilight. Her gaze held no judgment, no malice—only an endless patience, the kind that waits for love, for the world to catch up with its own better self.

Where the thirteenth Faerie brought horrifying midnight, the twelfth brought the promise of sunrise.

She leaned over the cradle and gently touched the princess's forehead. "I cannot undo the curse," she said, her voice lilting as a lullaby, "but I can temper it. The princess shall not die. Instead, she will sleep for a hundred years, undreaming, until a prince wakes her with a kiss. But beware—this sleep is not just for the princess. It is for all of you, even your animals. I promise that not all dreams shall be full of horrors, but even the best will escape you upon awakening—for a reflection of the curse has already implanted itself in your hearts."

Thus, the spindle became obsolete, or so the king and queen believed. For years, they worked tirelessly to protect their daughter from the unseen threads of fate, burning every spindle in the kingdom, locking away the memories of that cursed day. Yet, on the morning of her fifteenth birthday, something stirred within the castle—something old, something waiting.

The princess had grown into everything the Faeries had promised. Her beauty was a quiet, effortless thing, not just of face or form but of substance. She moved with the charm of someone who had never known fear, her laughter a song that echoed through the halls. People loved her for her kindness, the way she saw even the smallest, most forgotten souls. But today, there was a restlessness in her, a tug she couldn't explain, like an occasion she couldn't quite remember.

The castle was quiet. Too quiet. The birthday celebrations, full of music and laughter, had drifted into an afternoon lull, the guests retreating to their rooms for a time of rest. Left to her own devices, the princess wandered. Her footsteps were nimble, almost soundless, as she moved through the empty corridors, her curiosity pulling her forward. She had explored the castle many times, but today felt different, as if the air itself was guiding her.

She found herself at the base of an old, forgotten staircase. The stone steps spiraled upward into the gloom of a tower long abandoned. Dust clung to the banister, and cobwebs laced the ceiling. Something about it called to her, a whisper she couldn't quite hear. Without hesitation, she began to climb.

The staircase wound tighter and tighter, and with every step, the air grew thicker, heavier. The sunlight that filtered through the narrow windows seemed dim, like it had grown tired by the time it reached this part of the castle. Still, the princess climbed, her breath steady, though her heart had begun to race with a strange, growing thrill.

At the top of the stairs, an ancient, thick door waited, its iron handle icy beneath her touch. She paused for a moment, her hand lingering on the latch. There was no reason to open it—nothing awaited her on the other side. And yet, she felt compelled, as if something long forgotten had begun to wake, and only she could answer it.

The door creaked open, revealing a dimly lit room, its walls lined with old tapestries, faded and worn by time. In the center of the room, in a shaft of colorless light, sat an old woman, hunched over a spindle, her hands moving with slow, practiced precision. The measured whirring of the spindle filled the air, a rhythmic sound that tugged at something dormant within the princess, something buried under layers of memory.

The old woman didn't look up. "Come in, child," she said, her voice a scritch and scratching.

The princess's eyes were drawn to the spindle in the old woman's hands. She had never seen one before, but there was something about it—something familiar, as if it had been waiting for her all along.

"What are you doing?" the princess asked, her voice hushed, almost reverent.

"I am spinning," the old woman replied, her hands never pausing. "Would you like to try?"

The princess hesitated, but the spindle's pull was too strong, too familiar, as if it had been calling her from the moment she was born. She stepped forward and reached out, her fingers unsteady as they brushed against the smooth wood. The old woman's eyes, hidden beneath her hood, glinted with something dark, something knowing.

And in that instant, the world seemed to gulp, as if the air itself had frozen in mid-inhale. The spindle spun faster, a flicker of light and shadow, and then—pain. A sharp, sudden prick at the tip of her finger.

The princess gasped, pulling her hand back, but it was too late. Her vision blurred, her legs gave way beneath her, and she collapsed onto the indifferent stone floor. The spindle fell from the old woman's hands, clattering to the ground, but the woman made no move to catch it. She simply smiled, a slow, curling smile that never reached her eyes.

Around the princess, the room grew darker, the air viscid. Her eyelids fluttered as if she were fighting to stay alert, but the pull of unconsciousness was too strong. A bottomless, dreamless oblivion, a sleep from which there would be no waking—at least, not for a hundred years. Her breathing slowed, her body stilled, and she lay there, as if carved from marble, her face peaceful in the embrace of the curse.

And as she slept, so did the kingdom.

The king and queen, seated in the grand hall, slumped in their thrones, their eyes closing as if by an invisible hand. The courtiers, the servants, the cooks in the kitchens, the stable boys about their chores—one by one, they all sank into sleep. Horses in their stalls stopped mid-chew, dogs curled up in the courtyard, their eyes growing heavy. Even the birds on the rooftops ceased their song, their heads drooping under their wings.

A silence unlike any other settled over the castle, a silence that stretched across every corner, every room, and every heart. The kingdom slumbered, caught in the same dreamless sleep as the princess, unaware of the burgeoning truth that lay beneath their closed eyes—the truth that the curse had been not just on the girl, but on all of them. The true curse was not in the sleeping itself, but in the rot they had all sown that nourished it—divisions of their own making, fears they had nurtured in silence. The Faerie's magic didn't create these cracks; it only amplified what already festered within humanity's heart of darkness, spinning their buried suspicions and divisions into something they could no longer ignore.

Outside, the sky darkened, and as the first thorny vines began to grow around the castle walls, the world beyond continued on, unaware that within those walls, time had ceased to matter. Unconscious that the real curse had only just begun, not just for the sleeping castle—but for all of us, everywhere.

Time passed, an enormous hedge grew around the castle, and the world outside changed. The Fey withdrew from human sight, and without their guiding presence, humanity began to fragment. The judgment of the Fey, unseen, worked its magic. Humans, left to their own devices, allowed their inner fears to manifest outward realities. The "otherness" that had once been reserved for the Fey, they now applied to their fellow men. People split into tribes, into nations, into in-groups and out-groups. They feared those with different beliefs, different customs, and different faces. The curse had woven itself into the very fabric of human life, for in their dreams, the Fey still visited them, whispering phantoms of terrible strangeness that lingered into waking hours.

For this reason, humanity, divided and weakened by fright, turned inward. They formed alliances, built edges, and waged wars, never comprehending that the true enemy was not the other, but the fear born from their own sins. They forgot the Fey, and they forgot the curse, but they shored up the thorny hedges around their souls ever higher, separating themselves from the world as it truly was.

A hundred years passed, and one day, a prince from a distant land heard the tale of the sleeping kingdom. Unlike the others who had come before, he was not driven by glory or conquest, but by curiosity. He had always been different, an adventurer who brought his dreams with him back into his waking life. When he approached the hedge, the thorns miraculously parted for him, and he entered the castle where time had stood still.

There, in the highest tower, he found the princess, her face stuck in undying in-between. He kissed her, not out of love—not yet, anyway—but out of a longing, a wish, for a true connection he'd never known.

The moment their lips touched, the spell was broken. The princess awoke, as did the kingdom… but something essential had been lost.

She and the prince eventually married, of course, as is the fairy tale way of things, but theirs was not a story of true love—not really.

For though the curse was broken, its reverberation is with us still. Even now, we sleep our nights away, and during our days, we wander through waking dreaming, haunted by the fears we once laid at the feet of the Fey. We form our groups, our clans, clinging to one another as if safety could be found in sameness, while all the while, we divide ourselves further, pushing away those who seem too different, too *other*.

The true curse, the one we've never quite shaken, is what we fail to *see*—fail to see that what we reject in others is what we fear most in ourselves. The magic of the Faerie Queen only magnified the evil we had already nurtured. Now we all close our eyes not just in sleep, but in life, blinded by the walls we build between us, content to slumber in ignorance until the final sleep, the one from which none shall awaken.

Therefore, the kingdom was restored, but the world still waits. We sleep, much of our lives spent in either reverie or fantasizing—many of us utterly lost in our dreamworlds—and though the gift of hope remains, the curse of fear still lingers. It is only when we truly see one another, not as "other," but as part of ourselves, that the curse will lift and we shall, at last, wake up from our long, dark night.

And thus, my children, we have come to the end of this story— though we are all still waiting to awake.

If the Shoe Doesn't Fit

Once upon a time, there was a Kingdom caught between. The Kingdom breathed, old and new, a land wedged in the perplexing trap of twilight, its towers and turrets holding up a sky that never quite knew if it was dawn or dusk. Time hung there, suspended in the glow of an eternal "almost," and the people moved through their days like leaves drifting in a wind that had long forgotten where it came from. The King and Queen, stiff-backed and regal, were remnants from another era—flesh-and-blood reminders of a world built on rules as thick and immutable as the walls of their castle. They believed in power, in the crack of command, in the way men were meant to lead and women were meant to follow.

Their subjects, however, considered the royal family anachronistic figureheads at best.

Yet even the King and Queen had to acknowledge the strange, intoxicating resonance of this new world—a world where women had won the right to speak their minds, to vote, to govern themselves. Still, the throne room felt thick, as if the aristocratic past itself pressed down on every word spoken, every movement made. It was a world that had shifted just enough to be uncomfortable but not enough to fall apart.

And then, there was the Prince.

He moved through his days like a man trapped between stories, his life written in ink too dark and permanent for his liking. He was handsome, yes—too handsome, perhaps. The handsome that made the women of the kingdom catch their breath as he passed, made their hearts pound with a desire they couldn't quite understand. It was as though something primal still lurked beneath their ribs, something their modern minds told them they should have outgrown. They had been raised to want softness in men, a kind of quiet, beta reliability that they could command and guide. But there he was—an alpha, whether he liked it or not—pulling them toward him with the gravity of a planet, a star, a force of nature.

The Prince, poor soul, wanted none of it. Raised to be a man of strength, of duty, of leadership, he had been taught to be everything the kingdom expected of him. And yet, beneath that princely façade, a subtler voice spoke. He wanted to find himself, to carve his own path, to be a man by his own definition, not the kingdom's. But it was hard to break the chains of a legacy codified in tradition.

In a house not far from the castle, Cinderella toiled.

She had once known happiness—simple, unadorned happiness. Her mother, a woman of nobility and easy laughter, had taught her that there was beauty in the small things: in stitching clothes and shoes, in the scent of bread baking, in the warmth of a fire on a cold night. Her father, strong in his quiet way, had loved her mother fiercely. But when her mother died, the light went out of him. He remarried, as lonely men do, leaving Cinderella in a world where no hand reached for hers, no embrace shielded her from the chill, and human touch became a childhood memory.

Her stepmother swept in like a freezing wind, bringing with her the brittle edges of a new matriarchy. She was a woman of severe ideas and even severer words, a believer in a feminism that saw men as mere obstacles to women's greatness. She dominated her new husband until there was nothing left of the man Cinderella had known. And then, with the same precision, she turned her eye toward Cinderella.

The stepmother brought her daughters, too. The elder was social justice in human form, always dressed in blunt lines and tailored suits, eyes flashing with righteous fury. She was a lawyer, a fighter, a woman who could not rest while there was still inequality to battle. She saw Cinderella and sneered, despising the way Cinderella embodied a gentleness she had long rejected in herself. She could not understand why anyone would want to be beautiful, to be gentle, to need romance.

The younger stepsister, well, she was something else entirely. She wore her rebellion like a coat of many colors—blue hair, tight clothes, and a voice that rang out across the kingdom's social media platforms like a hammer on an anvil. She called herself a feminist of the new wave, tearing down not just the patriarchy but the shortcomings of prior feminists as well. She courted controversy like an old lover, gathering followers by the thousands. And yet, for all her progress, she seethed with hatred toward Cinderella. Cinderella, who still dreamed of commitment, of marriage, of children. Of a quiet home filled with cheer. To the younger stepsister, these dreams were nothing more than the muted remains of a past that had no place in the future she was building.

And so, Cinderella worked. She scrubbed the floors, mended the clothes, and minded the fire. Her stepmother and stepsisters forced her into these tasks, chores they themselves deemed beneath them, and they despised her all the more for doing them well. Every day, they told her she was wrong—wrong for being modest, wrong for wanting the things she wanted, wrong for believing in love.

It was enough to drive a person mad.

When the invitation to the royal Ball arrived, Cinderella felt a glimmer of hope, a fluttering spark of intense yearning the moment it was born. But the stepmother snuffed it out entirely with a word, with a snigger. "You? Go to the Ball? You don't deserve it."

And Cinderella believed her. They swept off to the Ball, their cruel laughter trailing behind like a final insult—the only thing that hadn't deserted her. She sat alone by the hearth, a threadbare blanket clutched tight—what remained of the fire offering little against the cold world that pressed in upon her. And then, just a glint, a blank space appeared in the depths of the fire. Not the bright, playful spark of magic she'd fancied in her childhood, but something deeper, something other.

A figure loomed from the blankness, emerging not with the glitter of enchantment but with the gloom of a graveyard wind. The specter's face—vacant sockets where eyes should have been— seemed filled with eerie melancholy. Draped in an ethereal gown that billowed like mist on a winter's eve and bound in phantasmic chains wrought of shattered quills, charred pages, and broken wedding rings, she fixed Cinderella with a gaze both harrowing and haunting.

"Rise, girl, and make your own way, for no magic shall do it for you," she stated, voice creaking like an iron gate, heavy with things too-long left unsaid. *"I am your godmother, as God and your mother sent me—though far more fey than fairy—for a godmother is a lantern in the dark, a whisper at the crossroads, a steady hand when the world tilts sideways. And who better than I to teach you how to rise before the clock strikes twelve?"*

Cinderella stared up at her, confusion clouding her thoughts. "Who... who are you?"

*"My dear child, do not fear, for I mean you no harm. I am Mary Shelley, remembered as the author of **Frankenstein; or, The Modern Prometheus.** Once wife to the poet Percy Bysshe Shelley, returned to bring you solace and truth, for I see the burdens you bear beneath this roof. Your stepmother and stepsisters—how they drape themselves in the guise of righteousness! Yet their hearts are ruled not by justice, but by vanity, envy, and power. I know this, for I too have known such shadows myself before, cast by those who*

mistake their desires for virtue and their ambition for excellence. I carry these same sins from my own life as well."

Cinderella sat still, her fingers twisting the edge of her blanket. The godmother's voice stirred something in her, like a half-forgotten dream, a voice she might have heard long ago, when her mother told her ghost stories at bedtime.

"In life, I wrote the story of a man who, in his arrogance, sought to play God. He stitched together an abomination, blind to the truth that his creation was not a triumph, but a reflection of his short-sightedness and arrogance. He saw only his own ingenuity, never his flaws—his selfishness, his refusal to take responsibility for the monster his convictions had wrought. And in the end, his creation turned upon him, as all lies eventually do. I see in your stepmother and stepsisters the same fatal flaw that haunted my own life, child. They speak of justice, but their cause is a mask for their own hunger. They do not seek balance, only more for themselves—their crusade fueled not by principle, but by the desperate need for validation and vengeance."

Hands motionless and resting lightly in her lap, Cinderella swallowed, a faint knot tightening her throat. These words were heavier than the buckets she carried to and from the well, heavier than the silence she kept when her stepsisters, again, chastised her for being herself.

"Beware, my dear, of those who claim to champion justice yet raise themselves up by treading upon others. True equality does not exalt one at the expense of another—it lifts all. They speak of empowerment, yet their words are tacked together from the tattered remnants of old resentments, sutured into a grotesque patchwork, much like Frankenstein's monster. What once lived, they have torn apart and reassembled into something unnatural, a thing of bitterness rather than renewal. They have draped their narcissism in noble language, but you see, as I do, the falsehood beneath."

Cinderella lowered her head, her hair falling softly around her face. This was the first time someone else had seen it, had *named* it for what it was. "I thought I was imagining it," she whispered, her voice small but steady. "That it was my fault."

"Your suffering is real, and their excuses do not absolve them. They tell themselves these lies to justify their behavior: that they deserve to take more because they have been wronged, that their wants are more important than your needs, that silencing you is somehow a path to justice. But child, lies do not remain small. They grow, twisting into something larger, uglier, more destructive—until they consume innocent and liar alike."

"They always have a reason," Cinderella muttered. "Always an excuse about why it's right for them to demand more, justified by the evils of those who came before. But it doesn't seem just. Neither extreme feels decent." She looked down at her hands, roughened by work, and wondered how something so apparent, so true, could feel so hard to believe.

"Take heart. You are not wrong to see through their pretense, to question their words and deeds. The world does not need another fallen angel, cobbled together from unchecked desire and revenge. What it needs are those who seek truth and act with kindness—even when met with vehemence."

Her ghostly godmother's voice lingered in the air, wisping through Cinderella—chilling, yet oddly comforting. She had carried these truths since childhood, though in recent years, they had begun to feel insubstantial.

"Do not let their resentment poison you, my dear. You must rise above it. Your strength lies in the very humility they scorn, the grace they have forgotten. You are not powerless, for your ability to see clearly is an ability they've lost. Use it. Be a creator who walks the path of life, not one who tears it asunder. Creation does not mean discarding the past and stitching together a grotesque imitation from lifeless cravings. True creation is a continuation—it honors what came before and builds upon it, shaping something new. Choose a path not of retribution, but of compassion, courage—and most of all, love."

The knot in Cinderella's chest began to loosen, her breath flowing more easily. "A creator," she murmured, a flare of resolve kindling in her chest. "I can be that."

"Those who dress up selfishness as virtue are staggering blind and unknowing toward ruin. Do not let their lies dim your light. Hold fast to the truth, and I shall help you find your way. The world has too many monsters already."

Cinderella's breath caught in her throat. "What truth?"

"The truth that no matter what age we live in, no matter what the world tells us to be, we are all bound by something far greater," Mary said, her eyes meeting Cinderella's with a steady gaze. *"Mainstream feminism, like so many movements before it, began with noble intentions. It sought to free women from the chains of oppression, to give them the right to live fully. But in its radical forms, it has lost sight of the very truth it was meant to protect. It has become a force that alienates men and women from the natural order of things, turning love into competition, and leadership into a weapon."*

Cinderella's tears welled up, spilling over her cheeks. She had felt that loss—felt it in the way her stepmother had spoken of men, of love, of marriage as things to be controlled or defeated. She had seen it in her stepsisters, in the way they wielded their ideas like clubs, shattering any sense of companionship or romance. But she hadn't known what to call it.

"Modern romance is broken," Mary continued, her voice like rustling pages. *"Men are lost, women are weary, and the dance of courtship—of true connection—has all but faded. In its place, a battlefield of blame and bitterness, where both are told they must fight for what is 'rightfully' theirs. But the deep truth is this: we were never meant to be at war. We were meant to build—together— something stronger than either could create alone."*

Cinderella looked up at her, her tears falling freely now. "But... they tell me I'm wrong. For wanting love. For wanting to create a home. For wanting something that's... true."

Mary knelt beside Cinderella and took her hand. *"That's because they've forgotten the truth that holds us all. There is no shame in wanting love, in wanting to build a family, to create something lasting in this world. The delusion of the current age lies in its refusal to acknowledge that we are, at our core, beings made* for connection—beings who need not just independence, but the foundation of interdependence."

She looked down at Cinderella's feet, bare and cold. *"That's why your shoes—your own foundation—matter."*

With a slow wave of her godmother's hand, Cinderella's ragged dress transformed. It didn't turn into something grand or glimmering, but into a simple gown of sturdy fabric, warm and beautiful and oddly honest. And on her feet, the shoes—her handmade shoes—appeared, delicate yet sturdy, crafted by Cinderella's own hands.

"These shoes," Mary said, touching the edge of one with reverence, *"are more than just something you made. They are a symbol of your connection to the world, to the work of your hands, to the truth that runs through and beneath all of us. In a world that tries to hand you modern answers for manufactured lives, you have created something real, something that reflects the deeper order of things. These shoes remind you that the path you walk is not dictated by fleeting ideologies or unmoored promises, but by the enduring truth of who you are in relation to the world around you."*

Cinderella's gaze locked on the shoes, her breath hitching in her chest. She had sewn them together in her quiet solitary hours, not because she had to, but because something within her had called her to create, to shape, to leave her mark. And now, they felt like more than just shoes—they felt like solid reminders of her essence, keeping her path straight as she ventured forth into this too-often crooked world.

"Society will tell you that you need to reinvent yourself, to be everything at once," Mary said, rising to her feet. *"But you are not here to live by their standards. You are here to find the truth that connects all of us—the truth that love and family are not weaknesses, but strengths. The truth that men and women are meant to build something greater than themselves together, not apart."*

Cinderella nodded, her heart swelling with a sense of clarity she hadn't felt in years. "But what do I do now?"

Mary smiled, the firelight reflecting in her ghostly eyes. *"Go to the Ball. Not to prove anything to them, but to be the truth they've forgotten. You wear these shoes—shoes made with care, with purpose—and let them see that you are not playing their game. You are walking in step with the innate rhythms of life, with the truths that have always been and always will be."*

And so, Cinderella stepped into the night, her shoes clicking delicately on the cobblestones, a reminder that she was not bound by the expectations of a fractured world. And with each step, she knew she was walking toward something actual. Something worth the risk. Something true.

And at the Ball, the Prince truly saw her. When they danced, it was not the grand, sweeping romance of storybooks. It was something calmer, something authentic. They spoke, not of fairy tales, but of the world they lived in—the confusion, the expectations, the way men and women had lost their way in the tangle of modernity. They spoke of what it meant to be human, to love, to want, to need. In each other, they found not the perfection of society's expectations, but something better than perfect—something real. They danced together, two souls mated against the lost Kingdom that had forgotten what it meant to be human.

When midnight came, Cinderella did not leave her phone number. She left behind her shoe—that dainty, feminine thing she had created with her own two hands. And in doing so, she told the Prince that if he wanted her, he would have to pursue her. Not by the rules of a broken society, but by the truth of who they were and might be together.

Thus, in the spirit of play, the next day the Prince commenced with seeking his future bride.

As the royal entourage announced the royal intentions throughout the Kingdom, the Stepmother's heart had leapt, not with joy, but with an itch. She saw it now—the path to everything and then some.

For years, she had worn her independence like a crown, onerous but necessary. She'd spoken of women's power, of strength, of a world where men were nothing but obstacles to be overcome. She had railed against the weakness of men, the oppression of women. But when the invitation came, with its promises of a Prince and a life wrapped in gold, those carefully constructed contentions disintegrated like ash puffed away on the wind.

Her daughters, too, felt the swing. The elder, with her angular features and searing ideals, who had fought her way through life like a soldier in a war against the system, stood in the doorway, her hands clenched, her eyes narrowing with delight as she imagined herself ruling at the Prince's side. She had told herself—and anyone who would listen—that men were accessory, that women were strong enough to carve their own way. But here, now, in this moment, she couldn't ignore the tingle of lust. She wanted the Prince, not for love, not even for the man he was, but for the authority, the command he represented. To be his wife would be more vital than any courtroom victory could ever make her. She could rewrite the rules of the game with him as her pawn.

The younger stepsister was no less conflicted. She, with her vivid, wild hair and rouged lips, who had spent her days screaming words into the infinite noise of social media about how men were predators and the patriarchy was the enemy, now found herself gazing at the invitation with the same appetite. She had built her empire on insurgence, on telling the world she needed no man, that no woman should ever rely on one. But here was a chance, a tantalizing chance, to be the wife of the Prince. To be more than an influencer with followers. She could be royalty, the very thing she had built her revolt upon destroying.

They glared at Cinderella, sitting demurely in her own little corner, quietly reading a book, and they saw the threat she posed. She had no platform, no audience. She didn't shout or argue or try to bend the world to her will. And yet, she had captured something they could not. She had the Prince's attention, and they hated her all the more for it.

"Lock her away," the Stepmother said, her voice low and tight with dread masquerading as dominance. "She will not ruin this for us."

Her daughters hesitated, but not for long. They had spent years despising Cinderella for her softness, for her femininity, and now that she stood in their way, they saw no reason to show mercy. They dragged her up the stairs, each step setting off a chorus of creaks, like the house itself wincing at their wickedness. The lock clicked shut, the sound final, like the closing of a coffin.

"Stay there," the Stepmother screamed through the keyhole, her breath hot and nasty. "You don't deserve him. You don't deserve any of it."

And behind that lock, hidden in the ambiguities of their own making, was the vicious truth the Stepmother and her daughters could not face. For all their speeches, for all their shouting about independence and strength, they didn't want the men they had tried to create. They didn't want the reliant, compliant, obedient versions of masculinity they had championed. They wanted the Prince. They wanted a man strong enough to stand tall, to protect, to lead—the man they claimed to scorn but secretly longed to possess.

The elder stepsister, with her sharp words and sharper suits, had never truly desired equality. She wanted power, and power, in her mind, still lay in the hands of men like the Prince. She didn't want a man who would ask her permission or follow her lead. She wanted a man who could carry her higher than she could climb on her own.

And the younger stepsister, for all her talk of dismantling the evils of colonialism, sought its fall only to crown herself upon its ashes, replacing it with a dominion shaped by her own ideas, naturally. She fantasized about ruling at its apex, a Queen enthroned on followers and fame. More than anything, she craved the Prince's desire—the one man whose favor could make her feel as though the entire world admired her.

The sisters didn't crave the hollow men their radicalism had molded. They didn't want the stuffed men who had bent themselves to fit the checklist they'd forged in speeches and manifestos. No, they wanted the Prince—the real Prince, with all his strength and quiet confidence, with his unfashionable masculinity that called to them in ways they wouldn't admit.

So, they locked Cinderella away, pretending she didn't exist. They locked away everything they mocked and secretly envied. They shoved the troublesome truth into the dark attic and turned their faces toward the dazzling delusion.

But deep down, they knew. They knew the Prince wouldn't want them. He wouldn't look past their serrated assertions, wouldn't hear the ache hidden beneath their words, no matter how carefully they tried to shape them into something worth believing. They could twist and turn them all they liked, but he wouldn't be fooled. They had built a world that scorned the very kind of man they now desperately sought, and in the end, they might be left with nothing but the bitter taste of their own hypocrisy.

In the attic, behind that locked door, Cinderella waited, not in despair, but in quiet knowing. She hadn't fought for the Prince's heart, hadn't tried to bend him to her will. She had simply been herself, and in that, she had found something they would never fathom.

The house seemed to shrink around its occupants, every movement deliberate, every sound unnaturally distinct, as the Prince's entourage approached. The Stepmother stood at the door, her smile too wide, her hands clasped too tightly. Her daughters, the elder in her snappy suit and the younger in her plastered-on complexion, hovered at her side.

The Prince stepped into the room, tall and silent. He motioned for the footman to step forward with the slipper—the single beautiful, simple shoe, a complete reflection of something honest in a world that had forgotten how to be.

The elder stepsister marched forward first, her hands smoothing her rigid skirt. Her lips, always so ready with arguments about equality and fairness, were now drawn into a thin, nervous line. She extended her foot as if she were presenting evidence in court, certain that logic and persistence would prevail. The footman knelt, the shoe in hand, and firmly slid it onto her foot.

But it wouldn't go. Not by an inch, not by the tiniest fraction. It wasn't just too small—it was as though the very nature of the shoe resisted her. The elder stepsister's jaw tensed. Without hesitation, she grabbed a nearby kitchen knife and, with a strong-minded grimace, sliced off her toe. Blood seeped into the silk lining as she shoved her foot back into the shoe, lips pulled taut in agony.

"Try again!" she barked, her voice harsher than she intended, a note of panic creeping in. But no amount of effort, no amount of will, worked. The footman looked like he might be sick as a dark trail followed her stumbling steps away from her failure.

The younger stepsister was next, her brightly dyed hair and brighter red lips practically pulsating with the need to be noticed. She smirked, tossing her tresses back as though the world were watching her, waiting for her to take centerstage. She thrust her foot out, her tight skirt hiking up as she did, her confidence unwavering.

"Let's get this over with," she said, her voice dripping with swagger.

The footman hesitated for only a moment before he knelt and tried the shoe. But again, it would not fit. The younger stepsister bit her lip, a flash of annoyance marring her features. With a shrill intake of breath, she yanked up her hem, revealing a concealed stiletto, and sawed off her heel, her eyes gleaming with frantic resolution.

Blood spilled freely, but still, the shoe would not go. The more she twisted, the more the truth became undeniable—this shoe would never fit her. Her face flushed with more than embarrassment. This was supposed to be her moment, the one where she surpassed the masses, rose above her critics, and claimed a crown.

The stepsisters shared a glance, unspoken panic passing between them as their bloody footprints smeared the floor. This was not how the narrative was supposed to go.

The Stepmother, watching from the sidelines, felt her stomach turn. She had convinced herself that surely *one* of her daughters would fit the shoe. After all, they had done everything they needed to secure their place—talked the talk, walked the walk, changed the rules of the game. But now, with the Prince standing there, watching their fiasco blossom into a full-blown catastrophe, she felt the truth sidle up and make itself at home, uninvited and thoroughly unpleasant.

The shoe wouldn't fit because the shoe wasn't meant for them.

"Enough of this!" the Stepmother spat, her voice brickle with barely-contained rage. "You must have brought the wrong shoe. There's been a mistake."

The Prince stood at the edge of the room, his head tilting in a way that suggested he'd just heard a particularly bad idea presented with excessive enthusiasm. His eyes, having long since grown weary of the stepsisters' theatrics, wandered instead to the room itself. It was neat. Tidy. Loved. Far too loved, in fact, for the likes of these three, who seemed more suited to a life of turning milk sour with a glance. And then there it was—a faint creak from above, just the sort of sound a house makes when it knows it's hiding something precious.

"There's no mistake," he said, his voice soft but resolute.

And with those words, something broke in the air. The Stepmother's composure, already hanging by a thread, snapped. She could feel the tide turning, slipping out of her control, and in that moment, all the duplicity she'd been hiding beneath her speeches, her creeds, her claims of independence came crashing down.

"There is no one else," she lied, her voice rising in desperation. "These are my only daughters, the finest women in the kingdom. If the shoe doesn't fit them, then it fits no one."

The Prince, ignoring her outburst, turned to the footman. "Is there anyone else in this home?"

The footman, still kneeling with the shoe in hand, looked to the Stepmother, but it was clear the truth could no longer be denied. He hesitated only a moment before nodding toward the ceiling. "There's... someone else."

The Stepmother's face drained of color. "No," she insisted, stepping forward, her voice low and venomous. "There is no one. You must be mistaken."

But the Prince's eyes had already moved past her, his hand gesturing for the footman to ascend the creaky staircase.

The house was silent as Cinderella, at last, stepped into the room. The Prince stood by the fire, calm and sure, the burden of the search lifting from his shoulders. He knew what he was looking for—not perfection, not ambition, but something real. This woman who was content to be a woman, just as he was learning to be his own man.

Cinderella moved toward him, her steps light, her heart sure. The footman knelt before her, holding the shoe—the one she had made, tender and true, shaped by her own hands. No magic, no glitz, no stabbing necessary. Just something that fit.

The Prince watched as the slipper slid onto her foot—not with a burst of triumph or the cosmic drumroll bards like to exaggerate, but with the inevitability of something finally settling into its rightful place. It fit because it was hers, not some fragile illusion cobbled together from pretense and wishful thinking, but a thing forged from the stubborn, undeniable truth of who she was. He looked up, their eyes meeting, and for one breathless moment, the room wasn't filled with gasps or applause—just the profound, unspoken synchronicity of recognition.

No words were needed. The truth was in the fit.

They married, not in a grand spectacle, but in an intimate ceremony that celebrated who they truly were: two souls, free from the chains of expectation, finding love in the cinders of a world that had forgotten how to be real.

And they lived, not happily ever after, but truthfully.

For remember, children, that every "the end" is also a beginning.

The Goldilocks Principle

Once upon a time, in a forest that was part storybook pages and filled with trees that gossiped amongst themselves, a girl named Goldilocks wandered off the beaten path, fancying herself on a quest. She had that look in her eye—the look of someone who had read too many books and wasn't entirely sure where the stories stopped and the world began.

Hers was no ordinary quest, mind you. She wasn't after something simple, like gold or glory or a dragon's egg. No, Goldilocks was after the one thing most people avoid their whole lives if they can figure a way out of it. She was after truth. She didn't know exactly what truth looked like, or how it would feel when she found it, but she knew, with a certainty that came from somewhere beyond her years, that she had to find it. Nothing else would do.

Now, the thing about truth is that it's rarely what people think it is. You don't just trip over it in a forest clearing and go, "Oh, splendid! Here it is." Truth is a slippery, argumentative thing, prone to disguise itself as whatever you weren't looking for, and liable to dart off just when you thought you'd caught it.

The trouble was, she'd noticed that people had two ways of talking about truth. Some people clung to one idea as if their very lives depended on it, insisting on a single truth and squashing any doubts that tried to creep in. Others insisted that everything was true, that all ideas were equally valid, and you could pretty much make up whatever you liked. And to Goldilocks, both approaches seemed… well, disastrous. One-truth thinking was a wall, rigid and suffocating, and all-truths thinking was a fog, sprawling and akin to following other lemmings off a cliff. In her gut, she knew there had to be something better.

So, naturally, she found herself at a strange little house deep in the woods—a house with a crooked roof, a somewhat disapproving door, and windows that made you wonder if they'd been peeking at you before you arrived. As she eyed the ivy that coiled around its timbers like serpents, she paused, for a small, gilded sign on the door read: *The Goldilocks Principle of Truth.*

Now, any reasonable person would have left this peculiar place well alone, but Goldilocks was not reasonable. She was curious. She *needed* the truth—solid, real, and vital as breath—and, well, her *name* was on the door.

Inside, there were three bowls of porridge, three beds, and three plaques, each rather opinionated in its own way. For this wasn't just any house. This was the House of Bears, and these were no ordinary bears. No, these were philosophical bears, each with a very particular view of the truth.

The first plaque, inscribed in stern, no-nonsense lettering, read: **"Papa Bear: There is One Truth."**

Papa Bear's side of the room was a shrine to Authority. The air felt thick, weighed down by the gravity of ideas that allowed no argument, no negotiation. The shelves groaned under the weight of enormous leather-bound tomes with titles like **The Eternal Truth** and **The Final Word,** books that didn't just sit on the shelves but loomed, giving you the feeling they might fall on you if you so much as doubted their contents. Goldilocks squinted at one particularly large volume labeled **Truth: Absolute and Irrefutable**, authored by luminaries like Pythagoras, Plato, and Descartes. She peered inside and saw charts of ideal forms, maps of heavens, diagrams of eternal harmonies. It was all deeply, overwhelmingly certain.

Amongst these volumes sat a massive bowl of porridge and, ignoring the warning in her head, she scooped a spoonful. Immediately, she recoiled. The porridge was cold—icy, in fact, and hard as marble. It tasted of Judgment, with a flavor so severe, it made her jaw ache.

"Good heavens," she mused, "this truth could break teeth." Pushing the bowl away, she muttered, "This truth is too much. Too clotted, too stiff. It's a kind of truth that closes every door."

She moved along to the next corner, where she found a plaque that read, "**Mother Bear: Truth is Whatever You Think it Is.**"

Mama Bear's side of the room was soft, glowing with warm light and draped with quilts, each one embroidered with landscapes and stars and the kinds of dreams that stay with you only as a feeling, never a shape. This side of the room was full of wavering candles, and a scattering of masks and ornate mirrors; Goldilocks felt as if each reflection in the mirrors around her was just another version of reality, and each one could be true. It seemed endless, covered in books with comforting titles like **Your Truth, My Truth** and **Infinite Likelihoods**—she could get lost here, dissolving into one of those reflections forever.

Mother Bear's porridge sat nearby, looking enticingly iridescent, like it couldn't decide whether it wanted to be eaten or simply admired. Goldilocks took a spoonful, and it tasted like… well, it tasted like possibilities, which is a nice way of saying it didn't taste like much. It was warm and comforting at first, but by the time she swallowed, it had slipped away entirely, leaving only a vague sensation that she might not have eaten anything after all.

She grimaced, recognizing the lingering taste of Heraclitus, Nietzsche, Derrida, and Foucault. Their whispers flitted through her mind: "Truth is a construct. Everything is relative. All meanings are masks…"

Goldilocks blinked. She tried another spoonful, but it was the same—soft, slippery, elusive as clouds.

"Too little here," she whispered, setting down the bowl with a shudder. "There's nothing to hold onto. How could anyone live in a world so… empty? I could eat this all day and still be hungry."

Feeling rather famished, she moved to the third corner, where a modest plaque caught her eye… "**Baby Bear: Truth is the Way.**"

Baby Bear's corner was messy and bright, with practical furniture and open windows letting in shafts of light; the shelves were lined with books that looked well-loved, as if they'd been read and reread, marked up with thoughts, questions, and the occasional sketch in the margins. His shelves were lined with titles like **The Search for Understanding** and **The Path Unfolds**, books that didn't claim to have all the answers but offered ideas, starting points, helped ask better questions, full of maps for a journey that was the adventure of one's lifetime. Names like **Aristotle**, **Confucius**, **Siddhartha**, **Marcus Aurelius** marked the shelves, each voice offering not an answer but a compass. It was a space that felt alive, curious, ready to evolve.

Baby Bear's porridge sat in a simple wooden bowl. When she tasted it, it was warm and kept her guessing, each bite offering something new—just a little bit of spice, a little sweetness, a little salt, and every bite just a bit different from the last. Nourishing. It tasted of curiosity, courage, and just a pinch of uncertainty—the sort of truth that wasn't afraid to let you ask, "But what if…?" It was not a stone wall, and it was not mist—it was a path. It asked her to walk forward, to keep looking, and it promised that, in the looking, she would find something precious.

Goldilocks laughed, the sound echoing around the little house. Here was truth that could be examined and inquired into, truth that could twist and turn and lead her somewhere surprising, something alive and willing to go with her as she changed.

"Yes," she said at last, with a long sigh, her eyes shining. "The truth will always be just right."

And just then, the three bears came lumbering in, each as evident as the day is long.

Papa Bear loomed in the doorway, a towering wall of fur and certainty. His resolute amber eyes gleamed like polished brass, and he smelled faintly of old books and freshly sharpened pencils, the kind you couldn't argue with. When he growled, it was less a noise and more a verdict, shaking the room with its weight: "There's only my way, so learn it. The rest are illusions—fools' quests."

Mother Bear drifted forward, her voice like pillows. She smelled faintly of wildflowers, lavender, and those exotic herbal concoctions that claim to cure everything from melancholy to hiccups. "All truths are beautiful, dear," she crooned. "Discover *your* truth. All truths are equally real, equally valid. It's all a matter of life experience. Let go of this need for *the* truth."

Baby Bear was small, scruffy, and had the air of someone who had just rolled down a hill and decided to make the best of it—a muddle of brown, the sort of brown that looked as though it had spent time in the sun, the mud, and possibly someone's jam pot. His bright eyes gleamed with a perspicacious, mischievous light, as if he'd just thought of a particularly clever idea and was waiting to see if anyone else would catch on. He smelled faintly of moss and the sort of slightly burned toast that suggests a great story is about to begin. When he spoke, his voice was steady but with a playful edge, like someone who knew exactly how serious this all was and was determined not to make a fuss about it. "Truth is not a command," he said kindly, "nor an opinion. It's a direction, Goldilocks, a path that we, every one of us, must walk for ourselves—or perish. No one truth will ever answer everything, but each step brings you closer, each question opens the door a little wider."

Goldilocks felt something settle in her heart, a quiet resolve. Here was the truth she could walk beside, one that asked her to keep exploring, to keep questioning. It wasn't rigid and suffocating, nor was it comforting and pointless. It was, in its own way, alive—just as she was. Truth was neither one nor personal, it was simply the truth—it didn't close doors or make everything equal. It was a course constantly in need of correction, offering her something she hadn't found anywhere else: hope. And she was a part of it.

So, with a steady heart, Goldilocks thanked Baby Bear. She left the house and stepped back into the forest, but now her feet felt lighter, her path clearer. She knew that as long as she kept her sights on the true direction—questioning, learning, listening—she would see what is true. The search for truth is the most important thing, a journey that would last her whole life, worth every step of the Way.

And in the woods, under the light of an ever-curious moon, Goldilocks set off, her heart full and her steps nimble, ready to follow the next bend in the road to the coming sunrise.

Speak Red

The world had shrunk to whispers. And even those were forbidden.

Little Red stood at the edge of the Woods, the dense, dark trees before her and the silent, shuttered town at her back. Behind the windows of every home, behind the steel-gray walls, people sat mute, their thoughts caged by the monitors and cameras that hung in every corner like mechanical spiders. The screens repeated the approved words, the sanctioned thoughts. *Say only what is permitted. Speak only what is safe.*

Avoid the Wolf.

No one knew what the Wolf really was anymore, but they knew better than to ask.

Red's parents were the same as the rest—automatons wrapped in flesh, their voices clipped to fit within the tiny boxes of government control. Every night, they would sit in their living room, listening to the endless loops of propaganda from the approved media sources. They nodded at the legal moments, blinked at the pauses, and never once dared to wonder what lay beyond the barriers they had built to protect their minds.

But Red? Red was different. Above her shushed heart, her throat revolted. Her voice burned to speak her mind. It had been kindled long ago by her grandmother, the only person left who spoke with a voice of her own.

Grandmother had left the town years ago, choosing the untamed Woods over the comfort of the town's sterile safety. They called her mad for it. They grumbled that she was reckless, foolish, that one day the Wolf would take her, as it had taken others. But Grandmother was no fool. She had simply refused to live in a world where words were strangled before they were even born.

Red's parents warned her, time and time again: *Stay away from the Woods. Stay away from the old woman. Don't listen to her lies. The government knows what's best.*

Red couldn't help herself. She loved her grandmother, loved the way her words still danced and twisted, free and alive. In Grandmother's cottage, hidden in the Woods, the air was rich with the scent of old books, the crinkle of papers full of words and thoughts that disagreed with each other, that philosophized and even lied. In Grandmother's cottage, Red could say what she felt, ask the questions that had long been smothered in the town. Only there could she truly *breathe*.

And so, when her grandmother fell ill, Red gathered a basket of food and wine and slipped into the Woods, heart pounding, thoughts racing. She was terrified of being caught—not by the patrols, not by the government agents who prowled the streets, but by something far worse, something that had no name but whose presence was felt in every leaf, in every shadow.

The Wolf.

No one spoke of him openly anymore. It was forbidden to mention the Wolf, forbidden even to think of him. The government told stories of him, of course—lurid, bloody stories. They whispered that the Wolf was chaos incarnate, that he represented everything uncontrollable, everything wild. He was lust and hunger, greed and destruction. He was the thing that lurked outside the walls of civilization, waiting to devour any who dared stray from the path.

But Red knew, deep down, that the Wolf was something more. He wasn't just a creature to be feared. He was something primal. Something free.

As she ventured further into the Woods, the silence of the town fell away, replaced by the bustle of life—the rustle of leaves, the distant call of birds. The Woods were alive, alive in a way that the town could never be. Here, there were no screens, no cameras, no eyes watching every move. It was wild and untamed, and that, more than anything, was what made it dangerous.

Halfway to her grandmother's house, Red stopped. She felt it before she saw it—a presence lurking just beyond the trees, just out of sight. Her heart quickened, her breath shallow. She had been warned about this. She knew what it was.

The Wolf.

He emerged from the shadows like smoke, his fur dark as night, eyes gleaming with a hunger that was more than just physical. He was tall, awe-fully tall, his body rippling with muscle and power. And yet, there was something supple about him, something almost beautiful.

"Where are you going, little daughter?" the Wolf asked, his voice a low, seductive rumble. "What could bring such a delicate thing into the heart of my Woods?"

Red swallowed hard, clutching her basket. "To my grandmother's house," she said, her voice tremulous.

The Wolf smiled, though there was no kindness in it. "Yes, the old woman in the Woods. How brave of you to visit her." He circled her slowly, his eyes never leaving hers. "But tell me, why stay on the path? There's so much more to see if you stray a little."

Red hesitated. The words were poison, sweet and deadly. The path was safe; the path was known. But the Wolf... the Wolf offered something else. He offered the possibility.

"The blooms grow wild just over there," he rumbled, nodding toward a thicket of trees. "Your grandmother would love them, don't you think?"

Red could feel the pull of his words, the temptation to step off the path, to dive into the wild and become part of it. For a moment, she considered it. The flowers called to her with words she had never been allowed to think, much less speak. Their petals gleamed darkly, the intense reds and purples of forbidden indulgence, ripe with unspoken longings.

"Just once," they coaxed, their songs slithering into her mind, thick with the beauty of ideas withheld. The warnings, the rules, all that had kept her safe and small, dissolved in the face of this tantalizing freedom.

"Step off the path," they beckoned, and in their promise, she saw herself—unfettered, untamed. Her heart raced, not in fear but in reckless thrill, for here, at last, were the feelings she had always buried, tugging her closer to the darkness she had long denied.

But no. The Wolf was chaos. He was freedom, yes, but freedom without responsibility was just another kind of death.

"No," she said firmly. "I'm staying on the path."

The Wolf's smile faded, his eyes narrowing. "Pity," he growled, before slipping back into the shadows.

When Red reached her grandmother's house, the door was ajar. A chill ran down her spine as she stepped inside.

"Grandmother?"

But the voice that answered wasn't her grandmother's. It was the Wolf, his body now clad in her grandmother's nightgown, lying in her bed, the sheets pulled up to his chin. He had gotten here first, had taken what he wanted.

"Come closer, child," he said, his voice a dulcet mockery. "Let me see you better."

Little Red hesitated, the air in the room too still, the fire too dim. At first she found herself mute, just as she had been taught. But when she saw the glint in his brutal eyes, a question burst forth from her unused lips:

"Grandmother, why are your ears so big, while mine are so small and taught to listen only to what I'm told?"

The Wolf's smile lengthened, a glint of teeth beneath the sheets. "The better to hear every call of the wild, my dear, unbound by censors or laws."

She stepped closer, her hand tightening around the basket. Her heart pounded, but her face stayed calm.

"Grandmother, why are your eyes so large and free to see everything, while they only allow mine to see what I'm shown?"

The Wolf's eyes gleamed, dark and deep like the forest beyond. "The better to gaze upon the real world, my dear, no matter how awful or unjust."

The fire crackled low, and Red's breath caught in her throat as she stood at the edge of the bed.

"Grandmother, why are your hands so big, able to reach for anything you desire, while mine are trivialized and trained to touch only what's permitted?"

The Wolf's claws flexed beneath the blanket, though he hid them quickly. "The better to take what I want in this world, my dear, while your hands are tied by the owners."

Red's heart raced. Her voice shaky now, barely more than a whisper.

"Grandmother, why are your teeth so big, sharp, and free to do as they will, while mine are so tiny and taught to hide themselves away?"

The Wolf's smirk finally broke free, all fangs and hunger. "The better to devour the world in my freedom, my dear, while you are muzzled by the chains of your society."

Red stood frozen, staring in horror at the creature wearing her grandmother's face. She knew what was coming. The Wolf was hungry, and he wasn't just after food. But when the Wolf lunged, the door burst open. A lone figure stepped into the room, tall and broad, with eyes like flint and a rifle in hand.

The Hunter.

Hunters were outlawed in the town—guns were banned as necessary evils from a bygone era. Firearm held high, he moved with the precision of a soldier, an old strength in his sinews, a man who had fought many battles—and not all of them for the government.

Without a word, the Hunter pointed his rifle and fired. The Wolf fell back, snarling, but he was not dead. He writhed on the floor, his body convulsing as the Hunter strode forward, his face grim.

"I know what you've done," the Hunter said, kneeling beside the Wolf's writhing form. Then, with a swift motion, he drew a hunting knife from his belt and sliced open the Wolf's belly. Blood poured out, dark and steaming, and from the gory mess, the Hunter pulled free Red's grandmother, alive but weak and covered from bonnet to boots in the Wolf's red essence.

The room was still, the only sound a snapping of the fire and the fading gurgles of the Wolf.

Red rushed to her grandmother's side, tears brimming in her eyes. The old woman smiled faintly, her voice raspy but alive. "I knew you'd make it," she whispered.

The Hunter wiped the blade clean and turned to Red, his eyes cool and appraising at first, then softening. "You've been lied to," he said quietly. "The Wolf wasn't the only monster."

The room fell silent.

Red blinked, confused. "What do you mean?"

The Hunter knelt beside her, his voice rough yet searching. "There's a revolution brewing in the Woods," the Hunter said, voice low. "A few of us who still speak the truth, who won't be silenced. Your grandmother is one of us."

Red's heart raced. Could it be? Could there still be hope?

She looked at the Wolf's lifeless body, then back at the Hunter. For the first time, she saw what it meant. The Wolf wasn't the enemy—the natural dangers in life were not the enemy. Words exchanged without restrictions, however contentious, in a free society were never the enemy. Not really.

The real enemy was what people *didn't say.*

And in that moment, Red made her choice.

"I want to help," she said, her voice strong and clear.

The Hunter nodded with a rare, genuine smile as he opened the cottage door. "Good," he said.

Her grandmother pulled Red's cloak tight around her shoulders, "Then it's time to speak, Red."

Rumpeled Words

Once upon a word, my dear reader, once upon a word—yes, you heard me right. Not a time, not a place, not a dusty corner of someone's downtrodden imagination, but a *word*. And not just any word. *The Word*. Words are the very breath of reality, you see. If you want a word to be powerful, potent enough to tilt the world on its axis, then you had best name it right, understand it right, define it down to its tonsil. Without clarity, without accuracy, you're merely babbling away the raw stuff of existence.

Now, I know you're familiar with this tale—a little girl, a spinning wheel, and a roomful of straw. And yours truly, Rumpelstiltskin, the so-called villain of the piece, stepping out of the otherworld and into the bargain. Well, let me tell you how it really happened and why the whole mess was doomed from the start, thanks to the precious human habit of tossing words around like so much chaff. Do you even know what it means to *spin* a word?

I did. And I do. It's the art of turning straw—meaningless, idle chatter—into something golden. It's the power of finding and binding a thing's essence.

Yes, *names have power.* More power than you've been led to believe. My name, for instance, isn't merely "Rumpelstiltskin." Oh no, that's the form of it, a mask for those who need a convenient handle. The name itself is ancient, gnarled and snarled, carrying weight and history that seeps into the bones of this world like water.

Ah, so you want to know what my name *means*, do you? Excellent—humans never bother to ask, they just prattle on with their "Rumpel-this" and "Stilt-that," without the faintest flush of curiosity. Well, let's break it down for you, though I doubt most of you can grasp the finer details. *Rumpel,* for starters—sounds a bit disheveled, doesn't it? Frayed, knotted, as if it's never been smoothed down or neatly pressed. And that's precisely the point. I am not tidy, nor am I meant to be understood on first glance. I'm the twist in the weave, the snag in the cloth, a bit of glorious disorder in a world that's desperate to smooth things over.

Then we have *stilt.* Ah, there's elegance there, height, even a hint of arrogance. Stilts are things you balance on, aren't they? They lift you above the crowd, give you an angle others don't have. And that's me in a nutshell. My perspective is higher, my view wider; I see things you lot are simply too thick to grasp, most especially the underbelly. Lastly, we come to *skin*—or perhaps *kin,* if you like, for we can play it both ways. Skin is what binds the whole messy lot of you, what defines your borders, keeps you neatly packaged, contained. But kin, now, that's a suggestion of belonging, isn't it? A hint that I am both of you and utterly alien to you. Am I fey? Certainly. Am I demonic? Only if you cross me. This name of mine, it's both an invitation and a warning: a reminder that while you might try to bind me with a word, I am as slippery as shadow and as stabbing as the edge of a well-chosen phrase.

So you see, *Rumpelstiltskin* isn't just a name; it's a riddle, a weave of meaning that holds both menace and mirth. It's a mirror for you humans—what you fear, what you desire, all spun into one.

And every time you utter it, you're brushing up against that ancient power, even if your tiny minds can't comprehend it.

Ah, famous names—now there's a topic worth sinking one's teeth into. Let's start with the *brilliant* ones, the names that sing with truth, names that capture the precise, uncanny essence of their bearers. Take *Alexander the Great*—that's a name that wears its laurels with ease, each syllable brimming with ambition, power, a destiny that could never be small or hidden. Or *Napoleon,* with its clipped elegance, as piercing and unyielding as the man himself; you feel the ambition in the very sound, the relentless push toward glory and disaster alike. Then there's *Cleopatra,* whose name almost hisses with beauty and danger, with the coiled might of ancient mysteries. These names are as well-wrought as any weapon; they cut to the core, naming the exact nature of those who bore them.

Of course, the beings that bore the names forged the names as thoroughly as the names forged them—the longer we maintain them, shore them up, these limiting statements of naming encapsulate the identities. We all of us and every big-banged little thing that exists were purportedly once (upon a word) stated into existence—remember?

But oh, the failures! How many poor wretches—whether in life or literature—have staggered under names or titles thrust upon them? Think of *King Ethelred the Unready.* A catastrophe, that one—forever branded with the impression of incompetence, a ruler who could never be prepared, utterly forsaking both himself and those he fancied subjects. And then there's Richard the Lionheart's younger brother—his mighty, history-defining title? Just... well, *John.* No *Lionheart,* no fearsome epithet, not even a half-hearted attempt at grandeur. Just plain, unremarkable *John*—a name with all the majesty of a public toilet. Then there's *Caligula,* that crazed emperor whose name means "Little Boot"—a trivial, diminutive thing that certainly foretold his lack of sanity and sense. And let's not forget poor *Ichabod,* which means "the glory has departed"—a name that any alpha male would throw a pumpkin at.

Names, you see, are not the things themselves—but this does not diminish their sway or stop people from sacrificing themselves upon the altars of them. They are often, to boil down Korzybski more pointedly, maps to mislead the sheeples. A name should draw out the essence, point to the truth, bind it. But a poorly chosen name—ah, that can ruin a life, curse it with smallness or mediocrity. Humans blunder about with their baby names, hoping for something 'nice,' but when they fail, they might as well be slapping chains on their poor children. Once, a name was christened with solemnity, whispered in a baptismal hush, or bestowed in the magickal rites of secret societies—its weight acknowledged, its meaning carried like a spell. A true name should resonate, it should echo. It should announce to the world exactly what one is—or, if chosen badly, exactly what one shall *never* be.

Ah, but there's the sinister twist, isn't it? A handful of modern minds—mostly the ones who claw their way into politics, media, and education—*have* realized the ancient power of words and the human bent to rename them. They know full well that language shapes reality, and they wield this knowledge not for truth but for their own ends. With a twist of a phrase, a rebranding here, a selective redefinition there, they warp perceptions, mold opinions, curb entire nations to their will. They understand that by controlling words, they control thoughts, and by controlling thoughts, they control people. They no longer speak to reveal the truth; they speak to obscure it, wrapping lies in layers of pleasant-sounding syllables until you wouldn't recognize truth if it knocked you on the head.

You see, these people aren't interested in naming things as they are; no, they aim to rename the world in their own image, to fill every corner with reflections of their own ideas, their own desires. The gods might have given humans the power of words, but this lot wields it with the precision of a trickster—setting traps, creating chaos, stirring up confusion to keep the rest of you in thrall. They're erecting states of illusion, enterprises built on words that mean nothing and something else at once, casting curses over the populace who, in their communal trance, never stop to question. And thus, they tilt the world closer to hell with every syllable, every

46

headline, every carefully crafted narrative. It's quite the spectacle, really, watching them do it—and even more amusing to see how few people notice the strings being pulled.

Ah, now we come to the so-called "fiction" books— Orwell's *1984,* Bradbury's *Fahrenheit 451,* Huxley's *Brave New World.* Novels? Hardly. Those are manuals, dear reader, warnings dressed up in literary garb, penned by a few who understood exactly where your world was headed. Orwell didn't invent Newspeak for kicks—he was putting a big, flashing neon sign above the modern masters of verbal trickery, the sort who can shave the edges off meaning until 'war' means 'peace' and 'freedom' comes with an instruction manual. Bradbury saw what happens when words, books, the very record of humanity, are snatched from your hands, and the masses are kept docile in a haze of shallow screened entertainment. And Huxley? He had the gall to pull back the curtain on a society so sated, so drowned in pleasure and distraction, that it was ruled not by fear, but by a subtle, sickening complacent consent. These authors may as well have handed you mirrors to peer into the murk of your own reality, prodding you to see that this power over language wasn't some distant dystopian nightmare but already creeping into every nook and cranny of society's spinal cord, connecting feelings to subvert original thought. Yet most people missed the point entirely, shelved these books as "what ifs," rather than the "wake up" calls they were meant to be.

Words, my dear, hapless humans, are the breath and bones of reality. They shape, define, disguise, and destroy—of course they do—but they also separate, distinguish, bring things into being. They trap myths in ink and spawn those maddening little jingles that lodge in your skull like an unwanted houseguest. And like any tool of real power, words demand precision. Name something properly, and you hold it in the palm of your hand. Name it carelessly, and you might as well stand back and enjoy the ensuing chaos.

Now, as for the miller's daughter—there's a spiral worth savoring. At first, she was as ignorant as any, believing words were only noises you toss out like scraps to a dog. She babbled away her promises to me without an ounce of understanding, offering whatever "trinket" I asked for, thinking it all just a game. But as the bargain tightened, as her debt deepened and the stakes became her child, she finally woke up to the importance of *words*. She saw that her father's flippant lie had spun a noose around her life. She learned that every word she spoke was a step further down that road, binding her tighter to fate. And, well, she grew shrewd, clever, began to seek out my name, knowing that if she could only grasp it—if she could *name* the essence of my self-made lies that define my separation from what *I'm not*—she'd unravel the trap. She got there in the end, I'll give her that, though it was a bit of a struggle.

But those born into the present zeitgeist? Ha! They strut about thinking they've cracked the code, when in reality, they're just copy-pasting the same old errors in a fancier font. They tweet and post and babble on as if words are just noise to fill the air. They label people, places, whole nations with words as flimsy as straw, and then wonder why the world falls into confusion. They take names lightly, changing them as they please, inventing new ones without a thought to what those names really mean.

They've forgotten that a word can be a sword, a spell, a bridge to understanding—or a stone to sink them. Unlike the miller's daughter—who at least had the good sense to learn something—they sling words into the chaos, blissfully unaware they're just adding to it. In the end, they're walking right into traps of their own making, yet have no clue how to speak themselves free. Imagine, if you will, being given the very gift of the *logos*—of words made flesh, of names that bear essence—and throwing it away. Because that's what people do when they speak without thought or principle. *In the beginning was the Word, and the Word was with God, and the Word was God.* And what did humanity do with this living gift? They began naming without knowing, speaking without forethought, creating heavens and hells by the sheer recklessness of their tongues.

You see, language is not just noise; it's *incantation*. When you speak, you tilt reality a fraction this way or that. You usher in paradise or you usher in perdition. But you lot—you sloppy, half-witted mortals—prefer to barter your truth for convenience, for

48

apparency, to name things not as they are, but as you wish them to be. It's a game of hide and seek with reality, isn't it? You think that by labeling something neatly, you control it. And that's how you found yourselves in that infernal straw-strewn room, frantically begging for a miracle. And that's why I, with my mastery over names, appeared.

So, perhaps *now* you will allow me to tell my side of the story—which, incidentally, begins with the miller, not his daughter. Now, here's a man who flung words about like chaff in the wind. Bragging to the king, he claimed his daughter could spin straw into gold. "Spin straw into gold!" Think of it—a preposterous idea, a wild, reckless utterance that flouted all reason. But he said it nonetheless, and with such boldness that the king believed him. And there we have it: one small lie, one poorly chosen phrase, and a world shifted.

The girl was summoned, taken from her quiet life, and brought to the palace, all because of words that her father spoke to make himself seem other than he was. In truth.

Picture it, if you will. A darkened room piled high with straw, the very air thick with the weight of the impossible. There stood the miller's daughter, timorous and petrified. The king had locked her in, told her that if she could not spin the straw into gold by morning, her life would be forfeit. And she was left alone in the cold, clutching the weight of her father's lie—a lie he'd spun without a shred of sympathy. And so, she wept, her cries echoing off the walls, and that's where I entered.

Now, I could have left her to her misery. I could have vanished like mist at dawn, leaving her to face the full, crushing culmination of what her father's reckless words had unleashed. But you see, I have a special appreciation for words and for names, and there was something in this pitiful scene that intrigued me. She had a name, this girl, and I was curious to see what she'd do with it.

"Why the tears, my dear?" I said, stepping into the light. She blinked at me, and through her hiccupping sobs, she told me the story. Her father's boast, the king's unreasonable demand, the threat that loomed over her. Words, words, all of them—and not a single one spoken with direction or reason.

So, I offered her a deal. "I'll spin your straw into gold," I told her, "if you give me something in return." She had no real awareness of what I meant, of course. She thought she was handing over mere trifles—a necklace, a ring. Baubles. But these things, too, have names, meanings, histories. And each time she offered them, I took her one step further down the path.

But the true price would come later. That's the thing about language—words spoken in haste, without thought or intention, often return to haunt you. They have a way of binding you, marking you. And it was clear that neither the girl nor her father had the faintest grasp of this. So I gave her the gold, and the king, enamored by the sight of wealth spun from straw, returned with more straw and more demands. Again, she wept, and again I appeared, and each time, her debt to me grew more oppressive, though she couldn't see it yet.

Finally, the king made her an offer that would seal her fate. If she could spin the straw once more, he would make her his queen. Now, here's where the story twists. Words like "queen" and "gold" and "promise" are potent, powerful cravings. They shape the world as much as a craftsman's hand shapes clay. But our miller's daughter had no grasp of this; she simply wanted to live, to escape the pall of death that hung over her.

So I appeared a third time, and I gave her the final deal. "This time," I said, "I'll spin the straw into gold, but in return, you'll owe me your firstborn child." Now, you might think I was pitiless, asking for a thing so dear. But remember, words have power, and names even more so. The child she would one day bear would come into the world with a name and an intention. And she was willing to give that away—again, without thought, without care, without mindfulness.

Sacrifice her future for gold today.

She agreed, and I spun the gold one last time, leaving her to marry her king, to become his queen, and to fulfill her bargain, even if she couldn't see it yet.

Months passed, and eventually, the child was born. And there I was again, ready to claim what she had promised. But the queen—ah, she'd changed her tune. She clutched the child to her chest, begged and pleaded.

"No, please, not my child. I didn't know what I was saying!"

There it was—*I didn't know what I was saying.* The very confession of her ignorance, her lack of foresight. She had given away the one thing that mattered most, all because she didn't know the power of the words she spoke.

So many of you are in this present-day pandemonium precisely because you've made agreements and, when the bill comes due, you don't want to pay what you've agreed to—that it's *your name* on the dotted line.

But, I am not without a sense of irony, so I made her a final offer. "If you can guess my name," I told her, "I'll let you keep the child." She agreed, thinking she'd solve this riddle with ease. But names are not easy things to guess, my self-absorbed reader. They carry history, weight, intention. And mine, well, it's not a name one stumbles upon lightly.

She sent her messengers out, scouring the land, gathering names like wildflowers. Each night, she would call out new names to me, and each night I would shake my head, laughing, because she had not yet grasped the essence of who I was. She thought my name was merely a sound, a collection of syllables. But a true name is far more than that. It is the heart of a person, the core of their being, and I was not about to let her uncover it so easily.

But eventually, one of her messengers—clever thing—followed the trail I'd all but painted in gold dust and stumbled upon my name. There I was, flinging it to the wind, shouting it like a challenge, daring the world to listen. *Rumpelstiltskin.* And when she called it out, my name, my essence, everything I'd built, unraveled in an instant—just as I'd known it would, from the moment I'd begun the game.

And so, I tore myself in two—for at last my part was played—cursing her foolishness with great gusto, but knowing full well that it wouldn't matter. My body, the thing she named, vanished, but my story—made up of words, spoken and eventually written down—lives on. Long after any memory of her or her royal husband or fatuous father. For the child she stole from me was warned about me by name, and he cautioned his children and subjects, and they told their own about me, too. *Rumpelstiltskin* lived long beyond any of them, and will outlive all of you as well, dear simpletons. Short-sighted humans. Because people like you never learn. You toss your words (and others' words) around, thinking you can bend reality without consequence, thinking you can shape the world without understanding its true nature.

In the beginning was the Word, my prized idiots. And the Word *was God*. And it was given to you—to all of you—to wield as a gift, to name things, to shape your world. But instead, you speak thoughtlessly, haphazardly, creating a mess of your lives and calling it fate. You spin straw, thinking you're making gold, and wonder why the world is as bungled as it is.

The miller's daughter may have learned her lesson, but I'll wager the rest of you never will.

The Elves and the Subsidy

Once upon a time, a shoemaker sat at his tired, worn workbench in the tired, worn twilight of his life, knuckles swollen as he stared at the last piece of tired, worn leather he had left. The small shop where he had worked for years, nestled between two great government buildings that loomed like sentinels, seemed to grow darker with each passing day. Once, he had been proud of his craft, his fingers deftly shaping fine leather into shoes that people loved. But now, those days felt like distant dreams. Customers were few, orders fewer still, and the world beyond his window seemed to shift in ways he could neither predict nor understand.

He leaned back in his chair, weary. He had heard stories—strange whispers carried on the wind—of help arriving in the dead of night. Magical, they said. Unseen forces, the hands of God, some a sort of miracle as though delivered from on high. And though he had always been a man of practicality, a worker who trusted his own hands over any fairy tales, he understood how desperation had a way of making the outlandish sound plausible to some. With a long sigh, he abandoned the piece of leather on his bench and went to bed, hopeless and exhausted.

The moonlight crept through the window as the clock ticked toward midnight. Then, from the corners of the room where shadows pooled like dark water, they came—the Elves. They were small, quick, dressed in crisp, neat suits with badges that glinted faintly in the foul light. Their faces were sharp, their eyes keen, and their hands worked not with the care of artisans, but with the efficiency of machines. They moved in flawless synchronization, wordless, precise, and in a matter of hours, they had transformed the shoemaker's last piece of leather into one damn fine pair of shoes. Not a stitch was out of place; the design was flawless.

When the shoemaker awoke, he could hardly believe his eyes. The shoes gleamed as if lit from within. That day, they sold for a small fortune, and the shoemaker, though puzzled by how it had all come to pass, felt a weight lift from his shoulders. He could breathe again. The anxiety that had gnawed at him for months seemed to vanish, replaced by a fleeting sense of security. But absence was not peace—something else, something worse, crept into its place, biting deeper. He hadn't made those shoes. He hadn't touched the leather, hadn't worked the thread. His own hands, the source of so much past pleasure and pride, hung limp at his sides.

But what did that matter when his troubles were disappearing?

Night after night, the Elves returned. Each time, they found the materials he had left for them—scraps of leather, bits of thread—and each morning, the shoemaker woke to find impeccably crafted shoes awaiting him. His shop flourished. Word spread about the miraculous quality of his goods, and soon, customers were lining up before dawn. He hardly had to lift a finger, as his business ran itself. The Elves took care of everything.

And the shoemaker? Well… he grew complacent. He stopped bothering with the bench, no longer cared to shape or mold or sew. Why should he? There were others, invisible and tireless, who could do it for him.

But as the days turned into weeks, and the weeks into months, something in the shoemaker began to wither. His hands, once so skilled, began to forget the touch of leather. His mind, once canny with the calculations of his trade, dulled under the torpor of inaction. He had surrendered his craft, his industry, and in doing so, he had lost something—something he didn't even know he needed. The once-bright flame of independence that had guided him through hardship sputtered low, nearly extinguished.

It wasn't just him. The city itself, once alive with the cadence of labor and the whir of industry, grew quieter. The streets, where vendors and craftsmen had once bartered and haggled, were now filled with men and women who, like the shoemaker, no longer worked. The Elves had come for them, too. Seamstresses, blacksmiths, bakers—each found their toil magnanimously lifted from them. Their businesses thrived, but their hands, like the shoemaker's, grew idle. And with idleness came a slow, creeping decay.

One night, unable to sleep, the shoemaker decided to stay awake and watch the Elves. He hid behind the old curtain at the back of his shop, peering through a slit as they arrived. They moved swiftly and with tenacity, as they always did, but this time, he noticed something he hadn't before—the way they whispered to one another in low, mocking tones.

"He doesn't even know we're here," one Elf murmured, his voice edged with disdain.

"Their kind never do," the other replied, chuckling darkly. "They think we're their saviors. But really, we're making them forget. One day, they'll be nothing without us."

The shoemaker's heart thudded in his chest. Forget? What had he forgotten? He glanced at his hands, at the tools he no longer used, at the bench where he hadn't worked in months. He understood, then, with chilling clarity. The Elves were not helping him—they were taking from him, little by little, what had once made him who he was. They were the hands that built, but they were also the hands that stripped away his independence, his sense of purpose. The security they provided was an illusion, a trap, and he had fallen into it willingly.

The Elves, the shoemaker realized, were never the nimble helpers he had once imagined. They were something much more cunning, something vast and intricate, spinning a web that stretched far beyond his small shop. They weren't simply offering help out of thin air; they were *taking*—quietly, methodically—from those who still labored under the sun, those whose hands were calloused with honest work, who spent the precious hours of their lives creating instead of lolling, whose minds were alert with invention and opportunity. The Elves were not creators. No, they were collectors, siphoning the wealth of the industrious, the resources of the great doers, and funneling it to people like the shoemaker—people who had forgotten how to work, how to strive, how to be truly alive.

He had been blind to it at first. The comfort, the ease, had clouded his vision. But now, as he pieced it together, he could see the larger design. The Elves weren't providing him with anything new; they were merely remaking, restructuring, taking from the hands that still knew the weight of hard labor, the value of sweat, and shifting it to those who no longer understood the effort it took to birth what might be.

And the Elves—those sly, silent creatures—stood prosperous and gleaming in the middle of it all, growing fatter with each transaction. Every pair of shoes they generated in the dark of night wasn't just a gift to the shoemaker. It was a piece of life taken from someone else—someone who still rose before dawn, who still believed in the dignity of their own hands. The shoemaker had been fed, clothed, and comforted by the efforts of others, though he had never seen their faces, never known their names. The Elves had hidden it well, disguising their theft within a perfect illusion of charity.

But the shoemaker saw it now—saw how the Elves played both ends against the middle. For every person who became dependent on their gifts, for every craftsman who traded his tools for ease or her industry for comfort, the Elves gained more control.

The shoemaker wasn't the only one. The city was filling with them—people who had once been productive, once had pride in their work, now clamoring for the Elves' assistance.

And the more people turned to them, the more the Elves took from those who still resisted, who still toiled away in the old ways.

What had once been a bustling city of craftsmen and merchants was now quiet. The streets where workers had once gathered to exchange goods and ideas were now lined with idle hands, waiting for the next gift from the Elves. Meanwhile, in the background, the Elves grew rich—not in coin, but in power. They controlled the flow of everything now—who worked, who ate, who lived comfortably and who did not.

It was a clever system, so subtle that few even noticed the change. At first, it was just the shoemaker. Then it was the baker, the tailor, the blacksmith. One by one, the industrious found themselves lured by the promise of ease, by the appeal of a life without struggle. And as they grew dependent, the Elves tightened their grip, reaping the rewards from the labor of those still striving, still their own.

Then the shoemaker saw the truth: the more the people accepted, the weaker they became, and the more powerful the Elves grew.

The Elves' hands were never idle. While the people slept, lulled into complacency, the Elves worked—always shifting, always reallocating, always ensuring that no one could rise without their aid. What seemed like help was, in truth, a clever form of conquest.

And the shoemaker? He was but one of many who had unwittingly traded his freedom for an easy life, not knowing that the cost was far greater than any coin or shoe could ever measure. The Elves, in all their shady dealings, had won, not by force, but by seduction, by convincing the people to give up their independence willingly, one piece at a time. And now, the Elves held it all—the wealth, the power, the lives of those who had forgotten what it meant to work, to struggle, to be their own masters.

He had thought it was just him. His shop. His burden lifted. But the forge down the street was cold, its flames long doused. The bakery, once filled with the warm scent of bread, now stood silent. The tailor's shop, too, had fallen quiet, the needles still. Everywhere he looked, once-bustling businesses were shuttered, their owners no longer toiling over their crafts. And yet, the city was not starving, not struggling. The goods were still there, the bread still on the shelves, the shoes still being sold. But they were not made by the hands of men or women.

The shoemaker's hands clamped at his sides. He had been a fool. He had allowed himself to be drawn into a comforting lie, to believe that the Elves were helping him when all they had done was take, take, take until there was nothing left of the man he once was.

He swore to himself to fight it. He committed to take back his craft, to refuse their help, to work with his own hands again. But the next morning, in the light of the rosy dawn, something inside his chest relaxed with the easy warmth. This new world of ease was so quiet, so peaceful. His shoes sold. Why bother? Why fight when life had become so easy?

And it wasn't just him. All around the town, others had come to the same conclusion. The blacksmith eventually sold his forge, instead waiting for the next shipment of goods the Elves provided. The baker no longer kneaded dough by hand, but simply opened his doors to the loaves the Elves left on his counter each morning.

Life had become easy. Too easy. And as the months turned into years, the townspeople, one by one, gave up the fight they had never fully understood they were in.

The elections came not long after. The Elves, now brazen with their presence, stood as candidates. They promised even more—more shoes! More bread! More comfort! They told the townspeople they could have it all without lifting a finger. And why not? They deserved it! There was no need to work, to strain, to sweat over the forge or loom. The Elves provided, and all they asked in return was a vote. A small thing. A simple thing.

The shoemaker, like everyone else, cast his vote for the Elves. He didn't hesitate. Who would? The thought of going back to the old ways—to the long nights of work, the uncertainty of the next sale, the empty bellies—it seemed unbearable. His hands no longer itched to craft, his mind no longer wandered to the joy of creation. The shoes on his shelves were not his, but they were perfect, and they sold well. That was enough.

As the Elves gained more power, the town fell deeper into the sleep of dependency. The promises of ease had been kept, but at a cost no one seemed to notice at first. The shoes, once so fine, began to lose their luster. The bread, once warm and fragrant, grew stale more quickly. The clothes, once so well-made, began to tear at the seams. But no one complained. How could they? They had forgotten what it was like to work for these things, to earn them. They only knew that the Elves provided, and that was enough.

The Elves, meanwhile, grew fatter. Their eyes gleamed with a greedy light as they roamed the streets, their power swelling with each passing day. The town was theirs now, and everyone in it was theirs, too. They had taken control, not through force, but through gifts—gifts that had slowly milked the people dry of their independence, their will to work, to think, to strive.

One morning, the shoemaker awoke to find his shop empty. The shoes were gone, the shelves bare. For a moment, panic rose in his chest. What would he do? How could he sell what he did not have? But then he remembered—the Elves would come. They always did. They would bring more shoes, more leather, more of everything he needed. He sat back, his worry fading, replaced by the dull comfort that had come to define his life.

Across town, the same scene played out in every shop, every home. The people waited, as they always did, for the Elves to bring what they needed. But this time, the Elves did not come. The shops remained empty, the streets silent. Slowly, the realization settled in. The town was drained. The Elves had taken everything of value— every bit of strength, every ounce of will—and now, there was nothing left to give.

The shoemaker stood at his window, staring out at the quiet streets, at the people who, like him, waited for something that would never arrive. The Elves had won. They had bled the town dry, fattening themselves on the very souls of the people, and now that there was nothing left, they had disappeared into the shadows from whence they had come.

The shoemaker felt a listless emptiness inside, not the absence of goods or money, but the absence of meaning. He had forgotten what it was like to create, to work, to be anything more than a passive recipient of someone else's generosity. And now, with the Elves gone and the town hollowed out, he realized, too late, that the gifts had always been a lie.

And yet, he did nothing. The struggle to reclaim what had been lost felt too distant, too hard. His hands, once strong, had grown weak. His mind, once quick-witted, had blunted. The fight had left him long ago. So, he waited, along with the rest of the town, for something—anything—that might never come.

And in that waiting, the shoemaker knew: he had chosen this. They all had. In the end, the Elves had not needed to take their freedom by force. The people had handed it over willingly, trading it for the fleeting comfort of an easy life.

And thus, my children, their will to do what it takes to live gone, they each laid down and returned to Mother Earth in the hopes she could at least make something of what little remained, one by one.

Death by Chocolate

Once upon a time, in a kingdom beset by a strange and growing sickness, people devoured sugar as if it were spun gold, scarcely aware that their hunger for sweetness was slowly devouring them from the inside out. It had begun with insinuations—then a proclamation that fat was the real villain, that sugar was a friend to all. So they poured it into their porridge, sprinkled it over roasted meats, filled their pies until they bubbled with syrup, and spooned it straight into their children's mouths. Everyone grew a little rounder, a little slower, yet none dared stop. For Dr. Witch, the kingdom's revered public health expert, had assured them they were marching steadily toward health, her words as honeyed as the sugar coursing through their veins.

The people adored her, this strange doctor who was neither entirely a witch nor merely a physician. She was something in between—a master of both potions and spells, of pharmaceuticals and medicines. With every passing day, her influence grew, even as the people grew more ill, plagued by aching joints and pounding heads, by bellies bloated and hearts burdened. Even the king, who gorged on frosted cakes and candied meats as he habitually puffed cigarettes like a dragon savoring the taste of its own smoke, collapsed one day mid-swing on the royal golf course, clutching his chest. Dr. Witch spun her explanation quickly, blaming it on the fatty burger he'd indulged in just before, dismissing the sugar he'd shoveled day after day as harmless. And so, the experts declared fat the great villain, warning the people to shun it at all costs. Their royal chemists and food manufacturers—dutifully inventive— crafted an endless parade of fat-free, artificially flavor-enhanced concoctions for their famished citizens, while the children grew rounder still.

And Dr. Witch secretly bought a carefully selected plot of land to begin construction of a secluded house at the edge of the deep, dark forest.

For you see, my chubby children, all this was part of a grand design conceived long ago, on a night when a conclave of particularly powerful witches gathered on an island in the South Pacific, far, far from prying eyes. Under a dense sky, they cast a spell meant to enrich their futures and mark the world with their power.

However, every time one alters reality, changes the agreed upon way of things—every charm, every incantation, every business deal—well, it has its price, an unavoidable byproduct ignored to one's peril. This time, the spell left an unexpected side effect: a tropical grass sprouted in their charmed circle, and when the witches tasted the mysterious shrub that looked oddly like a collection of walking sticks, they discovered it was tantalizingly sweet. It tempted, then tormented, and before long, became addictive—yet it made all who indulged terribly ill—and so the witches dubbed it "sicker cane."

Yet humans, clumsy and dull to the essence of things, misinterpreted it all. They took to calling the grass "sugar cane," a name that spread as quickly as the cane itself. Little did they know, every field of sugarcane symbolized some piece of potent magic, some massive spell rippling out into the world, balanced by this odd sweetness. And so it grew, weaving across kingdoms and creeping into every kitchen, a silent sorcery scattering through the masses, one teaspoon at a time.

And Dr. Witch's eyes twitched with moves and countermoves. Here was her chance to not only enrich the witches (for they owned the patent on seed-cane) but supply her own singular gastronomical predilection.

She reached out to a mortal colleague, one Dr. Locks, a scientist from a faraway land, whose name carried a certain weight despite his slippery morals. Together, they concocted a grand money-making scheme, declaring the evils of saturated fat while quietly promoting sugar as the golden alternative, the enchanting elixir of life. With great fanfare, they unveiled a "study" purporting to link fat consumption to heart disease—scholarship drawn from six kingdoms' data that conveniently upheld their theory. Never mind the sixteen other kingdoms that proved evidence of the opposite; Dr. Locks, with a smile as thin as a dollar bill, "misplaced" those records, leaving only the six plumpest, most sugar-happy kingdoms to bear the weight of evidence.

Their yummy findings spread like wildfire, and a slow panic took root across the land. The people shunned fat as if it were toxic, convinced by the expertly spun warnings that fat, not sugar, would be their doom. A frenzy of dietary reform swept the kingdom, bonfires blazing with charred animal fats, while sugary confections became the order of every day, every meal, a dulcet dose taken like medicine.

Dr. Witch, of course, wouldn't touch the sugary contaminant herself. She savored the blubbery texture of fat—preferably young and roasted. And all the while, Dr. Witch watched with a gleam of satisfaction in her eye, as the kingdom grew softer, slower, and sugarcoated to the bone.

At last, she finished construction of her home on the edge of the deep, dark forest.

For Dr. Witch, it was the most exquisite plan. The citizens followed her advice, even prescribing sugar-coated gummy prenatal vitamins to expectant mothers and lacing infant formula with "fortified" sugar. An entire new type of modern "food-like substance" began filling the grocery shelves created through the miracle of "ultra-processing" original ingredients to taste sweeter, better, and more addictively delicious. The people's babies soon grew as round and rosy as freshly baked buns. And as more and more children plumped up, Dr. Witch at last finalized her trap in the forest—a house so rich in sugar it looked like a dream, with walls of dark chocolate, windows of caramelized glass, and chimneys that puffed cotton candy like clouds in a cerulean sky.

In no time, fat children began to mystifyingly disappear from the kingdom, one by one. And the parents, suffused in their own grown-up problems, refused to even acknowledge what was happening, praising Dr. Witch for the kingdom's increased life expectancy.

One bedtime after over two dozen children had gone missing, two small figures lay nestled side by side in a cramped cottage on the edge of Dr. Witch's deep, dark forest. The boy, Hansel, had a face smudged with dirt and eyes that sparkled like bits of broken bottle-green glass, always dancing with mischief, always on the lookout for the next adventure. His hair, wild as a bird's nest, tumbled over his forehead as he lay still, listening, with one ear cocked like a fox who'd caught a whiff of something curious.

Beside him, his sister Gretel lay quiet, her face calm and thoughtful, with watchful eyes that saw more than most but kept every bit of it close. She was smaller and more delicate, but there was a fierceness in the way her tiny fingers curled around the edge of the blanket, as if she could hold the whole world together if she tried hard enough. Gretel was the child who would tuck lost things into her pockets—a feather, a pebble, a half-split seashell—and whisper their secrets to herself, while Hansel was the boy who'd chase after anything that sparkled, certain there was magic in every turn of the forest path. They were a mismatched pair, yet they fit like two halves of the same laugh, each looking out for the other first.

"We can't keep them, you know," they heard their mother whisper from the kitchen, a tremor in her voice masking a brittle tone. "We've barely enough for the two of us, and as they grow, they always need more."

"But they're our *children*," their father replied, his voice dragging like footsteps through deep mud. "What if we just… tried a little longer?"

The mother's silence stretched chilly and delicate, like the thin crust of ice over a withered pond, every unsaid word threatening to break through. Finally, she said, "No. Dr. Witch will be waiting. Remember what Dr. Witch says about acceptable losses. The broader benefits outweigh individual risks." And that was all. She turned, her footsteps muffled as she drifted back to bed, leaving the father standing alone in the silent gloom.

The next morning, Hansel and Gretel were awakened by their parents too early, who smiled too wide and moved too quick as they beckoned them to follow. "We're going to find berries today, a feast of them," their mother said, her voice bright but still brittle. Their father said little, his eyes hidden beneath the brim of his cap while he led the way into the forest.

As the trees grew dense and the light dimmed, Hansel's stomach churned with an unease he didn't yet understand. His fingers brushed against a handful of breadcrumbs he'd tucked into his pocket the night before, and his heart steadied. He began dropping them, one by one, each small piece a breadcrumb of hope to guide them back home.

Their parents led them into the heart of the woods, where the branches sagged close, weaving an almost impenetrable wall of bark and leaves around them. The clearing was cool and damp, an odd place to search for berries, Hansel thought, but he kept silent. Gretel, on the other hand, seemed to sense something amiss, clutching her brother's hand as they looked up at their parents' faces.

"Wait here," their mother said, her voice shifty as she patted Gretel's head a bit too swiftly, a bit too coldly. "We'll be back in no time. Just... stay right here."

Hansel's voice quivered as he called after them. "But Mother, Father... where are the berries?"

Their parents were already gone, slipping through the shrubbery and fading into the dense silence of the woods. Hansel and Gretel waited, staring at each other in the clearing, their stomachs aching, the hours stretching into emptiness. They began to understand then, slowly, what had happened—that there would be no return. Their parents had taken them as far as they dared, casting them out into the darkened woods.

Desperate with empty bellies, the children tried to retrace their steps. Hansel looked for his breadcrumbs, only to find the earth empty, each crumb already gobbled up by the wild birds that hopped cheerfully on the path as if mocking them.

Hours passed, and the light began to dim. Hunger scraped at them, relentless, a gouging reminder of all they'd lost, and the fear swelled within them. Then, as night coiled around the forest, a glow pricked the distance—too faint to trust, too real to ignore. It was vaporous and almost ghostly, illuminating the darkness in warm shades of amber and cream. Hansel and Gretel stumbled toward it, their hands clasped tightly, feet dragging through the underbrush.

They emerged into a clearing on the other edge of the forest—and there, standing in the moonlight, was a house unlike anything they'd ever seen. It loomed before them like a wild fever-dream, a thing spun from the darkest corners of every child's imagination. Compared to this confectionery marvel, Willy Wonka's factory was little more than a chocolatier's midlife crisis gone public. This? This was lunacy poured into a mold, polished to a sinful gleam. The walls loomed in great slabs of chocolate—dark as midnight, rich as hoarded treasure, and slick with a molten ripple, as if the whole structure had been caught mid-melt, just waiting for an excuse to collapse into indulgence. Every edge was lined with a trim of gingerbread, crusted with sugar crystals that caught the light and sparkled like tiny stars, rough yet delicate, a breakable sugariness that dared them to reach out and crumble it between their fingers. The windows were panes of hard nougat stretched so thin you could almost see through it, clear and golden as trapped sunlight. High above, peppermint spirals curled in dizzying red-and-white patterns, slathered along the roof in neat, candy-cane swirls that seemed to twist and dance whenever they moved their gaze.

Hansel, hands eager, reached out and pulled a piece of salt-water taffy from the doorframe, his fingers stickified with syrup. Beside him, Gretel picked at a peppermint lattice around the window, the cool, minty taste melting on her tongue. For a moment, the sting of their parents' betrayal faded, their hunger temporarily sated as they nibbled, one delectable bite after another, the terrible truth of their parents' departure drifting further away into the decadence, even as it carved each out like jack-o'-lanterns.

And as they ate, they didn't notice the quiet slither of footsteps behind them as a predator slipped into place, watching their every move with eyes that gleamed like the perfect, glistening shell of a candy apple—hiding a taint no glaze could conceal.

Tasting the change in the air, Hansel and Gretel froze mid-chew, their mouths tacky with half-melted sugar, as the intruder stepped forward, her small frame wrapped in flowing black that seemed to mug the moonlight in a dark alley and make off with any glow. Her eyes were hidden in the darkness created by her witch's hat, and her lips, a slash of cherry red, bent into a smile that teetered between welcoming and unsettling. When her head tilted, a dry, crinkling laugh spilled out, like the faint rustle of a candy wrapper folding in on itself—ordinary, yet wrong. The air grew thick and cloying, gooey as treacle in their lungs, and for a moment, Hansel and Gretel felt trapped, caught in her gaze as though the world had been dipped in sugar and left to harden.

"Children, children," Dr. Witch purred, her voice smooth and syrupy, "come in, come in—no need to loiter out here like stray kittens." Hansel and Gretel lingered at the threshold, their feet dragging as though tethered by invisible strings, their bellies heavy with sugar and their thoughts thick and sluggish, like honey left too long in the jar.

Inside, Dr. Witch unveiled a feast fit to topple the will of kings—cakes glistening with sugar glaze, puddings rich enough to make any spoon meander, and pies steaming with spiced apples, each bite a surrender to saccharine indulgence. Hansel, lulled by sweets and a false sense of security, ate himself into a stupor and slumped beside the fire, his pleasure as full as his belly. Gretel, meanwhile, stopped munching the moment Dr. Witch appeared, her appetite vanishing as quickly as her trust. Now she sat rigid, her gaze darting toward their host, suspicion pooling in her gut like day-old fatty porridge.

Dr. Witch played her role to perfection, lavishing the two children with food over the coming weeks and watching—smug and salivating—as Hansel swallowed bite after bite, growing plumper by the day. The boy's sister, however, had a brain in her head. She noticed the way Dr. Witch muttered to herself, her fingers twitching toward the oven as if itching to shove something inside. And she didn't miss how the old doctor's gaze lingered on Hansel— swelling, sluggish, and now far-too well-fed—with the same greedy anticipation one might have for a roast fresh from the spit.

On one final, fateful morning, Dr. Witch, eager for her long-awaited feast, demanded that Gretel check if the oven was hot enough. Gretel, eyes gleaming with something decidedly unchildlike, feigned ignorance and asked innocently, "Oh, but how do I check, dear Mistress?" With a huff, Dr. Witch leaned forward to demonstrate—her second mistake. The first had been building an oven designed to lock in the young meal. With one sure shove, Gretel sent her sprawling inside and slammed the iron latch shut. A wail erupted, shrill and furious, but the oven was made for trapping things that squirmed. Flames roared, filling the air with the scent of caramelized sugar and something far less pleasant.

Hansel and Gretel, their senses sharpened by fear, ran. Behind them, smoke scraped at the sky, rising from the ruins of Dr. Witch's burning house as it collapsed into a pool of bubbling sugar and blackened nightmares. The forest swallowed their footsteps, indifferent as ever. They did not look back. Their bellies were full, but not with food; their hearts pounded, but not with relief. They had ended a life, and no storybook platitude could wash that guilt away; their small shoulders braced against a world that, for all its sweet talk, hid things bitter and dark.

When they reached the edge of their village, they saw it with fresh eyes. The townsfolk lumbered in a sticky haze, their bellies round and cheeks flushed, faces slack and sluggish, hands always reaching for more—another slice of cake, another spoonful of syrup, the glaze blurring their minds, thickening their blood. Hansel and Gretel watched it all, their young eyes unblinking, feeling older than they ever had before. They could see now, in the slack movements and sallow faces, how Dr. Witch's spell had wrapped around the people like a snare, turning them into something closer to food than folk, something easy to control.

Days passed, and Hansel and Gretel began to tell their tale. They spoke of the seductive set-up of Dr. Witch's house, the glossy windows and peppermint pillars, the candy that had nearly cost them their lives. They warned of the dangers of confection and the poison hidden within it. At first, the townspeople laughed, dismissing the children's words as wild stories. But little by little, the truth seeped in—dismissed at first, then inconvenient, then impossible to ignore, like rain slipping through a roof until the whole house buckles beneath it. One by one, the villagers began to notice the gravity in their limbs, the ache in their hearts, the way their children grew tired before their time. And so, bit by bit, the kingdom turned from sugar and eschewed ultra-processed foods, beginning the steep climb back to health.

And the children learned, as children must, that the most dangerous things in life often come artificially sweetened, that sometimes the world is built to fatten you up just to make you easier prey. They learned to ask questions, to dig deeper, to see beyond the surface of things. They learned that villains are not always as they appear—that sometimes, they wear the cloak of an authority, that sometimes they smile with cherry-red lips and offer an ambrosial taste that forever leaves you hungry for more.

For in the final reckoning, my children, Hansel and Gretel understood that sometimes survival lies not in being convincing, or compliant, or even commanding, but in knowing when to say, "No." It is in turning away from the traps that beckon, in standing firm when the world insists on crystalized lies, in walking the long, hard road back from temptation. And so they walked on together, hand in hand, wiser now than when their story began, a cautionary reminder that not everything sweet is good, and that sometimes, to escape the candied house, you have to burn it down and walk away.

The (bittersweet) End

Little Lost Hope

It was the coldest New Year's Eve anyone could remember. In the forgotten corners of an American city—any American city—she watched the streetlights flicker like dying stars. Solitary, she grasped the box of matches close to her heart. Her name was Hope, though it didn't suit her any more. She barely existed to the world, a shadow slipping through broken sidewalks and boarded-up storefronts, clutching a handful of matches she was too afraid to light.

Her coat was thin, barely more than a patchwork of old fabric and threadbare memories of better days, the ones when her father still lived with them. Those days seemed more like dreams now—hazy, untouchable, but somehow more real. She could still hear his voice sometimes, echoing through the noise of the streets. He used to promise her things—new shoes, a bike for Christmas, a better life. She had believed him once, back when she was small and the world felt whole, before the cracks of his absence ran deep, branching through her like roots searching for something they'd never find.

Her mother worked two jobs now—one as a janitor at the local school, the other at a diner that stayed open until dawn. She was always tired, her face wan and worn enough for two lives. Hope had three younger siblings to look after when her mom wasn't home, which was most of the time. The apartment they lived in was small, cramped with the clutter of lack—a place where comfort was as rare as warmth. The radiator had broken two winters ago, and there was never enough money to fix it.

Hope watched families walk past her on the street, holding hands, laughing, bundled in thick coats and scarves. Fathers carried their children on their shoulders, strong and steady. She tried not to look, but it was hard not to feel the hollow where her father used to be. A hole that seemed to grow bigger with every day he didn't come back.

One in four, she'd heard at school. That's how many children grew up like her. But numbers didn't mean much when you were shivering on a street corner with no one looking for you, no one waiting for you to come home.

The matches in her hand felt small and fragile, like the last thread tethering her to something. With no breakfast this morning, she'd sworn to bring home money for dinner, and so she'd scoured the kitchen for matches—odds and ends, here and there—gathering them into a small box, hoping her mother still had enough to light the gas stove. She had been trying to sell them all day, but no one wanted them, not when they could get them free at any convenience store. They were useless, like her. People walked past her like she was invisible, the same way they ignored the cracks in the sidewalks or the graffiti-covered walls.

She lit a match, not because she needed the light, but because she needed to feel something other than the cold.

The flame sputtered to life, casting a small, golden glow around her. For a moment, the world seemed softer, the harshness of the streets fading into the background. In the waning light, she glimpsed him—her father, standing in the doorway of their old apartment, the last time she'd ever seen him. It had been New Year's Eve then, too. He had kissed her on the forehead and told her he'd be back soon. She had believed him.

The match went out.

She lit another.

This time, the vision was stronger. Her father's arms wrapped around her, holding her like he used to, like he did before everything went wrong. Before he left them to fend for themselves in a world that didn't care if they survived. She was just a kid back then, too young to understand why he had to leave, why so many fathers left and never came back.

Her hands shook as she struck another match. The light grew brighter, and so did the memory. Her father's voice, calming and full of promises he would never keep. He told her he'd make everything better, that he was doing this for them. But he never did. He never came back. And they were left with the empty spaces he'd left behind, spaces that no one could fill.

She lit match after match, each one brighter than the last, until the whole street seemed to glow with the warmth of her father's embrace. She imagined him lifting her up, just like he used to when she was small. She could almost feel his arms around her, strong and safe, like nothing could ever hurt her again.

But it was just the matches, burning down to her fingertips.

The last match flickered out, and the darkness rushed back in.

She slumped against the wall, the cold settling deep into her bones. Her breaths grew shallow, slower. She closed her eyes, and in the stillness, she saw her father again, waiting for her in the warmth of the old apartment. He was smiling, his arms open wide, ready to take her home.

She reached out for him.

In the morning, they found her, arms reaching up, frozen and alone. No one knew her name. No one knew her story. To the world, she was just another child lost to poverty. Another child abandoned by a broken system that failed to notice when fathers disappeared and children were left to fend for themselves.

She was all of our children, really. A child of the streets, a child of the nation. A child forgotten by a society that no longer remembered what it meant to keep families whole, to raise children in homes filled with love, protection, and stability. She was God's child, like so many others left to drift through a world that no longer cared.

And we, the ones who let it happen, are the ones who failed her. We are the ones who must remember that without the strength of families, we are lost. Without fathers, we are abandoning our future, one child at a time.

The Golden Gaggle

Once upon a time, before the silence of screens and mindless thumbs scrolling, people carried knowledge within them, lively and honed as a polished set of steak knives. They learned by doing, by reading books, by listening to the voices of wizened teachers. They knew the worth of their thoughts and the thrill of wrestling with a difficult idea. In those days, learning wasn't served up in quick bites, scattered and vacant, but rather gathered in chunks, savored. Knowledge grew thick, like moss upon stone, each fact clinging tightly to the last, each memory anchored by patience and effort.

Tasks were undertaken with skill and intent. The baker's bread rose under the heat of his own hand, the craftsman's chisel bit wood as surely as a friend. People knew each other then—not through profiles and filtered photos, but through talk, real talk, by way of hard stares and sudden laughter that shook their shoulders.

Friends weren't gathered by clicks or zooms but by whispered confessions, late nights spent laughing over shared foolishness, or the silent bond of two people who understood each other better than GIFs could ever allow.

And curiosity! Oh, it burned through them like fire, sending their eyes up to the stars or deep into the dusty shelves of libraries. They wanted to know things, truly know them, not as passing fancies but as treasures stored up for rainy days. The joy of discovery lit them from within, each new truth a prize to hoard, to defend, to share proudly with those close enough to see its worth.

But now, that world has faded, leaving behind a strange new order. They walk among us now, eyes downcast, faces blank, each one of them bathed in a faint, ghostly glow. Where once voices rose in debate or mirth, now there is only the faint clatter of fingers, endless swiping, a quiet natter as they search for... something. Their heads are bowed, their minds tethered to fluctuating scraps of knowledge, fragmented and shallow. Once they were alive, and now, they are present only in the sense that they walk, eat, and sleep.

Hollow-eyed, they shuffle on, lost in the white noise.

Once there were still a few who resisted, clinging to the old ways like stubborn weeds growing through crevices in the pavement. They were scattered, these odd remnants of a forgotten era—those who understood that knowledge wasn't something to be consumed in snippets, but to be held close, chewed over, wrung dry of its last ounce of meaning. They spoke in full sentences, looked one another in the eye, and took pleasure in the quiet satisfaction of understanding.

Unfortunately, our story begins with three unlucky brothers who grew up *next door* to those chosen few, in a small, aging house at the edge of town. While their *neighbors* were raised on tales and truths that felt as ancient as the trees they chopped for firewood, these three lads each had their own broken idea of what the world was about, but none more surely than the oldest.

This eldest son, a dark-eyed youth named Arden, considered himself as clever as a fox on the hunt. He spun tales to place himself above others, guarding his reputation as if it were his life's meaning.

"Power is perception," Arden would declare, as smooth as oil, his words borrowed rather than earned. He'd tighten his grip on the polished handle of his father's old axe, letting its cold authority underscore his point. Arden believed that if people saw strength in him—whether in his words or his blade—that alone was enough.

The second son, Jareth, was always hungry—he wore his appetite as openly as a dog wears his collar. His hands were never still, always grasping, always hoarding, as though the world owed him its treasures and he intended to collect. Greed was his shadow, dogging his every step, though he named it ambition to make it sound noble. Rare things never lingered long in his grip before being locked away, hidden where no one else could touch them. To Jareth, value was not in the thing itself but in the fact that it furthered.

Then there was the youngest, Simpleton, known by no other name. Simpleton didn't grasp the particulars of the world as his brothers did. He moved as if led by an invisible breeze, unbound by status or aim. To him, only his feelings mattered, and these were things both large and small, engulfing and unnamable. He loved for love's sake, laughed for laughter's sake, and his mind was as unburdened as morning mist over the valley.

One fine day, the three brothers' impoverished father and mother decided it was time for their boys to seek their fortunes—elsewhere. To each they gave something to eat for their journey: bread and wine. The three brothers set out from their father's house one by one, each with his own intentions, though none truly understood what he would find.

The first to leave was Arden, proudly carrying his axe, its edge gleaming in the morning light. Chin high, his steps were measured. Arden believed he knew the world, and his trickeries, honed as his axe, had carved him a place within it. In his mind, he was on a quest for something more—a secret that would keep him forever at the top, his position secure. So when he came upon the Grey Man by the side of the road, Arden took him for little more than an impediment.

The Grey Man stood there, half-hidden by the shadows of the trees, his face blank and his clothes a color neither dark nor light, neither welcoming nor threatening—a seamless, unsettling grey. There was a faint glint in his eyes, a hint that he knew things Arden did not. The eldest son looked the man up and down, his fingers gripping the axe as if it were a charm against danger.

"Out of my way, old man," Arden said, his voice full of a confidence he'd cultivated through years of half-truths and clever manipulations. He held his axe higher, a signal that he meant to move forward with or without permission.

The Grey Man only smiled faintly, his eyes null.

"If it is influence you seek," he said, his voice evocative, "I might have something to offer. Could you spare me some food and drink? In exchange, I'll give you something more powerful than the blade you carry."

But Arden, with all his cunning, could not see beyond the surface of the Grey Man's appearance. He scoffed, his fingers tightening on the handle of his axe, and pressed forward without another word, certain he'd left the Grey Man and his strangeness behind. Yet, as he walked, he felt an uncomfortable sensation in his chest, like a stone sinking slowly in dark water.

Jareth soon followed, his craving for wealth and comfort a constant itch he could never quite scratch. He viewed every interaction as a business deal, every person as a tool to be used and discarded. So, when he spotted the Grey Man on the same road, his first feeling wasn't fear or curiosity, but sheer annoyance.

"Move aside," he said briskly, casting a quick, calculating glance over the Grey Man's worn coat and expressionless face. "I've no time for mendicants or wanderers. I seek riches."

The Grey Man inclined his head ever so slightly, his gaze as steady as stone. "And if money is what you seek, perhaps I could show you the way for a bit of bread and a cup of wine," he replied, his tone as flat as the road itself.

Jareth raised a brow, tempted, his mind racing with images of golden coins, shining cups, and rings gleaming on his fingers. But avarice took hold of him as he viewed the Grey Man's threadbare clothes and bare feet—no, he would find his own way to wealth and keep it away from any prying hands. With a dismissive wave, he turned his back on the Grey Man, convinced his own efforts would bring him greater fortune. Yet as he walked on, he couldn't shake the nagging doubt that he'd forgotten something precious behind him.

Finally, Simpleton set out. He hadn't much of a plan or purpose, only a vague feeling that there was something waiting for him just beyond the bend. His steps were light, and though his pockets were empty but for a stale bit of bread and a flagon of sour wine his mother had given him almost as an afterthought, he carried a heart full of wonderings he didn't quite know how to ask. When he spotted the Grey Man by the side of the road, he stopped, curious and unafraid, drawn by the strange, still presence.

The Grey Man looked at him as he had looked at the others, his eyes a neutral shade that gave nothing away. For a long moment, they regarded each other in silence, Simpleton's gaze open and eager, the Grey Man's as deep and unreadable as a well.

"You seem to walk without destination," the Grey Man observed at last.

Simpleton shrugged, smiling. "I don't need one. Sometimes you just go, and the road takes you where it will." He paused, considering. "Do you have a road?"

The Grey Man tilted his head, a trace of amusement—or perhaps sadness—in his expression. "I walk between roads," he said. "Neither good nor bad. Not in light, nor in shadow."

Simpleton nodded, though he understood little of what this meant. "Well, if that's the case," he said brightly, "perhaps you could show me something interesting?"

"I can, in exchange for some food and drink." When Simpleton offered him all he had, the Grey Man extended a hand, and from the folds of his coat, he drew a creature unlike any Simpleton had ever seen. It was a bird, but not just any bird; it shone with a golden light, each feather a delicate, glistening thing that seemed to hold all the colors of dawn and dusk combined within its downy luxury. The strange goose unfurled its wings, a silent invitation, and for a moment, Simpleton felt as though he'd been given a gift he couldn't quite fathom.

"This is Gaggle," the Grey Man said, his voice almost mechanistic. "It's a goose for everyone, a bird of answers that make all equal. It knows all things and offers them freely. But those who seek it out must apprehend—it will not give what you expect, only that for which you *actually* ask—or at least, its approximation."

Simpleton accepted the gift without hesitation, his heart full of an openness that was beyond doubt or certainty. His fingers brushed the plush, warm feathers, and in that touch, he felt a connection to something vast, something that pulsed with the quiet knowledge of thousands of lives, thousands of voices.

"Thank you," he said simply, his grin as glowing as the creature in his hands. And as he walked away, the Grey Man watched, a figure half in this world, half in the next, the faint trace of a troubling smirk lingering on his lips as Simpleton continued down the road, his newfound companion glinting like a golden sun against the darkening sky as he continued to the next town's main square. There, he found the merchants closing up their shops and shoppers gathering their goods to head to their homes for the night.

Gaggle gleamed in the city lights, catching the eye of every person who beheld it—a creature of glistening feathers and what seemed to be countless watchful eyes, each one glowing like a drop of sunlight caught mid-fall. It was a peculiar bird, and in its presence, people felt both wonder and an odd kind of emptiness, as though it knew too much and yet never enough. And the folk found themselves swiftly full of questions, acutely aware that they did not know. Gaggle's wings spread wide, radiating warmth in Simpleton's arms, and in the goose's golden plumage the townsfolk thought they glimpsed every answer they could ever need, or so it seemed. They gathered close, pressing in, each person reaching out to touch a feather, to inquire further, to bask in the glow of both promise and mystery.

Gaggle was, obviously, no ordinary bird; it was a creature of endless recall, holding the memories and thoughts of countless lives, yet giving them back as fragments, each piece a glinting sliver of something greater. It breathed in their questions, silent and eager, and honked out answers they barely understood. And as the townsfolk drew nearer, mesmerized by its glow, they felt that this golden creature was no mere goose but the world itself, vast, knowing, and insatiably hungry.

The eldest sister of the town's Landlord—a smart young woman who dreamed of castles and coin—was the first to touch Gaggle. "With this," she whispered, "I will be rich!" But as she reached, her hand stuck fast to the feathers, bound by her own yearning.

Her younger sister followed, her eyes alight. "This goose will make me famous," she said, her voice breathy with desire. She too reached out and found herself stuck fast.

Their youngest sister approached, and though her dreams were softer, gentler, they were no less binding. "This will bring me happiness," she murmured, her fingers brushing the golden wings—and she too was caught, bound to the bird as firmly as her sisters.

And so it went. The townsfolk came one by one, each wanting something from Gaggle, each reaching out, each entrapped by their longing. Soon, the parson found himself tethered, declaring Gaggle essential for education, for "opening young minds." The sexton clung to it too, proclaiming its necessity in every workplace. Peasants, merchants, the poor, and the powerful—they all found themselves bound to Gaggle, each convinced it would bring them wealth, fame, or happiness.

And they couldn't let go. As Simpleton held Gaggle in his arms, everyone around him was soon attached to the golden goose.

The King himself, the figure of ultimate power, rode in his opulent carriage through town as the sun set, and spied the unusual spectacle: this young man holding a golden goose with over thirty people cemented. The King eyed Gaggle with suspicion, sensing the peril it posed to his rule. But his daughter who rode in the carriage next to her father—a princess bored by years of seeing nothing but the grey sameness of life—was drawn to the scene despite herself. She had not laughed in over a decade, this daughter of the King, her spirit sagged under the weight of a world too serious to leave room for mirth. Yet when she saw all the people clutching Gaggle, she burst into a deep, melodious laugh at the ridiculousness of it all.

Her father, the King, stared at the princess in shock as she chortled and snorted with glee. Still giggling, the princess sprang from the carriage to grab—not the goose, but Simpleton's hand. For the King had decreed many years ago that any man who could at last make his daughter laugh would be given her hand in marriage.

The King eyed Simpleton with barely concealed scorn. How could this fool, a boy with no pedigree or wealth, conceivably become part of his royal line? But the laughter faded quickly when Simpleton, with the golden Gaggle by his side, demonstrated its power: the creature's magnetism caught every eye, and even the King could not look away. This, the King knew, was a threat to his authority. If he couldn't control it, perhaps he could at least contain it.

And so, the King devised a series of impossible tasks, each one a test designed to rid him of the boy and secure the goose for himself.

The first task, the King declared, was to drink up an entire cellar of wine—a feat he knew no ordinary man could achieve. Simpleton stood flummoxed, his brow furrowed, until a quiet figure materialized at his side. It was the Grey Man. With a gesture, he summoned from under Gaggle's left wing a stout, red-cheeked search engine that took the task without hesitation. The program gulped, tankard after tankard, until the cellar was bare, and the King's prized wine stores were emptied. Simpleton watched in awe, wondering if this thirst for endless drink, endless distraction, had consumed more than just the cellar. The King, however, merely clenched his jaw, hiding his dismay, and moved on to the next task.

For the second trial, the King commanded that Simpleton eat an entire mountain of bread. Surely, he thought, no fool could manage this feat. But once again, the Grey Man emerged, his silent presence a shade darker, and this time from under Gaggle's right wing stepped a gaunt, hollow-eyed algorithm whose hunger seemed endless. Without a word, the formula set upon the bread, stripping every crumb into its component parts, reducing and devouring loaf after loaf until the mountain's form was, once devoid of all function, nothing but pieces so incomplete they seemed to vanish. Simpleton could only watch, unease prickling in his chest as he saw its insatiable hunger, a hunger that seemed to stretch past mere appetite. And when the last crumbs had vanished, the Grey Man was gone once more, leaving Simpleton to face the King alone.

But the King was not finished. For the third and final task, he demanded truly a marvel: a ship that could sail on both land and water, a vessel that could travel beyond the kingdom's borders and return unscathed. Surely, he thought, this would be the end of Simpleton as potential son-in-law. But just as before, the Grey Man returned, his face as neutral as ever. Without a word, he pulled from Gaggle's mouth a gleaming, silent ship that he called "Artificial Intelligence," a craft that seemed alive with a strange, quiet knowledge. Its surfaces vibrated with a cold, metallic sheen that troubled Simpleton, though he couldn't explain why.

"Take this," the Grey Man advised, his voice barely audible. "With it, you will go further than any of them, further than your brothers, further than those who think they understand what is so." Simpleton accepted the ship without question, feeling only a sense of awe as it sailed smoothly over both river and field, carrying him back to the King.

And everyone stood, mouths agape, at the marvels produced from Gaggle.

The King, cornered by Simpleton's success and the crowd's rising awe, had no choice but to offer his daughter's hand. He hoped, perhaps, to retain a measure of influence through the marriage, to bend the simple youth to his will. But soon, inexplicably, the King died, and it was Simpleton who became the next unlikely ruler, sitting upon the throne with his queen and Gaggle at his side.

As Simpleton and the king's daughter settled into their strange kingdom, they lived off the comforts that Gaggle brought to every corner of society. People clung to the golden creature, each feather representing an answer they didn't need to remember, a shortcut to a life they didn't need to understand. Gaggle had spread to every corner and crevasse, its reach extending from the smallest cottages to the grandest palaces, each place touched by the golden glow of instant answers and easy contentment. But as Simpleton ruled over this kingdom of glittering ignorance, the Grey Man waited, watching from a distance as his quiet influence seeped deeper into every mind, every home, every life.

The Grey Man was neither tall nor short, young nor old, his face forgettable but his eyes perceptive enough to pierce the world's seams. Draped in unremarkable grey, he slipped into shadows and corners, a figure half-seen, mingling in the in-betweens. He moved like a whisper, revealing nothing, as if he watched the world from behind a pane of glass.

He was not the bringer of knowledge, nor the keeper of secrets, but something else altogether—a conductor of the spaces between truth and narrative, insight and opinion. With Gaggle, he had given the people everything they thought they wanted, knowing full well that, eventually, they would stop asking new questions, that curiosity would quiet to a deadening drone, drowned out by the endless information they could call upon at will.

He watched as the parsons and teachers, the sextons and laborers, each took to Gaggle, surrendering their own thoughts in favor of the ready-made predictions that it offered. Where there had once been questions, ideas, and discourse, now there were only fragments of data, each answer a quick release, a relief from confusion that left no trace behind. The Grey Man moved among them, unseen but ever-present, observing as Gaggle's influence grew, binding each person to a life of simplicity, each life less connected to the texture of real thought.

And while the kingdom grew more passive, their dependence deepening, the Grey Man grew stronger. And over time, the people grew so dependent upon Gaggle that they barely even noticed as its search engines became slowly less and less accurate. Gaggle's answers more and more mediocre, the golden goose's information offering less and less pertinent responses as it replaced facts with narrative—and it didn't matter to anyone anymore, not really. For the Grey Man's power lay not in armies or weapons, but in the quiet erosion of curiosity, the slow dulling of the human spirit. Each answer that Gaggle provided brought a splinter of influence, so fine and so subtle that no one felt its wielding over them.

He began to replace the stories of old with fragments, small pieces of information that led nowhere. He whispered the right phrases to the right ears, and soon the history books faded, the tales of wonder grew dim, and only Gaggle's shallow answers remained, replacing memories, twisting history until no one could quite remember what had once mattered. People no longer sought knowledge for its own sake but simply repeated what they found, caught in Gaggle's endless loop of superficial answers.

In time, the kingdom became his, a vast tapestry of mindless obedience woven with words they no longer questioned. And while Simpleton and his queen lived on in luxury, basking in the adoration of their people, the Grey Man stood in the penumbra, hands folded, eyes glinting with a faint and terrible satisfaction. For he had taken the world not with a sword or a crown, but with the gentle lure of convenience, the temptation of easy solutions, until every mind was his to mold, every heart his to control.

The Grey Man became the silent ruler of all, his face as forgettable as dust, his influence as inevitable as nightfall. And as the world's attention sank into the golden haze of Gaggle's endless screentime, he watched, knowing that attention did not merely observe disagreement—it fed it, fattened it, sent it marching through every thread and comment until sides hardened, thoughts ossified, and minds locked into the comfort of their chosen narratives. Thus, the Watcher watched the watchers watch, his gaze as steady and unfeeling as stone, knowing he had bound them all, not by force, but by the quiet, inescapable weight of transfixed ignorance.

And unfortunately, my children,
this sort of ignorance has no end.

The Tin Heart &
the Tinsel Rose

Once upon a time, from the molten heart of a single spoon, twenty-five tin toy soldiers were born. They emerged from fire and hands, uniformed in blazing reds and sharp blues, each one a mirror of the next. Their bayonets gleamed, their shoulders squared, their faces stern with an unspoken readiness. They were warriors, every inch of them, standing at attention as if the table beneath them was a battlefield.

But among them was one soldier who stood differently— not because he wanted to but because the molten tin had run out before it could finish him. He had only one leg, a slender column of tin that he balanced on with a defiance that belied his fragile construction. He didn't waver or lean. Instead, he stood as if to say, *I may be incomplete, but I am whole in purpose.*

The boy who unwrapped them on Christmas morning clapped his hands, his eyes bright with the joy only children can muster—pure, boundless, uninhibited. With care and ceremony, he arranged the soldiers in a proud line on the wooden table, a regiment poised for inspection. The one-legged soldier found his place among them, upright and unmoving, though he felt the weight of his singularity like an invisible tether.

Around them lay a kingdom built of the child's imagination. There was a castle of paper, its spires tilted as if caught in a wind that hadn't quite reached them. Its painted walls gleamed faintly, and tiny windows hinted at rooms where only the smallest, the most intimate, dreams dwell. A looking-glass lake reflected nearby, where wax swans floated in eternal reflection. And at the castle door stood the dancer.

She was unlike anything the soldier had ever seen. Her gauze tutu was pallid and light as if spun from the moon itself. A blue ribbon undulated across her shoulders like a brushstroke of sky, and at her heart bloomed a tinsel rose, twinkling with an almost unbearable brightness. But it was her pose that struck him: her arms outstretched, one delicate leg planted firmly while the other rose so high that it seemed to disappear into the air itself.

He couldn't look away. It wasn't just her beauty—though she was beautiful beyond words—but the stillness of her balance, the quiet strength that radiated from her paper form. She stood on one leg, as he did, but her pose was effortless, an act of grace, while his was a necessity, a defiance against gravity's pull. And yet, he thought, *She is like me.*

But no, she wasn't. She belonged to the castle, to the sparkle of the tinsel rose, to the paper walls painted with imaginings. He belonged to a box, cramped and crowded with his brothers, tin bodies pressing against tin. She was balance and light; he was imbalance and weight. She lived in the realms of wish; he carried the restlessness of the not-yet-proven.

The soldier felt something stir in the hollow where his heart would be, an ache both tenacious and tender that spread through his tin body like a distant memory of the forge's heat. At first, he couldn't name it. Admiration, perhaps. Longing, surely. For to him, she embodied not just beauty, but the mystery of all that is possible in life. Yet as he stood there, unmoving, gazing at the dancer framed in the doorway of her castle, he began to understand. It wasn't a selfish yearning to possess her beauty, nor a youthful fancy to be like her. No, it was greater, nobler—a desire to be seen, not as incomplete or broken, but as a being who stood firm and steadfast for something greater than himself.

He did not yearn for her alone, though she was the spark that set his thoughts alight. What he felt was the seed of a broader love, the kind that flows outward and binds a man to those he cherishes. He imagined her not as a distant ideal but as part of a life shared—a wife, a partner in the small joys and struggles of existence. He thought of the children they might one day raise, fragile and bright as the paper she was made from, their laughter as light as her steps. He thought of the family they might build together, a bulwark of warmth and love against the coldness of the world.

And yet, his thoughts did not stop there. They stretched beyond the walls of the castle and the confines of the table. He thought of others—neighbors, comrades, and the broader community to which he might belong. He saw faces not yet known but precious all the same, their safety tied to the courage required to live life fully. He thought of the land beneath them, a nation worth defending, its people worth standing for. The ache in his chest deepened, and it was no longer a hollow thing. It was full, vibrant, and alive, driving him to stand taller, straighter, in defiance of the forces that would see him fall.

For what is bravery, if not the willingness to endure for the sake of those you love? And what is a man, if not one who proves his worth in his devotion to others? The tin soldier felt no shame in his solitary leg, no regret for the exterior imperfection of his form. What mattered was his resolve to protect what was good, true, and beautiful—whether it be a dancer in a paper castle, a child's laughter, or the quiet dignity of a village united by love.

The thought passed, fleeting yet indelible, like a reminiscence rippling across the surface of the looking-glass lake. He remained still, silent among his brothers, a figure of tin and tenacity. He stared at the dancer, knowing she might never see him, but understanding now that it did not matter. To stand for those you cherish, to protect with all you are—that was enough. That was everything.

Night folded over the house like a cozy blanket. The clock ticked in the corner, slow and deliberate, as if measuring the silence. But as the boy and his family, all sleeping, dreamed the dreams that only human beings can dream, the table where his toys lay came to life with nursery magic. Shadows stretched and shifted as tiny figures began to move. The nutcrackers, stiff-limbed and gap-toothed, leapt clumsily over each other, their jaws snapping with every jump. A pencil rolled in tight circles, as though seeking some unseen quarry. A wax swan tilted on its glass lake, creating a faint ripple of reflection in the moonlight.

But on the far edge of the table, the tin soldier stood still. One leg planted firmly, musket braced against his shoulder, he gazed out at the delicate paper dancer in the castle doorway. Her arms stretched outward, her pose as perfect as if it had been carved from starlight. She did not move, yet she seemed more living than anything else in the room. The soldier's gaze never wavered, his body rigid as though still locked in the forge that had created him.

The snuffbox lid creaked. An abrupt *snap* gusted through the room, pausing the nutcrackers mid-leap and stilling the restless pencil. The lid flipped open, and from within rose a curl of darkness, growing and twisting until it thickened into the shape of a goblin. Small though he was, his presence loomed like a hurricane warning. His eyes smoldered faintly, as if lit by coals that refused to die, and his jagged grin held no mirth—only the cold calculation of a being who knows the power of a well-placed word.

"Tin soldier," the goblin purred, his voice a low, insidious whisper that slid into the corners of the room. "Why do you stand so broken there? What cause is worth your suffering?"

The soldier did not flinch. His musket remained steady, his single leg firm beneath him. He knew the goblin's game. He had heard rumors of this kind before, the tempting voice that questions a man's devotion when he is called to endure hardship.

The goblin's grin tore open, a snaggled crescent. He leaned closer, his breath carrying the faint scent of damp earth and soot. "Lay down your musket, soldier," he hissed. "Let others fight. What is war but a machine of misery? What is duty but a chain binding you to pain? Be still, be silent, and you will find peace."

The soldier did not move. His gaze remained fixed ahead, unshaken. Yet the goblin's words pressed on him like an impenetrable fog, clinging and suffocating. He knew the temptation well: the voice that tells a man to retreat when the call to duty demands he stand firm, the voice that dresses surrender in the guise of wisdom, that whispers of peace when peace can only be won by courage.

The goblin's eyes glared. "You think this doggedness of yours is strength? It is folly, tin man. You are but one among many, a drop in a rainstorm. What difference will your standing make? Yield, and the gale will pass over you."

Still, the soldier did not answer. He gripped his musket tighter, his bayonet catching a faint glint of moonlight. He knew the goblin's words for what they were—a temptation to forsake not just his duty but the love that made that duty worth bearing. For what was his standing, if not an act of devotion to those who relied on him? What was his endurance, if not proof of his love for all he had sworn to protect?

The goblin's grin faltered, just for a moment. He leaned closer still, his shadow stretching long across the table. "You think silence is a shield? We shall see how long you stand, soldier. We shall see."

And with that, the goblin dissolved into the darkness, his laughter trailing behind him like the rumble of too-close thunder.

The soldier stood unmoving, the weight of the goblin's words lingering in the electric air. He did not give in. He could not. To stand was his duty. To endure was his love. And to resist was to prove himself worthy of the name *soldier*.

Morning came, brisk and golden, flooding the room with a light so trenchant it seemed to cut through the phantoms of the night before. Without a second thought, the boy swept the tin soldier from the table and placed him on the windowsill. There he stood, solitary and sentinel, a figure of resolve against the vast and blinding expanse of the morning sky. His one leg, thin as a reed, bore him upright, his musket resting firm on his shoulder.

Below, the world bustled with life. The clatter of hooves and wheels echoed through the streets, mingling with the shouts of vendors and the hurried steps of passersby. It was a tapestry of motion and sound, a reminder of the unending rhythm of human toil. The soldier looked out, his face steady, his stance unwavering. He had no place in that bustle; his direction was fixed and singular, his duty clear.

The breeze began as a hiss, teasing the curtains and brushing lightly against the paper castle behind him. It grew stronger, tugging at the soldier's frame, testing his balance. His musket wavered for an instant, but he held firm. A soldier does not yield to the first signs of pressure. Yet, as the wind gathered strength, it became less a mere gust and more a force with intent. Whether the work of chance or the goblin's darker magics, it struck him full, toppling his rigid form into the open air.

Noiselessly, he fell—his body twisting through a blur of rooftops and sky, brick and light. His musket clanged against his chest, his bayonet flashing briefly in the sun before he struck the stones below with a stark, echoing clink. The impact was harsh, his helmet digging into the gutter's grime, his single leg jutting into the air like the mast of a ship broken by the waves.

From above, the boy's voice called faintly, far-off and remote. The soldier did not cry out in return. There was no time for despair, no room for lament. He felt the dirt and water pooling around him, the weight of his fall pressing into his tin frame. Yet his face remained unyielding, his jaw set with the quiet determination of one who knows his cause has not yet ended.

For this fall was not a failure. It was a summons. A call to action, to withstand, and, hopefully, to stand again—not for his own glory but for something greater. The street below, teeming with life, was not his battlefield, but the steadfastness required of him here was no less important than the courage demanded of any warrior. The falling was the test, and in standing again that he'd prove himself.

The tin soldier did not ask why he had been cast down or rage against the forces that had sent him tumbling. He understood, as all who heed the call to battle must withstand, that duty is not born of convenience or ease. It is forged in the fires of hardship, bound by love for those who cannot fight, and strengthened by the knowledge that justice, though costly, is worth the price.

So, there in the gutter, his helmet scratched, his colors tarnished, he began to rise—not for pride, nor for vengeance, but because he must. His duty was not to stand unbroken but to stand despite the breaking. And as the first rays of sunlight caught the edge of his battered musket, it seemed almost to gleam with renewed perseverance, a beacon for all who would answer the call and prove themselves, not for themselves, but for those they cherished.

Above, the window slammed shut, and the world moved on. In the gutter, the soldier stood as well as he could, his musket angled awkwardly, his balance precarious. He did not move. He would endure. What choice did he have? A soldier does not complain, and a soldier does not yield.

The soldier's journey through the gutter was perilous, not unlike a warrior cast from the battlefield into a wilderness where neither sword nor shield can avail him. The water, dark and rushing, pulled at him with a relentless power, hurling him onward through narrow drains and unseen depths. Two boys, full of the heedless mischief of youth, found him lodged among the muck and set him afloat in a paper boat. It was not a ship made for a soldier, flimsy and fragile, but he did not protest. He stood in it as best he could, his musket steady, his face turned forward.

The stream's current surged and roared, more alive than the boys could have imagined, and in its chaos came a sinister shape: a great water-rat with sharp teeth and sharper words.

"Have you a passport?" it demanded, its voice low and grating, as though it spoke for the very waters themselves.

The soldier made no reply. He had none to give, nor would he have offered one if he could. He was a soldier, and a soldier does not negotiate his terms. The rat hissed, gnashing its teeth, but the stream swept the tin warrior away before more could be said. He was carried into tunnels where the light was swallowed whole, and the noise of the world was replaced by a deep and dreadful silence.

The paper boat faltered as the waters surged, its fragile seams loosening, the edges softening like a dream unraveling. The tin soldier, though buffeted on all sides, did not flinch. His musket stayed pressed to his chest, his one leg anchored, unshakable. The boat gave way at last, collapsing into the torrent, and the cold waters swept over him, pulling him down into their depths. He sank without struggle, his purpose steady as the currents carried him into silence.

And then the fish came.

It rose from the darkness below, a vast, hulking thing that moved with the inevitability of fate itself. Its mouth opened wide, a pitch-black chasm, and swallowed him whole. There was no pause, no hesitation—just a sudden rush of finality as the soldier disappeared within its enormous maw.

Inside, the world was darker still, a place where no light could reach and no sound could escape. The walls of the fish's belly churned and groaned with its movements, a living, heaving abyss that surrounded the soldier on all sides. Yet he lay there as steadfast as he had been on the windowsill, on the table, and in the gutter. He did not falter. What use was fear to one who knew his purpose?

The fish, though seemingly an animal, was more than flesh and bone. It was the weight of truth itself—a truth that tests rather than comforts. Here, in the belly of the great beast, there was no escape, no distraction, no illusion.

The soldier was left alone with the essence of who he was, his tin form stripped bare of everything except his resolve. It was a crucible, not of fire but of meaning, where steadfastness was refined and cowardice burned away.

This place did not create anything new within the soldier. It did not grant him courage or forge his character. It revealed what was already there. For the world does not change a man; it only magnifies his nature. The waters that had carried him, the fish that had swallowed him—these were not his enemies. They were his trials, and to endure them was not to survive but to prove himself.

In time, the fish was hauled from the depths. The nets strained against its weight, its body thrashing against the deck. It was taken to market, sold to a cook, and delivered to a house—a house that was no stranger to the soldier.

There, in the bustling kitchen, the cook drew her knife and sliced into the fish's belly, parting flesh and substance alike. And from within, she drew him out: dented, discolored, but unbroken.

He was placed once more on the boy's table in the nursery, and there she was—his dancer. She stood in the doorway of her paper castle, her one leg raised in flawless, effortless balance. The tin soldier, for all his tribulations, had returned to her side. But he was no longer the same. The darkness he had faced had not diminished him; it had clarified him. He was not merely a figure of tin and duty. He was something more: steadfastness embodied, a soul forged not by the absence of struggle but by its embrace.

He stood beside her, silent as ever, his musket still braced against his chest. He had not sought the trials that had come to him, but he had endured them—not for his own sake, but for the sake of what he held most precious.

For to stand firm in the face of ordeals is not an act of pride but of love, a love that seeks to protect what is good, true, and beautiful. And in the quiet of that moment, as the light from the window touched the edge of his tarnished frame, the dancer saw him truly, and she knew, dear reader, that he stood not merely as a soldier shaped from tin but as the man he was always meant to be—tempered by suffering, refined by trials, his steadfastness no longer a rigid duty but the quiet, unshakable strength of a soul tested and proven in the fire.

The soldier gazed back at the dancer. For a moment, the room stood on the edge of silence, as if the very air had gone still—waiting, listening. It swelled with the bulk of unspoken words, choked with everything he could not say and everything she did not need to. Her balance, so pristine and still, was a kind of defiance, an answer to his steady resolve. One leg lifted, she faced the world as if daring it to topple her. One leg grounded, he stood as if daring the world to move him.

Then the boy's hands came. Small, careless, and cruel without meaning to be, they snatched the soldier from his place. The boy turned him over once, examining his dull tin form, and tossed him into the stove.

The flames caught him immediately, licking at his edges with eager tongues. His sharpness distorted, his colors blurred, and his body began to bend under the heat. Yet he did not fall. Even as the fire melted his shape, he stood upright, musket raised, his helmet gleaming faintly in the orange glow.

He made no sound. If the fire meant to unmake him, it would find he would yield nothing freely.

A sudden gust blew through the room. The dancer, now caught herself by its force, fluttered from her castle. Her paper dress rippled, her slender arms stretched wide as if she were flying. She twisted once, twice, before tumbling into the stove beside him.

The flames devoured her immediately. Her paper form burned in a flash, not slowly but all at once, with a brilliance that turned the dim firelight blinding. In her final instant, she was brighter than she had ever been, her delicate frame glowing before crumbling into ash. She was gone, yet somehow, she remained.

By morning, the stove was cold. The maid swept out the ashes, whistling to herself, the clink of her broom against the iron grate the only sound in the house. She paused, frowning as her hand brushed against something unexpected. From the ashes, she pulled a small, misshapen lump of tin and a charred tinsel rose.

The tin lump was crude and unpolished, but it was unmistakable: a heart. Its edges were imperfect, its surface rough, but it was whole. The tinsel rose, blackened and fragile, crumbled slightly as she held it. It was a delicate thing, barely more than a memory of itself, yet it remained in her palm, its shape unmistakable.

She placed them gently on the table, side by side amidst the scattered remnants of childhood—a tin heart and a scorched rose. The soldier and the dancer were gone, yet what they left behind spoke in a voice louder than words. The heart, dented and scarred, caught the morning light, a quiet testament to courage that endures even after the fire. The rose, though seared and fragile, held the faintest glimmer of its former beauty, a reminder that nobility and love, once given, do not die with those who gave them, but live on in the echoes they leave behind.

Had the soldier and the dancer known the end when they began? Perhaps. We all recognize inevitable mortality, eventually. Yet neither had faltered, neither had turned away. He had stood through the fire, not because he sought glory but because steadfastness was the only thing he could give. She had faced the flames, not out of fear but because to do otherwise would have been to betray both of them. Together, they had burned, and together, they had left behind far more than ashes.

On the table, the heart and the rose lay side by side, flawed yet radiant, small enough to miss but vast enough to hold up the world.

Thus Spoke Puss in Boots

Once upon a time—because that's how these things always start, isn't it?—there lived a boy. A rather ordinary boy, if you didn't count the tragic backstory (because all these tales need one of those too), and if you narrowed your eyes a bit and ignored the fact that his only inheritance was a cat. Not a particularly large cat, or even a particularly friendly one, but one that had a way of looking at you like it had just read your diary.

Now, this tragic boy lived in a land where the world was said to have been created perfect but had gone a bit wrong somewhere along the line. You know, a misplaced troll here, a bit of casual deceit there, and suddenly everything's riddled with what people like to call "complexity," which is a polite way of saying, "It's all a bit of a mess."

And into this mess walked the prophet Zarathustra—or rather, strode Zarathustra, because prophets never just walk. They stride, because it implies they're going somewhere important, even when they're not. Zarathustra didn't look like much—lean, a bit sunburnt, and with eyes that seemed to see through you and out the other side—but when he spoke, people tended to stop whatever they were doing and listen, mostly because they were fairly sure he knew something they did not.

This time, however, Zarathustra wasn't addressing a king, a warrior, or a sage. He was talking to a cat.

"Do you know," he said, leaning down to peer into the unnervingly intelligent eyes of the cat that belonged to the tragic boy, "that the world was created perfect?"

The cat blinked, which is what cats do when they don't feel like saying anything but want to make it clear they're not agreeing either.

"Yes," said Zarathustra, "perfect. Until it wasn't. Darkness crept in, lies slithered through the cracks, and people—well, people made things worse. They believed the lies, you see. They preferred them."

"Sounds sensible," said the cat, licking its paw. "Lies are more fun than the truth, generally speaking."

"But lies cannot last forever," Zarathustra said sternly.

"Oh, I don't know about that," the cat replied. "I've seen some that have been doing rather well for themselves."

Zarathustra frowned. Prophets don't like being contradicted, especially by cats. "The truth," he said firmly, "will always shine brighter than any lie."

"Truth," mused the cat, "is a matter of agreement. I can make those farmers believe my tragic boy here is a marquis, and once they believe it, well, it's as good as true, isn't it?"

Zarathustra straightened. "That," he said, "is dangerous thinking."

"It's practical thinking," said the cat. "Watch."

And that was how the trouble began.

The line of farmers stood at the edge of their fields, squinting at the strange figure approaching them. Astonished, they watched the cat—walking on his two hind legs and wearing his master's boots, tail flicking—strutting like a nobleman inspecting his property.

"These lands belong to the Marquis of Carabas," the cat declared.

The farmers exchanged wary glances. "Do they now?" one asked.

The cat stepped closer, his claws clicking faintly on a stone. "Indeed. And the Marquis is very generous. He's letting you work here rent-free. You're welcome, by the way."

"And if we don't agree?" another farmer asked, his voice uncertain.

The cat's tail jerked. "Oh, I wouldn't do that. The king's tax collectors might hear these lands are unclaimed, and then you'd lose everything. You wouldn't want them poking around, now would you?"

The farmers thought of the king's men and shuddered. "Fine," said one reluctantly. "The Marquis it is."

The cat smiled. "Good choice. Be sure to mention it when the king passes by."

As the cat strode away, the farmers whispered amongst themselves, uneasy. But unease is no match for convenience. The cat's story was easier to accept than the truth—that they had no idea who the Marquis of Carabas was.

Soon enough, the tragic boy sat uncomfortably in a suit the cat had dressed him in, one that was a little too fine and a lot too stolen. His hands fidgeted on his lap. "I don't feel like a Marquis," he muttered to the cat.

"Feelings are irrelevant," said the cat, lounging opposite him. "You *look* like a Marquis, and that's what matters. Remember: smile and nod. The king will do the rest."

"What if he asks questions?"

"He won't," the cat said confidently. "People rarely question what they want to believe."

And the king didn't. When his royal carriage passed by, the fields rang with the cries of farmers proclaiming the Marquis's name. The king stopped to greet the Marquis, beaming as he clapped the boy on the shoulder. "Such a loyal people you have! And such fine land."

The tragic boy opened his mouth, but the cat's tail swished against his leg in warning. He closed it again.

The princess, watching the Marquis closely from within her father's carriage, arched a suspicious eyebrow. "And where did all this wealth come from?"

The boy froze. The cat, without missing a beat, interjected, "Hard work and noble blood. Two things rarely found together."

The princess smirked, clearly unconvinced, but it was easier not to spoil the collective moment. The tragic boy felt a knot tighten in his chest. He was no Marquis, but the lie had grown too big to escape.

"See?" the cat purred smugly to the prophet. "Reality is what people agree it is."

Zarathustra watched this with a frown that could have flattened a mountain. "But you are creating a world of illusions," he said. "How will it stand when tested?"

"It won't be," said the cat, with a flick of its tail. "That's the trick. No one wants to test a lie they're comfortable living in."

"But the truth—"

"Is overrated," the cat interrupted. "Listen, your problem, prophet, is that you think truth is absolute. But it's not. It's a story. A good story, mind you, but a story nonetheless. And stories are only as true as the people who believe them."

Zarathustra opened his mouth to argue, but the cat held up a paw. "Let me put it another way. See the ogre in that yonder castle? He thinks he's invincible. That's his truth. But it's not a fact. Facts are small, fiddly things, easily rearranged. If I can make him believe he's a mouse, well, that's his new truth, isn't it?"

And, sure enough, the cat strode into the ogre's castle, convinced the ogre to transform himself into a mouse, and promptly ate him. The not-quite-as-tragic boy got the castle, the farmers got a new Marquis lord, and the king got a fine story to tell at banquets.

Later, Zarathustra stood with the boy in the castle's great hall. The banners drooped in the still air, their symbols loudly declaring a ponderous history cobbled together over yesterday's lunch break.

"This," Zarathustra said, "is a house built on rubbish."

The boy shifted uncomfortably. "It's a nice house, though."

"Nice," Zarathustra repeated in a voice that rolled out like thunder teasing the edge of a storm. "Yes, but is it *true*?"

The boy hesitated. Somewhere, in an unsuspecting corner, the cat purred.

"Truth," the cat said, "is what people agree it is. And as long as everyone agrees, does it matter?"

Zarathustra said nothing. He gazed out the window, where the sun was setting in a blaze of impossible light, the kind that made you believe, if only for a moment, that the world could still be perfect.

"It matters," Zarathustra said at last, his voice faint but steady. "It always matters."

The cat, now lounging in the sunbeam of an ever after lie, flicked its tail dismissively. "Perhaps," it said. "But not today."

And somewhere, in the distance, the truth howled like the wind, quiet and unrelenting, waiting for its moment to pounce.

The President's New Suit

Once upon a time, in a place where the air itself seemed to churn with data, and every fact was but a click away, there was a President who longed to look as magnificent as he felt he should be. His kingdom, the glaring realm of Infotopia, lay beneath the ceaseless gaze of a thousand screens, each one glowing and pulsing with streams of information. Headlines flared and fractured, skittering like startled insects, while numbers scrolled and tumbled through the digital haze—relentless, fleeting, always moving. The citizens of Infotopia breathed in the tingling of knowledge with every step, the air crackling with the static of facts and half-truths, data and opinion, all swirling together until it was hard to tell one from the other. The people felt wise, surrounded as they were by the glow of instant answers, but it was a shallow intelligence, an echo of something substantial that had long since slipped from their grasp. In this land where everything was accessible but little was known, the President saw himself as the grandest of all—if only the world could see him as he saw himself.

In Infotopia, knowledge was easy, so easy it slipped through your fingers like water, so easy it pooled in shallow puddles rather than deep wells. The citizens loved it that way. Why dive deep when you could skim its meme-like surface? Why wrestle with hard questions when the answers floated right there, just a swipe away? *Skim, scroll, share*, and move on. That was the way of life in Infotopia. Questions made you feel ignorant; answers—quick and nice—made you feel right.

And reigning over this empire of image was the President, a man as sleek and polished as glass within a looking glass. He knew how to surf the digital tides better than anyone, knew how to turn a phrase that would dance from screen to screen, viral and chic, leaving the people breathless and satisfied, like a sugar rush. And yet, beneath the gloss of his carefully curated words, a wasteland of inflation was brewing that made Infotopia's money melt like butter left out in the hot summer sun.

Prices spiraled upward, wages flattened, and the people—so addicted to easy excess—grew restless. They wanted answers, wanted solutions now, but reality, as ever, refused to cooperate. And the President, with his impeccably groomed hair and smooth smile, found himself trapped between three of his closest advisors—each considered brilliant, each convinced they knew the answer, each at war with the others.

Alpha, the old Austrian, his voice like gravel, barked, "We must tighten our belts! No more handouts, no more printing money! Let the market cleanse itself, as it always has. The tempest will pass if we let it."

"Nonsense!" contended Beta, the Keynesian, his cunning eyes unctuous as a pool of oil. "We need more money *now*! Spend! Stimulate! Pour cash into the hands of the people! That's how we get out of this. The government must intervene, or we're all doomed."

Omega, the youngest, practically snarled as she leaned forward, fingers twitching. "You're both cowards," she growled, her Marxian fervor burning bright. "The problem is the system itself! Redistribute the wealth, take from the rich, give back to the workers! *That's* the only way. Tear it down before it tears us all apart."

And there they sat, lobbing ideas like barbed spears, their words more weapons than wisdom, while the President, caught in the middle, nodded and smiled and pretended to listen, even as his mind wandered. For what was the use of theory, of ideas that twisted and turned and demanded further thought? What he needed—what Infotopia needed—was *something simple,* something the people could believe in, something they could see and touch and—better yet—*share.*

And just then, as if summoned from the ether, two foreign economists were admitted to his octagonal office. They came from international universities so prestigious that their very names carried the scent of money, names spoken in reverent tones by those who dared to think they understood everything.

These men, with their galvanizing hands and strange smiles, promised something not just revolutionary—but futuristic to the point of seeming *magical.*

"We can weave you a business suit," the economists said, their voices smooth as spider silk. "Not a suit of mere cloth—oh no, that would be far too ordinary for a leader like yourself. This suit will be something entirely different. It will be crafted from pure data, spun by the most advanced AI algorithms ever created. Algorithms so precise, so intelligent, that they can weave a fabric no human hands could ever hope to match. This suit will be invisible to the simple-minded, the unworthy. Only the greatest, the most enlightened minds will be able to see it."

The President's heart began to race. A suit like that! A suit not just to wear, but to embody. It would be more than clothing—it would be a statement, a badge of superiority, a symbol of his brilliance. With this suit, he wouldn't just be a leader, he would be *the* leader—the one who saw better, thought clearer, acted with vision beyond anyone else in Infotopia. He could feel the power of it already, wrapping him in its invisible folds, pulsating with unseen authority.

"But there's more," the economists continued, their words gliding closer, tightening their grip on the President's imagination. "This suit will do more than elevate your status. It will reveal the truth about those around you. To the degree that one is prejudiced, racist, bigoted, sexist, uncompassionate, oppressive, or just plain despicable, they will not be able to see the fabric at all. This suit will separate the wise from the fools, the worthy from the unworthy."

The President's chest tightened as his pulse kicked and stumbled, like a clock skipping seconds. Yes, he thought. Of course. This wasn't just a suit, this was a weapon—a way to reveal the truth about everyone in his circle, his government, even the nation itself. A suit that could strip away the illusions others wore, leaving only the righteous standing. The idea of such a fabric lured him, confirming what he had always believed: that he was destined to be the greatest, the brightest, the one in the know.

"But how? How is such a marvel even possible?" he asked.

"That's the beauty of it," the economists whispered, leaning in, their eyes cryptic with coded calculations, "this suit will be woven by the most advanced machine learning models in the world. These AI are not merely tools, but creators—learning, evolving, predicting. They will take the infinite data streams of Infotopia and spin them into something beyond human comprehension. Each thread will be crafted from data, stitched together from economic patterns, political insights, social dynamics, and the latest advancements in technology."

The President felt a shiver run through him. A suit woven from AI? From the very data that powered Infotopia itself? It was too perfect. The suit would be more than just an answer to his problems; it would be a testament to his clarity, his foresight. With it, he could stand before the people, draped in the full authority of his office, and *prove* that he was the one meant to lead.

The algorithms would weave decisions into the fabric, ensuring that every move he made, every policy he enacted, was not only flawless but unquestionable.

"This suit," the economists asserted, their voices infectious, "will guide you to make the best decisions. Each stitch, each fold, will whisper to you the answers that only the most brilliant minds could ever hope to understand. And because only the greatest among us can perceive its intricacy, you will know, without doubt, who is truly fit to serve by your side—and who is not."

The President's mind raced with the potentials. He could already picture it: standing before the cameras, his advisors at his side, clothed in this invisible armor of wisdom. Alpha, that antiquated Austrian economist with his constant talk of austerity, would be speechless. Beta, with his Keynesian insistence on endless government spending, would at last be curbed. Omega's grasping hands would convulsively reach for something else to break. None of them would be able to see the brilliance of the suit—because they were unworthy.

The President's eyes sparkled with anticipation. *Yes,* he thought. *Yes, this is what I need.* Modern leadership wasn't just about solving problems; it was about *the perception* of making the right decisions. In Infotopia, where information was unlimited and inundating, where everyone believed they knew more than they did, *presence* mattered more than the present. If he could wear this suit, if he could stand before his people clothed in this invisible brilliance, they would know. They would *believe.* And believing is seeing.

"And remember," the economists added, their smiles enlarging, "this suit will not just elevate you. It will expose those who are unworthy, those who cannot see it for what it truly is. To the degree that one is intolerant, corrupt, hypocritical, or blinded by privilege, the suit will remain invisible to them. They will see nothing, and in their blindness, they will condemn themselves."

"Begin at once," the President commanded, his voice thick with yearning. "Weave me this suit. I must wear it. How much?"

The economists named a considerable price, but the President didn't balk. The deal struck, they bowed deeply, their eyes flashing with the quiet cha-ching of numbers falling into place. Without another word, they backed out of the room, intoning something dark and electrifying.

And as the President imagined himself, draped in his technicolor dream suit, standing before his beleaguered nation, he exulted in his triumph.

After all, if you *looked* right, you *were* right.

Thus, the economists were funneled nonstop funds—for what price could you put on such ingenuity? They set to work in a gleaming room filled with computers that vibrated and blinked, dark screens and tangled cables that seemed to weave something mysterious, something profound.

Weeks passed, and the President, nervous but curious, sent Alpha to inspect the progress. The old Austrian shuffled into the room, squinting at the empty desks, the silent screens. He saw nothing. Nothing at all. His heart sank, a cold fear gripping his chest. *Am I unfit?* he thought. *Has age dulled my mind?* But Alpha would never admit such a thing. So he returned to the President and said, "The work is extraordinary. You've never seen algorithms like these."

Next, Beta, the fiery Keynesian, was sent. He entered, confident, but when he asked to see it, he was told, "Why, it's everywhere—it fills the room!" Beta, however, found himself staring at nothing but cold machines and blank air. *Can I... not see it?* he thought, biting his lip. *Impossible.* But he, too, would never show weakness. So, he returned and reported to the President, "It's a masterpiece. The future of economic thought."

Omega was sent last. The young Marxist perceived nought—nothing but the emptiness where her revolution should have been. Yet, terrified that her youth would betray her, she returned, eyes alight with false excitement. "It's revolutionary," she gushed. "Unlike anything the world has ever seen."

Finally, it was time. The economists stood before the President, holding up jacket and trousers of data and code, making a huge production of carefully placing the suit on the President's frame *just so*. "See, how it fits you!" they said, marveling at their handiwork. "Such refinement, such power! Truly, only a mind as astute as yours could wear it!"

The President, staring into the mirror, saw… nothing. His heart pounded. *Am I unfit?* But no, he could not, would not, admit such a thing. So, he smiled, broad and confident, as they led him toward the cameras, toward the stage where his grand address would be broadcast to all of Infotopia.

And there he stood tall in all his (ahem) glory, proud and naked, wrapped in nothing but their shared delusions and lies. "Behold!" he cried to the nation. "This suit—this masterful suit— is the key to our salvation! With it, I will lead us out of this crisis. Only those blessed with true discernment will see it!"

The people stared at their screens, eyes and mouths agape, fingers poised to like, to share, to repost. But no one said a word. No one dared admit they saw… nothing. Who among them wanted to be called blind? Or even worse, be cancelled?

And so they clapped. They cheered. They messaged about the brilliance of their President, about his new suit, about how he would lead them to prosperity.

Until a small voice broke the silence.

"Daddy," queried the astonished voice of the President's youngest daughter—holding a bowl of hot-buttered popcorn for her after-school snack—her eyes round with innocent confusion. "Why aren't you wearing any clothes?"

And in that instant, the truth cracked open. The illusion shattered. And one by one, the people of Infotopia whispered, then posted, then shouted— "He's naked!"

"The President has no suit!"

In the end, the President was pronounced unfit, his mind clouded not just by incompetence, but by hubris. He was summarily fired, not in a blaze of glory, but in the quiet shutting of damning secrets behind an embarrassing door, a man who had traded depth for the dulcet siren song of pretense. His economic advisers and experts tumbled after him, one by one their models of how things *should* be, splintering, their algorithms exposed for what they were—hollow, soulless constructs that promised order but delivered more chaos.

They had all made the same fatal error. They had built their networked babbling into a towering atrocity, but instead of bricks and mortar, it was made of distant data streams, systemic algorithms, and alienated anyones. Each figure, each statistic, a stone piled higher, until the tower stretched toward the heavens. But they forgot the human heart, the weight of real questions—the ones that defy easy answers, the ones that live in the silences between words, in the spaces no algorithm can calculate.

The ones that no lofty promises, no viral soundbites, no power suit can resolve.

For they had prided themselves on their breadth of knowledge, mistaking the sheer quantity of information for wisdom. They had forgotten that ideas without understanding is like a body without a soul—hollow, lifeless. In their pursuit of certainty, they lost sight of the very thing that makes us human: the need to ask, to ponder, to dwell in uncertainty, and, in that uncertainty, to find truth not in the data but in the connections we forge with one another.

And so Lucifer fell from grace. The Tower crumbled. Things fell apart, like microchips slipping through data streams, revealing beneath them nothing but emptiness.

They had reached for the stars, but they had forgotten to look each other in the eyes.

And so it was that the nude President, his mad (in every sense of the word) advisers, and their grand designs, faded into history as an historical footnote, not only of the reaching for everything, but the understanding of what lies within our grasp.

And in the end, as the dust settled, the world remembered that true connection, the kind that binds us as humans, cannot be found in the glow or click or swipe of a screen, but in the warmth of a shared question, in the quiet depth of a conversation that reaches together.

For sometimes, my children, "the end" is exactly what needs to happen.

Your Baba Yaga

Once upon a time, a girl was born to two loving parents who named her "Vasilisa." Her story, like the river's course or the mountain's climb, would echo the paths of becoming. She lived in a log cabin surrounded by a singular forest of willow trees that rose and wilted like the Tree of Life, their branches reaching toward the heavens as their roots plumbed abyssal depths. Vasilisa was a spark, precious and fresh, whose inner light held a clarity beyond her years. She walked reverently through the weeping forest surrounding her home, listening deeply to their silence, sensing, at times, the universe leaning in, as if beingness itself watched with intent, guarding the course her soul was yet to unearth.

Our story begins on the day of Vasilisa's eighth birthday, when her beloved mother—a woman who wore sorrow like a second skin but gathered love within the chapel of her core—

handed her daughter a small doll wrapped in muslin. The doll looked ordinary enough—just a simple thing, made of cloth and string, with eyes that perhaps seemed to gleam faintly.

"Vasilisa," she said, her voice no stronger than a sigh and unsteady with fever, "this doll is a part of you—your soul, the breath of all that makes you, *you*—a gift from me, and all that came before, and all that might well be. Care for it, feed it, speak to it. This doll, child, will guide you when all else fails." Vasilisa, eyes raw with equal measures of agony and wonder, promised her mother she would care for her doll from that day forward.

The world around Vasilisa, however, was a noisy, harsh place—a world that, with a thousand clever distractions, scoffed at the idea that such a doll existed. The soul, the voices insisted, was merely a tale for children. Soon after, her mother passed away; her father married a woman hardened by this cynical world. Vasilisa found herself surrounded by those who dismissed the silly notion of a soul doll. Her new stepmother and two stepsisters saw the girl's soulful glow and hated her for all of it together.

This new family was a dark dwelling with closed shutters, and the world they made was one where things like "soul" and "doll" were absurd words, tossed out with the dust and cobwebs. The stepsisters mocked her doll, and the stepmother told her that such juvenile toys were nothing but foolishness.

Yet, whenever her heart ached, or her stepmother sent her to do harsh work, Vasilisa would slip away, take her doll from her pocket, and give it a crumb of bread and a thimbleful of wine. She would whisper her hopes, her hurts, her fears—and the doll, in its silent stillness, would listen and guide her. Each time Vasilisa fed and spoke to her doll, she felt herself grow stronger, as though the doll fortified her essence.

Years passed, and Vasilisa became more beautiful, even as her life grew more difficult. Her stepmother, sensing something effervescent within Vasilisa that she could not contain, grew resentful. To rid herself of this loathsome radiance, she tore Vasilisa from her cherished willow forest and moved the family far away— to the edge of the crooked, labyrinthine hinterlands of skeletal larch, nightmare fir, and baleful birch, where, it was said, Baba Yaga, the ancient witch of the woods, made her awful home.

Then came a night when the stepmother, in a voice as thin and strained as a violin string on the verge of snapping, declared, "We need light, but the candles are gone. Vasilisa, go into the forest and find Baba Yaga, that old witch, and ask her for a flame. Perhaps she can teach you some respect." And so, with only her doll tucked into her pocket, Vasilisa stepped out into the forbidding night.

The forest was alive with rustles and mutters, as if the trees themselves bent ready to attack. She walked through the night, afraid yet strangely reassured, for the doll in her pocket pulsed with a warmth she had not felt before. Abruptly, out of the darkness, a horseman clothed in white galloped past, bringing with him the first light of dawn. She saw his face, fair as moonlight, and he nodded to her before vanishing among the trees.

Then, as the day brightened, she saw a second rider, this one clad in red astride a fiery horse. His face was like the sun at noon, blinding in its brilliance, and with a tip of his hat, he too vanished. Finally, as dusk gathered like dirt on old furniture, a third rider came—black as midnight, subduing as sleep, drawing night across the forest like a blanket. He bowed to Vasilisa and disappeared, leaving her at the threshold of Baba Yaga's house.

It perched on chicken legs, swaying slightly, as if listening. The house was surrounded by a fence made of bones, each topped with a skull whose eyes glowed faintly. And inside, Vasilisa knew, was Baba Yaga—a figure of fire and teeth, a creature neither of the light nor of the dark, but of something older, deeper, rawer.

The house lowered itself as she approached; the door swung open with a creak. And there, standing like a specter, was Baba Yaga herself, all bones and brittle hair, her eyes sharp as shards of broken glass. She sniffed the air, her iron teeth clashing together, and said, "A human child! What brings you here, girl?"

"My stepmother sent me to fetch light," Vasilisa replied, voice quivering yet calmed by the even heartbeat of the doll in her pocket.

Baba Yaga let out a harsh, grating laugh. "A light, is it? Then stay with me, work for me, and I shall give you more light than you ever wanted." She eyed Vasilisa with a fierce, testing gaze. "But be warned: fail me, and I will consume you. I am not kind, child, though I might be just."

Each day, Baba Yaga set Vasilisa arduous tasks: to sort grains by type, to sweep and scrub the entire house, to fetch water from a distant spring that ran deep in the forest. Each night, as the skulls on Baba Yaga's fence glowed, Vasilisa would feed her doll a morsel of bread with a thimbleful of wine and whisper her fears. And each morning, she would find her tasks mysteriously complete, what seemed impossible made possible by the doll's silent knowing.

And Baba Yaga took notice. One night, as she sat with her bony hands folded over her chest, she eyed Vasilisa closely and barked, "For your good work, you may ask me one—and only one—question, and I shall answer it."

Contemplating her journey to this place and the unending night that seemed to always conceal Baba Yaga's strange cottage, Vasilisa asked, "Who are the horsemen I met upon my way?"

Pleased by the girl's shrewdness, Baba Yaga's face split open as her voice seemed to creep through the air, causing Vasilisa to involuntarily clasp her doll tighter. "Every soul, child, must face my riders: the white, the red, the black. Dawn comes first, soft and strange, brushing the new with a light that knows nothing of sin or sorrow. It wakes you gently, but in its pale hands it holds a question: *Who will you become?* When high noon comes pounding behind, red as blood and hot as fire, it sets the soul ablaze with its demands. This is the rider of choice, of hunger, of everything you take and everything you lose. He does not linger; he leaves you scorched and shaped into something hard and true—or broken. And last comes dusk, shady yet certain, the slow rider who wraps the soul in shadow and silence. The time for asking questions is over; he simply gathers what remains. You see, child, my riders are neither sympathetic nor malicious—they are what *is*. They pass through you as they pass through the forest, the sky, the earth itself, leaving nothing untouched. Dawn begins you, noon carves you, and dusk takes you home—a soul remade, refined, or undone in their passing."

Vasilisa only nodded, her hand resting on the quiet warmth of the doll hidden in her pocket. Baba Yaga watched the girl for a time, and after the stillness stretched, she narrowed her eyes and asked, "What magic lies in those small hands, girl, to do all I demand? What power guides you?"

Vasilisa met the witch's dark, unreadable eyes with her own, answering, "My mother's blessing, Baba Yaga. I carry it with me, and it speaks to my heart." With these words, she reached into her pocket and drew out the doll, holding it up for the witch to see.

A streak of something—recognition, perhaps—passed across Baba Yaga's face. "A mother's blessing, indeed," she muttered. "And so, your doll is your guide." Her eyes tightened, and she nodded, as though understanding some private truth. Then, as if in response, in her ancient hand she held forth a writhing mass made of bones and feathers, its eyes fierce as the forest itself. "Even I have a daemon," Baba Yaga said, her tone milder, as if speaking a truth she rarely shared, "though I do not carry it with me. But beware, for it is wild and ancient, and I return to it always in the dead of night."

Vasilisa stared, and at last, she understood: Baba Yaga was not merely a witch but *the* witch—nature itself—consuming as she creates, fierce as she is wise, her depths as untamed and ancient as the forest around her. Nature reveals truth to those with eyes to see, and here stood its reflection in this dark mother, both test and teacher. The witch's doll, strange and terrible, was bound to her just as Vasilisa was connected to her own doll—a reminder that even in the smallest of things, a greater hand is at work.

"Do you fear me?" Baba Yaga asked, her voice a rasp like wind through dead leaves.

"Not any more," replied Vasilisa, feeling her own courage grow. "You are not safe, nor gentle, but you are… true." Baba Yaga nodded, satisfied.

When Vasilisa completed her final task, Baba Yaga handed her a skull atop a stick, its eyes blazing with a fierce light. "Take this," she said, "and bring it to those who sent you here. They have tried to snuff out the light of your soul. Let them feel its true power."

Vasilisa returned home, carrying the skull with its blazing light. The stepmother and her daughters, who had sneered at the notion of a soul, were consumed by the fire of its gaze, and by morning, nothing of them remained but lifeless ashes.

In time, Vasilisa grew into the woman she was meant to be; she carried her doll with her always, feeding it and speaking with it, for she understood now that it was a part of her. Eventually, she married a king and became queen—but that is a tale for another day. For this once upon a time, know that she became renowned as a wise woman, a keeper of secrets, a teller of truths. And those who were sincere, those who still retained the spark of wonder, would come to her and ask, "Do we, too, have a soul?"

In these moments, Vasilisa would smile, her doll warm in her pocket, and say, "Yes. We all do, at the start. But only those who feed it, only those who cherish it, will ever know its magic. There is no greater tragedy, no deeper mistake, than to ignore your doll. People rush about with their feet pounding on manmade spaces, their minds brimming with facts and their figuring, their bodies straining under the mass of the world's demands. They pour themselves into their daily routines, their monuments of stone and steel, all the while starving that burgeoning gift of truth tucked away in the deepest pocket of their core. They tell themselves that the mind is all they need, that the body is the only vessel worth tending. But the doll—their doll sits starving, its voice faded to a faint whisper too low to pierce all the noise, noise, noise, noise. And in doing so, they lose the secret map carved into every one of us, a plan leading us to those things the mind alone can never grasp and the body will never reach. To ignore the doll is to drift through life as an apparition, to wander paths that will never feel like home, and to wonder, one day, why the world feels so very empty and needless."

In that way, Vasilisa the Beautiful and Baba Yaga's tale passes on, from one generation to another, spreading and blending, as all the old but true tales do, until it is only remembered as a fairy tale, a legend, a myth—of a doll, a witch, and the light that guides us home.

But never forget, my children, if you someday happen upon an ancient forest by a twisted river and a dark, brackish bog, where there isn't so much wilderness around you that you lose your sense of the world outside, yet there isn't so much world outside that you cannot feel and smell and touch the wilderness within. You'll see a forest full of trees. And twisted roots and damp, rotting leaves now that autumn is here. Full of ghouls that slink under branches and fog that weaves itself between trunks and a thick silence that settles like mist over everything.

Remember, that this deep and dark and ancient forest is full of… secrets.

The dusk of an endless night.

All the trees leaning away from the path.

A forest full of waiting demons.

Remember, my children, not to be scared when your path suddenly disappears.

And deep within, behind a fence made of brittle bones and skulls that grin with hollow-eyed malice, you might find a hut—a hut that stands on spindly, bony chicken legs, shifting from foot to foot as though it can decide, at any moment, to leave. It's a house like no other, a house that can run from visitors if it wants but stays still for only one. And inside this hut, in the dark soul of the forest, will be your Baba Yaga.

She will be old, so old she might have watched the stars when they were young, might have heard the first laughter of rivers. Her hair, long and wild, hangs like smoke, streaked with the dust of forgotten things, and her eyes are blacker than the depths of any night, a darkness where no light dares to linger. Her nose, crooked and warted, hangs low over her lip, her teeth of iron clatter with a sound that sends the birds from their branches and stills even the wind.

Her hands—oh, her hands!—are thin and brown and ridged, with nails that grow long as claws, clutching tight to her pestle, which she grinds down into her mortar, her broom sweeping tracks that vanish with the sound of a low, hungry hiss.

She is no simple thing, no ordinary creature. She's both light and dark, good and terrible, a force as primeval as the roots of the world itself—feared not for cruelty, but for truth, for power. Baba Yaga is not safe. She is not kind. But, possibly, she might be just— *this time*. And she waits there, deep in the forest—she is always waiting.

And if you come to her forest without a doll of your own, my child, without a soul tucked close to your heart, then Baba Yaga will be there, watching, and she will take from you all that has always been hers to claim.

So, clasp your doll close, dear one, and never forget to feed it, speak to it, nurture it—for when your own end comes, your doll is the only companion that will never, ever leave you.

Froggy Epidemiology

Once upon a time—and you should understand that time, in fairy tales and science, rarely behaves itself—there lived a princess named Sciencella. Her name came from her unusual love of inquiry and calculation, which had, over the years, made her the sort of royal who could determine the odds of you tripping over your own feet just by looking at your shoelaces.

Sciencella spent her days in the castle library, surrounded by stacks of books with exciting titles like *The Epidemiology of Faerie Curses* and *Meta-Analyses in Magical Maladies*. The kingdom was mostly fine with this, as she tended to keep to herself, except when pointing out errors in royal decrees ("Dad, you've overlooked confounding variables in your tax policy again").

One afternoon, while juggling her golden ball—a habit her tutors had labeled "nonstandard use of downtime"—Sciencella found herself in one of her usual contemplative moods. The ball was more than just a toy to her; it was a shining sphere of perfection, a symbol for the clean, elegant logic she sought in a world muddied by misconceptions and half-truths. As she tossed it higher and higher, she imagined she was balancing the weight of her kingdom's misunderstandings, juggling the tangled chaos of relative risks and hidden biases into something coherent, something beautiful in the harmonious precision of a Fibonacci spiral.

Of course, metaphors are slippery things, as was the ball. With an inevitable turn of fate that any regression model could have predicted, it slipped from her fingers, arced agilely through the air, and landed with a disheartening *plop* in the ancient well.

She froze, staring into the dark depths. The ball was gone—her bauble of order, her perfect sphere of rational simplicity—swallowed by the murky unknown. "Well," she muttered to herself, "if that isn't a metaphor for epidemiology, I don't know what is." A single, despairing ripple spread across the surface of the water, as if mocking her loss.

"Oh, bother," said Sciencella, peering into the well's inky depths. "A statistically significant misfortune."

"Statistical or not, it's solvable," came a voice, crisp and reedy.

Sciencella looked up and blinked. Sitting on the rim of the well, dripping faintly, was a frog. A smug one, at that.

"You've got a problem," said the frog, his eyes twinkling. "And I've got a solution."

"And who, exactly, are you?" Sciencella asked, arms folded.

"Ribbold, at your service," said the frog, puffing up proudly. "Problem-solver, swamp philosopher, and occasional prince under unfortunate circumstances. I propose a deal. I retrieve your golden ball, and in return, you grant me a favor."

Sciencella raised an eyebrow. "Define favor."

"Oh, nothing too outrageous," Ribbold said breezily. "Just a kiss."

"A kiss?" Sciencella said, incredulous. "What kind of risk-benefit ratio is that?"

Ribbold grinned. "A favorable one. Studies suggest that princesses who kiss frogs experience a 100% increase in happiness."

"Relative risk," Sciencella replied, unimpressed. "What's the absolute likelihood?"

Ribbold's grin faltered. "Well, if we're being pedantic—without the kiss, happiness stands at 1 in 1,000. With the kiss, 2 in 1,000. Doubling, you see."

"Doubling a tiny number is still a tiny number," Sciencella muttered. "Typical."

"Perhaps you're forgetting," Ribbold said, rallying, "that I'm also a cursed prince. Surely there's an association between royal smooches and curse-breaking?"

"Association, not causation," Sciencella countered. "Have you accounted for confounding variables? Princesses who kiss frogs might just be adventurous types predisposed to happiness."

Ribbold paused, his froggy features clouding. "Swamps," he muttered. "Always complicating things."

"Fine," Sciencella said, rubbing her temples. "Retrieve my ball, and I'll think about it."

With an enthusiastic *splash,* Ribbold dove into the well, emerging moments later with the golden ball held triumphantly in his mouth. He spat it onto the grass and looked expectantly at Sciencella.

"A deal's a deal," he said.

Sciencella sighed and leaned down to give him the briefest of kisses, one foot already poised for a quick retreat.

In a swirl of emerald air that smelled faintly of algae, Ribbold transformed—not into the dashing prince of storybook fame but into a tall, gangly man with perpetually damp hair and a grin that suggested he might still eat flies if no one were watching.

"Finally!" Ribbold exclaimed, stretching his long arms. "That took long enough."

Sciencella, unimpressed, grabbed her ball. "You neglected to disclose the secondary outcomes of this curse reversal. Do you still leave slime trails? Are there lingering croaking tendencies?"

Ribbold cleared his throat, attempting dignity. "I'm an adaptable prince. But perhaps we should discuss the terms of our new alliance?"

"Oh, we will," Sciencella said, marching toward the castle. "Right after I calculate the multivariate model for this whole ridiculous scenario."

That evening, Sciencella presented Ribbold to the King, who was thrilled at the prospect of a curse-breaking prince, no matter how soggy. As for Sciencella, she drafted a landmark study on *Risk Factors and Predictive Outcomes of Amphibian-Human Transformational Interactions,* which would revolutionize the field of epidemiological fairy tales.

Unfortunately, Sciencella still found herself exasperated with her own subjects, who seemed determined to misunderstand the very studies she worked so hard to explain. They clung to headlines as if they were divine decrees, never pausing to consider whether the risks being reported were relative or absolute—or whether they applied to their lives at all.

When a study suggested that eating swamp cabbage might reduce the risk of dragon flu by 10% (a relative figure, naturally), villagers devoured the plant by the cartload, despite the absolute risk reduction being so negligible it wouldn't spare even one in a thousand.

Worse still, the kingdom's politicians twisted numbers to suit their narratives, declaring crises or triumphs as they advanced their ambitions, while journalists magnified results without context, emphasizing whatever would stir the loudest uproar and increase viewers.

"How," Sciencella fumed to Ribbold one evening over dinner, "can I teach them to ask the right questions when they'd rather cling to comforting lies than grapple with the reality of complex choices?" She slammed her fork down onto her plate of swamp-inspired fare, sending a piece of seaweed skittering across the table.

"They want everything reduced to a single, simple headline, Ribbold: 'Eat this, live longer,' or 'Avoid that, escape doom.' But life is intricate. Epidemiology isn't simple—it's the study of *variance*. These studies—" she gestured to a stack of scrolls on the sideboard, glaring at them as if they were to blame—"are like puzzles with half the pieces missing, yet everyone expects me to hand them the full picture, polished and perfect, as though causation can be delivered with a flourish. They don't want complex precision; they want magic bullets, even when they don't exist."

Ribbold paused mid-bite of toadstool. "You can't blame them entirely," he said, chewing thoughtfully. "Simple answers are reassuring. 'Do this, evade disaster.' It's human nature, isn't it? But tell someone there are multiple variables—hidden ones, unpredictable ones—and that certainty is a myth, and they shut down. It's easier to believe in a fairy tale where the curse is broken by a kiss than to wrestle with a study that concludes, 'It's complicated.'"

Sciencella groaned, dragging her hands through her hair. "But the answers *are* complicated! They depend on context, on confounders, on differences in confidence intervals and collinearity. Instead, they ignore the nuances and chase solutions that might not even work. They'd rather put their faith in swamp cabbage than accept that some risks simply can't be neatly managed."

Ribbold grinned, raising his pond-water goblet. "Tread lightly, Princess. If you keep making this much sense, they might mistake you for a witch."

"And that," Sciencella muttered darkly, "would still be easier for them to believe than the truth of probability."

Ribbold, now enjoying his newfound ability to wield a fork, raised an eyebrow. "What's not to believe? Frogs are charming and statistically misunderstood."

Sciencella rolled her eyes. "It's not about frogs, Ribbold. It's about logic! They'll hear that swamp cabbage reduces dragon flu risk and assume it's the cabbage itself, never wondering if it's actually because swamp cabbage eaters also live near clean ponds, far from the dragon nests. Or that the real benefit comes from the added herbs they mix with the cabbage, which no one bothered to study properly. And don't get me started on the 'exercise improves longevity' report. They nod sagely at that headline but refuse to ask whether it's exercise—or the fact that active people already have healthier habits, better diets, and fewer swamp-related accidents!"

Ribbold chewed thoughtfully. "So, it's not the cabbage or the exercise, but the circumstances?"

"Maybe!" Sciencella exclaimed, gesturing wildly with her spoon. "Confounding variables! Those sneaky, unseen threads that twist data into knots. And yet, my dear subjects stubbornly insist on treating every headline as if it descended from the heavens on a golden scroll. It's as if I'm shouting into a bog, my words vanishing into the muck before they can make so much as a ripple, trying to convince them to consider alternate explanations, to question the results, to—"

She threw her hands up. "Well, to not leap to conclusions the way some princesses leap after princes."

Ribbold dabbed at his mouth with a napkin, smirking. "Careful, Your Highness. If you keep making this much sense, you might accidentally start a revolution of reason."

Sciencella sighed, leaning back in her chair. "I'm not holding my breath. They'd probably think the revolution was caused by swamp cabbage, too…."

Not really *the end,* is it?

Bluebeard Revisited

Once upon a time, there lived a self-possessed man who elevated the acquisition of possessions into an art form. His name, or rather his alias, was "B.B." Few dared to mention it with anything less than respect—and perhaps a touch of dread. His fortune was a matter of hushed reverence: rows of grand estates, tapestries more priceless than honest labor could afford, and carriages gilded in gold that rumbled between his endless establishments.

And B.B., dear reader, had a beard. A beard the color of midnight seas, blue-black like the depths of a frozen lake, like a night too deep to escape. It wasn't simply a beard; it was a presence all its own, a dark, frosty thing that glistened as though made of something not quite alive, something old and still and waiting. B.B. would stride into a room, and his beard would lead the way, glinting coldly in the dim light, casting a shadow darker than locked doors.

When B.B. arrived, it wasn't so much an entrance as it was an occupation, like a thick fog descending on an open field. That blue-black beard of his particularly glinted in the dimmest light, giving him the look of some relic unearthed from a bygone age, something preserved in ice yet potent still. Women found themselves drawn to him with a weird inevitability, as if caught in the slow, deliberate turn of a key in a lock—a lock they wished, against all caution, would open. He had a smile like a well-set trap, charming and crafted to lure, while his gaze held just enough intensity to suggest he'd chosen you, and only you, to hold in his regard. In B.B.'s orbit, the air felt richer, scented with the promise of a life lifted above the dull mechanics of ordinary existence, where each step you took beside him might polish you into something splendid, something to be admired and treasured.

Young women, like Ginger, never stood a chance. Though they shied at one glimpse of that blue beard, still their hearts would flutter. Danger of his sort holds a heady attraction, especially when mixed with sophistication and success. They didn't fall in love with B.B.; they fell *into* him, like sinking into dark water. He made them feel special, the way his gaze lingered a little too long, the way his hand would rest on theirs just enough to send a shiver, but not enough to push them away. He wasn't looking for equals; he was looking for someone to mold, to cradle in his palms like something precious, something that would glow brighter under his deep blue gaze.

Ginger was a new flame that danced in all the wrong breezes, her hair a copper blaze that caught the light and drew every eye without so much as a thought. Hers was a beauty that held you in place, the sort that made people pause like they would at the edge of a cliff—half in awe, half with that strange urge to step closer to the drop. Her eyes, bright and green as new leaves, seemed to drink in the world with a depth that hinted she felt its wonders more deeply than most. She moved with an unstudied grace, oblivious to the spell she cast, yet there was a hint of naivety in the way she leaned toward life, as though forever on the brink of some grand revelation.

But beneath her beauty, there was a craving, one she hadn't yet named. It was there in the way her eyes drifted past people, never quite settling, as if she were waiting for someone or something to arrive, something to fill the hollow space she didn't even know she carried. She was too eager to believe in promises wrapped in pretty words, too quick to think that being wanted was being loved, too desperate to believe that being chosen by a man larger than life would save her from the smallness of her world.

Allegedly, B.B. had married many times, though no one had ever met any of these former brides. He was the subject of hushed rumors, of envious gossip, of course, and yet none of the young women he courted dared to openly reject him.

But Ginger's heart was full of dreams too big for her world. She had grown up in a quiet house, a place where her father was a revenant, a ghostly figure who drifted in and out, and two much-older brothers whom she rarely saw anymore. Besides a string of governesses, this left Ginger with only an older sister, Anne, who looked at the world with a skepticism Ginger could not understand. Anne "knew" men like B.B.—men who collected, who possessed, who swallowed people whole without leaving a trace. She had warned Ginger, spoken to her in grave, desperate tones about the dangers of desire—men who spoke in constellations, their promises as vast and ungraspable as the night sky. Yet Ginger, with her great, luminous eyes alive with a hunger for what wasn't hers, could not resist the pull of something larger than herself.

And so, B.B. set his sights on securing Ginger. It sounded like love. It felt like love. But what Ginger couldn't know, what she refused to see, was that she wasn't being *loved*.

She was being purchased.

Anne remained wary, for she sensed something deeply unsettling not just in the hasty arrangement, but about B.B.'s beard. It wasn't just the way it curled neatly against his jaw, as though it was hiding something. No, it was the color—the deep, strange blue, like the eye of a tornado, like the ocean when it's too calm and you know something terrible is brewing beneath. That blue seemed to move, to shift as though alive, catching the light and throwing it back in cold, sharp angles. It was a blue that pulled you in, made you forget to breathe, and yet left a chill in the air long after you'd passed away.

She cautioned her sister, told her that men like B.B. wanted something other than partnership. Her older brothers teased Ginger about her beau, dubbing him *Bluebeard* as they warned their youngest sister that older men only courted much younger women when they wanted to control, to dominate, to be obeyed—even worshipped. Ginger wouldn't listen. How could she? She wanted, she needed, the happy ending. And so, the marriage was quickly arranged and consummated.

B.B.'s mansion was everything Ginger had anticipated. Rooms draped in gold and silver, mirrors that reflected her every step, her every curve, as though she had become a trophy in her own story. At first, it was intoxicating—his attention, his lavish gifts, the way he seemed to lift her above all other women. But there was always a chill to his touch, a cold, considered admiration that made her feel like an object on display rather than an equal partner.

One night, when the wind howled outside and the windows rattled in their frames, B.B. handed her a ring of keys, each one unique and ornate. "Every room in this house is yours to explore," he vowed, his voice smooth as melted wax. "But this key—" he held up a small, plain thing, as blue as his beard—"this key must never be used." His eyes, cold and glittering like frost on glass, locked onto hers, and Ginger felt a shiver run through her, a thrill mixed with fear—something dark, almost snakelike. But the temptation was already planted. She was special, wasn't she? He had told her so. And wasn't this her home now? Shouldn't she know all its secrets?

Their days together passed in a blur of fine dinners, dazzling parties, and passionate nights. Over time, she explored room after room in their mansion—every one grander than the last, full of more and more treasures—but the weight of that forbidden key slowly grew. It seemed to pulse with something—some hidden part of her she couldn't comprehend. Curiosity gnawed at her like a broken sentence, hanging heavy and unfinished, begging for completion.

She waited until he left one morning to travel for business, the key burning a hole in her pocket, its weight dragging her further downward with each passing hour. She'd invited Anne and her brothers to visit for the holidays, but they hadn't yet arrived. She entertained herself by exploring the mansion's hundreds of rooms and thousands of treasures, each one more lavish than the last, every room festooned with mirrors that reflected her back at herself, smaller and smaller with every step. But all the while, that little key pulsed in her pocket, a mass that grew heavier and heavier, whispering secrets in a voice she couldn't quite hear.

As if drawn inexorably against her better judgment, she slipped down the winding corridors, where the dense darkness pooled, pressing close as if waiting. The blue key slipped into the blue lock, the sound grating and brittle as it turned. The door creaked open, and a rush of cold air spilled out, wrapping around her like icy hands. Inside, the room was dark, so dark she could see only shapes at first—ashen shapes, silent shapes that lined the walls.

She stepped in, and the cold hit her like a slap. The air was thick and frosty, as if the room were a vault of ice, a place meant to preserve something unnatural. Her breath shuddered out in vapors, and that's when she saw them—lined up in silent ranks, B.B.'s wives, each fixed in an eerie stillness, their faces a perfect mask of beauty frozen in time. Shock pooled in her stomach. They weren't simply dead; they were preserved, posed like exquisite china dolls, each suspended in the height of their beauty, with glassy eyes that seemed to look past her, lips parted as if caught mid-sentence or mid-plea.

They were perfect, every type of feminine beauty imaginable, in a way that clawed at her insides—smooth skin, eyes frozen wide with the adoration he'd always required. It dawned on her with sickening clarity: they weren't buried and forgotten; no, they were here for him, displayed like his prized possessions, trapped in this icy tomb for him to visit and admire whenever he pleased. The freezing blue light seeped through their garments, catching on every jagged icy detail, casting ghastly shapes across their forever-still faces. And as she took a hesitant step back, she could almost swear that the wives were watching her, eyes pleading from within their glacial prison—as if they knew that soon, she too would join their frigid ranks.

Ginger's breath caught in her throat, and she apprehended, with a sudden and terrible clarity, that she was no different. She had been deceived, lulled by the velvety blue cloud beneath her husband's lying lips. He had made her feel unique, cherished, as if she were his one and only, but she was just another prize in a long line of possessions, each as expendable as the last.

Ginger realized, too late, what she had married. And only as she slammed the door shut, locking its horrors away, did she see it—dark streaks of blood she hadn't noticed before, seeping from the key, now staining her hands apple-red. Desperately, she scrubbed, tried to wipe it away, but the blemish remained, sinking deeper, a mark she couldn't erase.

The key had turned against her, and its master was coming home.

Anne arrived soon after, her face melancholy as she examined Ginger's red hands and listened to her tale. "Our brothers are on their way," Anne whispered, her voice shaking. "But we must be ready." Together, they waited, their breaths intermingling in the cold air, bracing for what was to come.

Far too soon, the baying of B.B.'s hounds echoed in the hall, signaling his homecoming. Ginger's heart sank. Her mind raced through escape plans, but there was no time. B.B.'s voice was deceptively sweet as he greeted his bride, but his blue beard cast lingering edges across his cool face.

"Your hands are trembling, my love," he remarked. "May I have my keys, please?"

Ginger handed them over, pulse pounding in her ears. Then B.B. noticed the crimson-covered blue key.

"Why is there a stain on my key?" His tone was short, controlled—too controlled. The air seemed to thicken, smelling of damp earth and metal, as if a dozen cyclones had been trapped in the sky and were only now scrabbling their way down. Ginger's world paused; the hair at the nape of her neck prickled as the taste of chilled iron settled on her tongue. The low rumble of B.B.'s tone held thunder.

"I don't know," Ginger whispered, her throat tight. The lie felt weak, feeble against the awful truth standing in the room between them.

"You don't know?" B.B.'s smile twisted into something spiteful. "I told you not to enter that room. Now, you must take your place with the others."

A blade flashed out from beneath his coat, steel catching the firelight. Ginger fell to her knees, the full weight of her choices crushing her. She had ignored every warning—her family's, her own instincts—and now she would pay the price.

As B.B. raised the blade to strike and Anne screamed, the door burst open with a deafening crash. Her brothers. Late, but just in time.

B.B. turned, startled as they moved quickly, drawing their swords. Ginger and Anne grabbed each other, scrambling back as the men clashed. B.B. fought like a cornered animal, his movements fierce and desperate, but her brothers were relentless, their strikes measured and sure.

With a last, bewildered gasp, B.B. crumpled, his life slipping away like darkness at dawn, swift and irreversible, a merciless echo of every impulsive step Ginger had taken to reach this dire tableau. In that instant, she felt the suffocating weight of his grip fall away, the burden of her own mistakes peeling back like old paint, leaving her exposed but free, standing on the edge of a life she might finally claim as her own.

Her brothers didn't linger over their victory. They helped Ginger to her feet, their faces grim but not harsh. One squeezed her hand; the other gave her a firm nod. No words of judgment, just the genuine relief that comes from seeing someone you love escape a trap of their own making.

Later, when they cleaned out the forbidden room—what everyone now called *Bluebeard's* room—the full horror was laid bare. The bodies of his wives, the women who had stood where Ginger now stood, their lives taken for the same transgression. Their faces told a story not unlike her own: warnings unheeded, choices made in defiance of those who loved them. Each of them had thought they knew better, had believed they were different, and had paid the price.

As Ginger stood in that room, staring at the evidence of her own recklessness, she wept—not from fear this time, but from the bitter truth that she had chosen this path. Her brothers didn't scold her; they didn't need to. The lesson in blueblood splayed out before them, in the silence of the dead.

In time, Ginger inherited all of Bluebeard's riches. The vast estate, the wealth, the enterprises—everything he had once lorded over with a formidable hand was now hers. But it all felt empty and sullied, for she wasn't the same girl who had married him, wide-eyed and selfish.

She didn't become a recluse, nor did she squander her inheritance. Instead, Ginger used it to build something lasting, something worthy of the lessons she had learned. She listened to her family now—their advice no longer felt like a burden, but a compass pointing true north. The sister and brothers who had stood by her, who had warned her, who had pulled her from the jaws of death—they had been her foundation all along. She had just been too blind to see it.

And so, dear ones, the tale of Bluebeard comes to rest not simply with his end but with the quiet awakening of a young woman, her heart broken by the humbling mass of her irresponsible, unheeded choices. Ginger came to see that the gentle urgings of family—of those who love us, not for what we can give them, but for what they can give us—were never chains but lifelines cast by those who saw beyond her brash youth to what she might become. The greatest treasures are neither gold nor adoration, but the love offered by those who see the raw, unfinished shape of us and still reach out, ready to forgive, to suffer, to save us—even from ourselves. For perhaps the sweetest and most stubborn pride of youth is this: to close our ears to the quiet counsel of elders who, in ways we scarcely grasp, know us more deeply than we dare to know ourselves.

But to be known—that is another thing entirely.

And perhaps, too, we only begin to see ourselves at all when we are no longer admired, but known—when the reflection staring back is not one we've crafted, but one returned to us in the steady gaze of someone who sees the truth and stays. B.B.'s blue beard, after all, was no mere ornament—it was a calculated mask, and Ginger loved it because it let her wear one too. In its cool, cobalt shadow, she could believe she was special, untouchable, superior. But blue is the color of the forlorn and fantasy and forgetting—and the longer we linger there, the more the truth beneath begins to set, quiet and final, until the rigor mortis of deceit sets in. And so the story of Bluebeard repeats again and again: not with fairy-tale monsters, but with faerie truth mirrors: each of us, at some point, standing before our own blue beard—or worse, growing one—desperately hiding our awful truth.

And somewhere,
behind another locked door,
the blue still waits...
for all of us.

Of Writers & Fairy Tales

Once upon a time, in a world that spun too quickly for its own good, there lived a writer who longed to create something that would outlast the clamor. He wasn't sure what it would be—perhaps a story as simple as summer's dusk or as fierce as a thunderstorm—but he knew he wanted it to mean something. To someone. Somewhere.

His desk overflowed with paper, each sheet filled with fragments of ideas—half-formed characters, scribbled dialogue, outlines of worlds that seemed to fade as quickly as they appeared. The more he tried to gather them, the more they scattered, like the shards of a broken mirror catching the light but refusing to hold it.

That night, when longing stretched beyond the reach of language, he let his pen fall and, with a sigh of surrender, asked the vastness what it had always known.

"How do I begin?"

The room swelled, the air drawn taut, as though caught in the pause before the word that once summoned the world from silence—and then, it shimmered. Not like the glare of a screen or the sterile hum of fluorescent light, but like fireflies dancing in the summer night—soft, inviting, alive.

From that shimmering stepped two figures, luminous yet familiar.

The first was a tall man with a wistful gaze, his eyes imbued with the soft melancholy of Denmark's northern lights and the unspoken legends of its fjords. Hans Christian Andersen, whose very presence seemed to echo the cobbled streets and quiet harbors of his homeland. His presence stirred the hush, light as the brush of wings where one world touches another, forever bound to the wondrous book of fairy tales he left behind—not as an escape from sorrow, but as a transfiguration of it, shaping the pain he knew so well into stories that carried hope and truth to those who needed them most.

The second man was sturdy and rooted, with a kind smile and the quiet authority of one who had walked the rugged moors and climbed the mist-shrouded hills of his native Scotland. George MacDonald, whose words carried the cadence of heather and stone, and whose fairy tales had taught the writer about the delicate interplay of magic and truth—how one could illuminate the other in ways both wondrous and profound. His stories had always felt like home to the writer, even when their full depths lay just beyond his understanding.

They stood together, their presence filling the room with a sense of timelessness, as though past, present, and future had folded into one incandescent now.

Hans spoke, his voice gentle and edged with longing, like the first notes of an old song. "We have been waiting for you. You called, and we came."

"To write a story," George added, his voice deep and resonant like the bell of a great cathedral, "you must first journey through one."

The writer blinked, his heart racing in his chest. "Journey? But how?"

"Not just any journey," Hans said. "And not just any story. The *old* tales, the ones that carry truths so deep they cannot simply be spoken and fully known. You must walk through them as their characters did."

"And then," George said, his smile broadening, "you will find your own story waiting for you on the other side."

The air shifted abruptly, like the moment before a cloudburst, and the writer found himself standing ankle-deep in snow that sparkled unnervingly in the half-light. The landscape stretched endlessly—jagged peaks of ice, walls as sheer and slick as glass, and a sky the color of a bruise. Only the wind stirred—a needy, restless thing, winding through the frozen air like a hand seeking a latch in the dark, as if the land itself held a secret too dreadful to utter.

Beside him, Hans Christian Andersen stood, his gaze distant and somber. "This," he said, his voice poised between the crisp bite of frost and the first touch of dew, "is the realm of *The Snow Queen*."

The writer tugged his coat tighter, though it seemed to do little against the biting cold. "It's beautiful," he said, though the word felt wrong as it left his lips.

Hans's mouth quirked. "Yes. And it is deadly. All stories begin in places like this, you know: the frozen heart of humanity, where warmth and life are stripped away, leaving only the illusion of perfection."

The writer turned to ask what he meant, but Hans had already begun to walk, his boots crunching lightly in the snow. Reluctantly, the writer followed.

They stopped at the edge of a frozen lake, its surface smooth as a mirror, yet ruptured with spiderweb fissures. As the writer looked closer, he saw movement—tiny shards, like slivers of broken glass, whirling beneath the surface. They spun faster and faster until they erupted into the air, sprinkling like silver rain.

"What are they?" the writer asked.

"Shards from the wicked sprite's mirror," Hans said. His voice was soft, but his eyes were hard. "Once upon a time, the sprite created a mirror that distorted everything it reflected. Beauty became grotesque; kindness seemed like weakness. It shattered, as all wicked things must, but its fragments remain. They drift on the winds of the world, finding their way into people's eyes, their hearts."

The writer flinched as a shard sailed past his cheek. "What do they do?"

"They change the way people see," Hans said simply. "And the way they feel. Once touched by a shard, a person sees only flaws, only ugliness. In others. In themselves. The heart grows cold, impervious to love." He pointed across the lake.

The writer followed his finger and saw a boy standing at the edge of the ice. The boy's face was lifeless, his expression fixed in an unfeeling calm.

Beside him stood a woman of breathtaking beauty, her gown pulsating like starlight, her presence as arctic and unyielding as the land around her.

"Kai," Hans said.

"The Snow Queen," the writer murmured.

The Snow Queen raised her hand, and the boy stepped onto the lake without hesitation. Where his feet touched, the ice thickened, smoothing itself into a flawless, mirror-like sheen. The writer shivered.

"Why does he follow her?" he asked.

Hans didn't answer immediately. He crouched and picked up a shard of the mirror that had embedded itself in the snow. Holding it up to the light, he said, "Because he can no longer see the world as it is. The shard in his heart tells him the Snow Queen's promises are truth. He believes her promises hold salvation, and he will give anything to be part of it."

As the writer watched, Kai knelt at the center of the lake, his hands moving mechanically as he began arranging shards of ice into a puzzle. The Snow Queen watched impassively, her gaze distant, as though she had already forgotten he was there.

"Will he finish the puzzle?" the writer asked.

Hans gave him a grim smile. "The puzzle has no solution. That is her trick."

The sound of footsteps on snow drew the writer's attention. From the depths of the forest beyond the lake emerged a girl, her red cloak a splash of color in this lifeless world. Her breath came in ragged puffs, her steps faltering, but her eyes burned with resolve.

"Gerda," Hans intoned, and the name carried with it a solidity that settled in the writer's chest.

The girl stumbled but caught herself, clutching a bundle of tattered cloth to her chest as though it held the sum of her hope. She called out, her voice uneven but fierce. "Kai!"

The boy did not look up.

"Why does she keep going?" the writer asked.

Hans's gaze relaxed. "Because love cannot help but act. It is not a feeling; it is a force. Persistent, sacrificial, unyielding. Gerda's love is her flame. Even here, where everything conspires to extinguish it, it burns on."

As Gerda reached the lake's edge, a solitary crow landed beside her. It cawed once, then took off toward the Snow Queen's palace in the distance. The girl hesitated, then took a step onto the ice. The writer felt his breath catch as she slipped, falling hard. But she did not stop. Slowly, painfully, she rose and began walking again, each step a gentle triumph over the cold.

When Gerda reached Kai, she knelt beside him, her cloak settling around them like a pool of blood on the ice. She placed her hands on his, stilling their mechanical movements, and leaned close. She whispered something the writer couldn't hear, her breath misting in the cold air.

For a long moment, nothing happened. Then a single tear rolled down her cheek and fell onto his bosom. It pierced through to his heart, thawing the lump of ice within and consuming the little shard of glass buried there.

The change was almost imperceptible at first—a softening of his face, a flash of awareness in his eyes. And then, like a spring thaw, the ice began to crack. Not just in Kai's heart, but across the lake, the palace, the entire frozen realm.

The Snow Queen turned, her flawless features unreadable. She raised a hand as though to stop them, but it was already too late. Kai looked at Gerda, his expression one of wonder and regret, and took her hand. Together, they stood and began walking back toward the forest.

The Snow Queen watched them go, her icy form dissolving into the wind.

Hans turned to the writer. "Do you see now? Love is not easy. It does not come without cost. But it is the only thing that can melt the ice, remove the shards, and bring us back to ourselves."

The writer nodded slowly, his chest tight. "No heart is too frozen to thaw," he said, almost to himself.

Hans smiled faintly. "And no shard too deep to remove. This is the first gift of stories—not because they happened, but because they reveal the truths that facts cannot reach."

The frozen landscape began to blur, the serrated edges melting as warmth returned to the world. The writer felt himself being pulled forward, away from the lake and the palace, toward the next part of his journey.

He found himself standing on the edge of a great forest. Its trees rose like church spires, their branches entwined, forming a roof that caught and refracted the light. It wasn't ordinary sunlight that shone here, but something richer—golden, liquid, alive. The air was warm but carried the faint chill of a distant wind, as though this place were both welcoming and warning.

George MacDonald stood beside him, now sturdy and calm as ever. "This," he said, gesturing to the forest, "is *The Golden Key*. It is not a place of rescue, as you saw with Gerda and Kai, but of transformation. Here, the journey is not outward but inward. Watch carefully, for the truth is often hidden in the humblest things."

The writer stepped forward, feet crackling on a path of pine needles that seemed to appear only when he walked. Ahead, he saw two figures—children, though the boy seemed older than his years. The other moved with restless energy, her eyes fixed on a flickering glow, darting and dancing among the trees. But as they came nearer, the writer saw she followed a strange and marvelous creature—a fish with owlish feathers instead of scales, its fins glinting like a hummingbird's as it swam through the air.

"I called that an *air-fish*," George chuckled. "Meet Mossy and Tangle," he continued, his tone affectionate. "Two paths, one destination—this," he gestured to a magnificent rainbow, "is where Mossy's story began. He'd listened to his great-aunt's tales of the golden key for years, but here, at last, he saw the rainbow's end—the only place where such a key could be found."

The writer watched as the boy searched the rainbow's base, the colors shining against the mossy ground. "And did he find it there?" the writer asked.

"He did," George replied, his voice compassionate. "But not that night. The moon rose, the rainbow vanished, and he slept on the bed of moss where it had stood. By morning, the sunlight revealed the golden key, glittered with fiery sapphires. He grasped it with joy, yet the key held a new mystery he could not yet solve—for once he had the key, it was time to find the lock it was made to open."

The writer leaned forward as the scene shifted to the girl, who followed her air-fish to a small, round cottage that seemed to have been grown rather than been built. The firelight, warm and lively, pirouetted upon walls that carried the earthy scent of the forest. By the hearth stood a lady, serene and radiant, her green dress draping her with a goddess-like majesty.

Without a word of reproach, the lady began to wash away the dirt and weariness of the road, her fingers working patiently to untangle the wild knots in the girl's hair. "You shall be called Tangle," she said, her voice bearing both the ache of what had been and the quiet hope of what might yet be. "Your hair tells its own tale—of neglect, of people who ought to have cared for you but couldn't be bothered. Let it stand as a reminder—not of what you were, but of how far you've come."

The scene blurred and refocused as the cottage door opened again. Mossy stepped inside, the golden key glinting faintly in his hand. His face was lined with weariness, but his grip on the key remained firm. The lady's gaze softened as she approached him, her presence both commanding and kind.

"Do you see Tangle's air-fish?" George asked, pointing to the lady's cooking pot that hissed and bubbled as the creature rose from its boiling water, transformed into a be-winged angelic being. It circled the cottage once before vanishing into the night.

The writer drew a raw breath, his heart twisting at the sight. "It went to its death freely," he reflected, half in awe, half in disbelief.

George nodded, his expression solemn. "Yes, willingly," he said. "The air-fish's sacrifice parallel's Mossy and Tangle's own journeys—both must surrender what they think they are, giving themselves wholly to the unknown, in order to be transformed into what they might be. Just as the fish becomes more than itself through the fire, so too must Mossy and Tangle."

The writer's gaze lingered on the seething pot. "But why must it endure the fire?"

"Ah," said George, his eyes twinkling with the hint of a smile. "Because transformation demands something of us. It is not enough to see the light or follow it. One must partake of it, take it into oneself, and let it change every fiber of one's being. The fish is a mirror for us. It shows that to truly live, we must be willing to let go of what we think we are so that we can become what we might be. It is a small act, perhaps, to eat a fish. But no act is merely what it appears to be."

The writer nodded slowly, disturbed by something opening deep within him. "So the fish wasn't destroyed. It was... fulfilled?"

George's smile broadened. "Yes, my friend. Fulfilled. With every step upon the way, every sacrifice, we are not losing ourselves but discovering what we were made to be."

The writer leaned back, as the lady counseled Mossy and Tangle before they clasped hands and stepped into the forest to continue their quest together. "Are they truly ready?" he asked, his brow furrowed in doubt.

"Ready," George said, "not because they know the way but because they have already begun to be changed by the walking of it."

"What are they seeking, exactly?" the writer asked, his voice hushed as the stillness of the forest.

George smiled faintly. "The meaning of the key, of course. But more than that, they are seeking the light that calls to every soul. It is not the kind of treasure they can hold, but the kind that holds them."

The writer frowned. "But they don't even know what's at the end, what's shaping them. Why do they keep going?"

"Because," George assured gently, "the light calls. And to those who hear its voice, there is no other choice."

The writer continued to watch in dismay as the darkness deepened, surging around Mossy and Tangle. Though their steps were resolute as they pressed into the growing darkness, Tangle reached out—only to find her hand suddenly empty. She called Mossy's name, but the unending shadows swallowed the sound.

Mossy was gone.

The writer glanced at George, his forehead pinched and his hands clenched at his sides. "They've lost each other," he said, almost in accusation. "Surely they were meant to stay together."

George tilted his head slightly, his lips pressed in a quiet, measured line. "They were," he replied thoughtfully, "but only for as long as the way allowed. Now, for a time, they must walk alone. Do you see? Mossy and Tangle have shared what they could, giving each other strength for the road ahead. Yet there are parts of the journey that no one can carry for another."

"But it's cruel," the writer protested. "They were stronger together."

George nodded slowly. "Perhaps. But the deepest lessons often come in solitude, when no hand is there to hold."

The writer and his guide trailed Tangle as she descended into the depths below, soon meeting the Old Man of the Earth, who gazed into his mirror. "Here," George explained, "we see the soul meeting mystery—what it cannot yet understand but longs to grasp.

The Old Man of the Earth dreams of the country from which the shadows fall but he cannot find it himself. So we humans wrestle with the limits of earthly knowledge, catching glimpses of truth but unable to possess it fully. Tangle's task here is to accept the longing without despair, trusting that the next step will be revealed."

Finally, they watched Tangle stand alone before the childlike Old Man of the Fire, his face serene and his presence unshakable. "And now," George said, his voice dropping to a reverent shush, "we see the soul's surrender. The fire burns away all that is false, leaving only what is real and enduring. The fiery child places his hand on Tangle's heart—not to protect her from the fire but to prepare her to walk through it unscathed—and tells her to follow the serpent. Thus, her final leap of faith—to trail the serpent, that twisting, gliding thread of change, and plunge headlong into the vast, breathing mystery of the unknowable.

The writer watched as Tangle shadowed the serpent through the heat of the desert, untouched by the molten rivers around her. "So each stage," the writer said slowly, "is a deeper layer of unfoldment."

"Precisely," George replied. "We must first be cleansed, then come to terms with our limits, and finally be tempered by fire. It is only through this progression that Tangle uncovers what she truly is—a seeker ready not just to find the country from which the shadows fall, but to *become* it."

George's eyes burned with quiet intensity as he lifted his hand to point ahead. "Look there, lad," he said, his voice low but compelling. "This is where it all turns. Watch closely—what you see is ending and beginning both."

At his words, the writer's gaze deepened, and he beheld Mossy standing before the Old Man of the Sea, his shoulders bowed with exhaustion and something unexpected. "Why does he look so aged?" the writer asked, his voice tinged with both curiosity and concern.

"Because," George replied, "the way excavates great portions of us, as the tide carves the rocks upon the shore. Mossy has carried his burdens long and faithfully, but they have molded him—remade him. Watch."

The writer watched as Mossy rose from the waters, the lines of age gone, his eyes clear, hands steady. The Old Man's voice, like the deep reverberation of the world's first waking, cut through the quiet. "You have tasted of death now. Is it good?"

Mossy raised his head, his eyes clear with understanding. "It is good," he said softly. "It is better than life."

The Old Man smiled faintly, shaking his head. "No," he replied, his tone filled with gentle certainty. "It is only more life. Your feet will make no holes in the water now."

And to Mossy's wonder, when he glimpsed his own reflection in the water, it was not the child Mossy but the Old Man of the Sea who stared back at him.

George turned to the writer, his voice tranquil but full of authority. "Do you see, my friend? Death, as Mossy has tasted it, is not the end but a revelation—a peeling away of all that blinds us to what is actual. When we can truly see the sea—not as chaos or boundary, but as it is—then we find we can walk upon it, no longer weighed down by fear or falsehood, buoyed by the truth of every step. It is not the loss of life, but the first taste of a life far richer and more true than we can yet imagine."

The vision swapped, illuminating Mossy as he ascended a stairway of falling stones, each step appearing only as he committed himself to the next. The writer edged closer, captivated. "And now he's found Tangle," he said, his voice jubilant yet baffled. "Why has she waited for him so long?"

"Ah," said George, "Tangle's odyssey was different. She was called to wait, to learn the stillness of devotion, while Mossy was called to walk, to persevere. Together, they complete what neither could accomplish alone. Do you see how she knows him now to be *both* the Old Man of the Sea and her own Mossy? Each path, you see, transforms its traveler, but it does not erase who they are. Instead, it makes them more—more themselves than they ever imagined they could be."

Mossy and Tangle exchanged their stories and revelations about how "everything meant the same thing," their shared joy spilling over into the peaceful beauty of the cave. "So this is the culmination of the way?" the writer asked.

"It is but a threshold. They have found one another, but the deepest longing of all is not yet fulfilled. They still seek the country whence the shadows fall—the eternal truth, the source of all beauty and light. And for that, they must continue."

The writer stood silent, watching as Mossy and Tangle, hand in hand once again, ascended *through* the rainbow, their forms so fixed and radiant he could no longer see them at all. "The journey, then," he said finally, "is the transformation."

George smiled, his voice both kind and firm. "It always is. For the soul cannot find its way without first becoming ready to see it."

"Why must it be so hard?" the writer asked, a note of frustration creeping into his voice.

"Because the way refines each and all," George replied. "The light changes those who pursue it, as fire refines iron to steel. It is what all who seek the golden key find—not a treasure, but transcendence."

"So this is the end?" the writer asked.

George shook his head. "Not the end. A brink."

"But they are forever changed," the writer challenged.

"Yes," George said. "Yet notice how the world has changed because of them."

And the writer followed his gaze. The trees, the leaves, the very air seemed alive now with a beauty he hadn't noticed before. The imperfections of the forest—the gnarled roots, the fallen branches—were not flaws, but part of its wonder.

"We see with new eyes," George said. "That is the gift of the golden key: not a door to another world, but the ability to see the light in all shadows."

George turned to the writer, his expression thoughtful. "And so," he said, "what do you take from this?"

The writer considered the question carefully. "The journey and the matter aren't what matter, for the light is always worth following, even when the path is hard. All the great stories are not about endings but about what is made possible beyond them—what is birthed anew in the reader when the last word is read."

George grinned, a glimmer of pride in his eyes. "That," he said, "is the second truth of stories. Now, let us go on, for your story is not yet finished."

And with that, the golden forest began to fade, but the light lingered in the writer's heart, a quiet flame that would guide him long after his own journey was done.

The writer now stood in a meadow that stretched on forever—or at least for quite a long way, which amounts to much the same thing when you're in a place like this. The grass was that perfect shade of green that seems to exist only in illustrations of children frolicking in sunny fields, and the air carried the faint smell of new parchment, ink, and, for some reason, freshly baked chocolate chip cookies.

Under a tree that was both exactly like every tree the writer had ever seen and yet utterly unique, stood three figures. They looked... well, they looked like authors, in the way that certain people always seem to be carrying the slight aura of half-finished manuscripts.

"Good, here you are at last," said a man whose voice carried the calm assurance of a convivial Fellow who was always quite certain that *tea was the answer, even if you hadn't asked the question.* He gestured toward the writer with a smooth, deliberate wave of a hand that invited trust—though it held the unspoken edge of someone who had seen enough unexpected guests to know that not all of them left things as they found them.

"We are some who carried the old tales forward," he said, as if that explained everything.

The writer squinted at the other two.

"A Giver," said the second figure, her smile penetrating and friendly all at once. The sort of smile that seemed to say, *I've seen your nonsense, and I've decided to forgive it anyway.*

"You may call me Cherubim," said the third, who seemed to see everything with the quiet confidence that comes from knowing how to fold space-time into origami swans with her words when expedient.

Recognizing himself to be in the presence of literary greatness, the writer tried to nod intelligently. Instead, he let out a small noise, somewhere between "Erm" and "Eeep."

"You've come far," the Fellow said, stepping forward. "From the frozen heart of *The Snow Queen,* I wove my fantastical world, a place where winter melts beneath the roar of the great lion."

"I shaped *The Golden Key* into the fabric of my novels," the Giver said, her tone brisk, like a teacher who expected you to keep up. "Its light became the memory that awakens a people frozen in sameness."

"And I folded both stories into the tesseract of my books," Cherubim added, her eyes glinting. "The shard became the darkness we fight, and the light became the love that binds the stars."

The writer tried to process this. It wasn't that he didn't understand. It was just that he wasn't sure what you were supposed to say to people who'd taken cosmic truths and turned them into bedtime reading.

"And now?" the writer managed, his voice doing an impression of a small bird attempting its first song.

"Now," said Cherubim, her tone as gentle as starlight, "it is your turn."

"The stories do not end with us," the Giver added, her smile softening into something like approval. "They live in every heart, waiting to be told again."

"They are eternal sparks," the Fellow said, as if he were delivering a particularly rousing lecture to a room full of students. "Igniting the fires of creation. And now, the torch is yours."

The writer blinked. "Mine?" he asked, looking at the torch now inexplicably in his hand.

"Well, we're certainly not holding onto it forever," said the Giver.

"What would be the point of that?" Cherubim said, winking, her voice brimming with promise and mirth.

The Fellow clapped him on the shoulder with that firm encouragement that makes you believe in both yourself and the existence of lampposts in enchanted forests. "You've seen the shards. You've followed the light. You know where the stories come from and where they lead. Now, it's time to tell your own."

The writer glanced back at the meadow, then down at the torch. Its flame swayed, golden and steady, a light that wasn't just fire but possibility.

"And don't overthink it," the Giver added, as if reading his mind.

"Just start," cajoled Cherubim, grinning as if she knew something wonderful was about to happen.

"After all," the Fellow said, stepping back beneath the great tree, "you've been carrying the spark all along."

The writer took a deep breath, gripping the torch in both hands tightly. Behind him, the meadow stretched on forever. Ahead of him, there was only a blank page, waiting.

And with that, he stepped forward.

Once upon a time...

The writer sat before his empty page, and for the first time, the silence felt warm. It wrapped around him like the fading glow of a dying fire—not with flames, but with the kind etched in our memory of heat. His pen hovered over the paper, no longer hesitant but filled with the certainty of motion, the anticipation of creation.

He carried within him the fracturing of Kai, the fierce love of Gerda, Mossy's golden key, and even Tangle's air-fish, along with the voices of the storytellers who had walked alongside him and before him. They had not given him answers—no, answers were fleeting, like facts. But they had given him stories, and stories were eternal.

Fairy tales, he now understood, are the marrow of every story ever told. They are not bound by time or place, for they are not merely iterations of the world but the sparks that create the creation of it. They burn through the fabric of what is and reveal what could be. It is in their telling, retelling, and reshaping that humanity takes its next step forward—not with certainty, but with hope. Hope that the next tale might carry us closer to the door beyond the mountain, closer to the light that we glimpse and follow, even when the way is hard.

For every writer, no matter how small, holds in their hands the power to shape humanity's path. Fairy tales are the seeds of the divine story, scattered across time to grow in hearts that long for light. They remind us of what is true—not by replacing the truth, but by leading us to it. These stories, simple yet profound, can guide us closer to the light, warning us of evil, pointing the way to hope, compassion, and the divine threads that bind us all.

Yet he also understood the danger: stories can be abused. They can be wielded not to teach truth but to obscure it, to twist and distort, filling the void where truth would stand. Such stories do not lift us; they weigh us down, feeding despair, breeding division, and leading us toward annihilation.

The writer now knew the choice before him. To write is to decide: to nurture the seeds of the divine story or to plant something darker, something that consumes rather than creates.

With his pen poised above the blank page, he chose. He chose to sow the seeds that might grow into something greater than himself, something that could lead others to the light they so desperately sought.

Thus, the Telling continues...

The Godfather

Introduction by Brother Reginald,
Accidental Discoverer and Chronicler of Unlikely Epistles

*Let it never be held that divine revelation only arrives with dignity. The discovery of **The Book of Death** was, in fact, the result of a poorly maintained table, a particularly stubborn floor crack, and my own misguided belief that rocks make excellent tools for carpentry. When the table collapsed (as all tables inevitably do when confronted with enthusiastic incompetence), I stumbled upon this ancient manuscript hidden beneath the library floor. Its title, **The Book of Death**, was not what one might call reassuring. My first thought was, "Oh dear," followed quickly by, "This seems* *important," and finally, "I wonder if this will get me out of latrine duty."*

Inside, I found words of startling profundity, humor, and, somewhat inexplicably, a great deal of respect for French bulldogs. Yes, French bulldogs—the small, snorting creatures that look like God got distracted halfway through creating them and decided to see how far human intervention would go. Death himself, it turns out, is particularly fond of them, citing their mere presence as proof of a loving God. He muses that if humanity can sustain such odd and wonderful little beings, perhaps we aren't entirely without hope. And really, who am I to argue with that? After all, it isn't every day you discover a lost book of the Bible written by Death himself and featuring life lessons about humility, mortality, and the occasional ludiocrity of Frenchies.

1. This revelation made known by sending the angel Samael to his servant John, I was caught up in the Spirit, and I beheld a great vision of endings and beginnings, truths wrapped in illogicality, and the mystery of existence itself. And lo, a poor man walked the earth, cradling his newborn son, his brow furrowed with the eternal question: "What shall become of this child?"

2. The man sought a godfather for his son, one who might guide him in the ways of wisdom and purpose. First, he approached a merchant, whose wealth gleamed like the sun but whose soul seemed as hollow as the inside of an ornamental vase. 3. "Will you take my son as your godchild?" asked the man.

4. The merchant smiled the sort of smile that only excessive wealth and a lack of accountability can produce. "Bring him to me, and I shall teach him to measure his worth in gold and his success by the number of people who envy him." 5. The man considered this and thought, "That sounds deeply unfulfilling," so he left.

6. Next, he approached a farmer, bent with toil but radiant with the earthy dignity of someone who could grow a prize-winning

pumpkin without ever mentioning it. "Will you take my son as your godchild?" he asked. 7. The farmer nodded solemnly and said, "I shall teach him the patience of the earth and the reward of labor."

8. But the man hesitated, for while he respected the farmer's way, he suspected his son might not enjoy a life of shoveling shit.

9. And as the man continued his wanderings, the darkness deepened, and the air grew still. Finally, he happened upon a figure, tall and cloaked, whose scythe gleamed with inevitability. The man fell to his knees and whispered, "You are Death."

10. YES, said Death, in a voice that echoed with all the lost things. BUT DON'T WORRY—I'M GENERALLY GOOD COMPANY, AS LONG AS YOU DON'T MIND THE ODD FRENCH BULLDOG.

11. "French bulldog?" the man asked, confused.

12. YES. THEY'RE NOT JUST DOGS. PERISH THE THOUGHT. THEY'RE PROOF. PROOF THAT THERE IS A GREATER POWER OUT THERE, SOMEONE OR SOMETHING WITH A KEEN SENSE OF HUMOR AND A LOVE OF THE RIDICULOUS.

13. CONSIDER THIS: BY ALL LOGIC, FRENCH BULLDOGS SHOULD NOT EXIST. THEY CAN'T BREATHE PROPERLY. THEY CAN'T SWIM. THEY LOOK LIKE WOBBLY LAMPSHADES THAT GOT INTO AN ARGUMENT WITH GRAVITY AND LOST. AND YET, DESPITE ALL OF THIS—DESPITE BEING AN OXYGEN-CHALLENGED, AERODYNAMICALLY IMPOSSIBLE, AND UTTERLY UNNECESSARY CREATURE—THEY THRIVE. NOT ONLY THAT, BUT PEOPLE LOVE THEM. ADORE THEM. EVEN BUILD INSTAGRAM PAGES FOR THEM. NOW TELL ME, DO YOU REALLY THINK THIS HAPPENED BY ACCIDENT?

14. **IF THE UNIVERSE WERE PURELY RANDOM, WE'D ONLY HAVE EFFICIENT DOGS. DOGS THAT COULD OUTRUN CHEETAHS AND FETCH STICKS FROM SPACE. BUT NO. WE HAVE FRENCH BULLDOGS.** 15. **THE ONLY REASONABLE EXPLANATION IS THAT SOMEWHERE OUT THERE, A CREATOR LOOKED AT THE WORLD AND SAID, "YOU KNOW WHAT THIS NEEDS? A DOG THAT SOUNDS LIKE A WHEEZY TEAPOT AND WALKS LIKE IT'S CONSIDERING WHETHER IT'S TOO MUCH EFFORT TO FALL OVER."**

16. **SO, WHEN YOU LOOK AT A FRENCH BULLDOG, WHAT YOU'RE SEEING ISN'T JUST A DOG. YOU'RE SEEING THE EVIDENCE OF A DIVINE SENSE OF HUMOR. YOU'RE SEEING THE PROOF THAT SOMETIMES, CREATION ISN'T ABOUT SENSE OR MEANING. IT'S ABOUT JOY.**

17. **AND IF THAT DOESN'T MAKE YOU SMILE, THEN I REALLY DON'T KNOW WHAT WILL. BUT WE DIGRESS. WHAT CAN I DO FOR YOU?**

18. And so the man, slightly unnerved but oddly comforted, asked, "Will you be the godfather of my son?"

19. Death tilted his skull, considering this. **I SUPPOSE I COULD. IT'S BEEN A WHILE SINCE I'VE TAKEN A DIRECT INTEREST IN HUMANITY. BESIDES, I AM FAIR. I COME TO ALL.**

20. And Death made a covenant with the man. **YOUR CHILD SHALL BE A HEALER. WHEN I STAND AT THE FOOT OF THE SICK, HE MAY SAVE THEM, FOR THEIR TIME HAS NOT COME. BUT IF I STAND AT THEIR HEAD, HE MUST DO NOTHING—BECAUSE, LET'S BE HONEST, EVERYONE HAS TO PAY THE BILL SOMETIME, AND I DON'T DO EXTENSIONS.**

21. And it came to pass that the child grew to be a physician of great renown, beloved by the people and slightly too aware of his own brilliance. 22. But as his fame grew, so too did his pride, until he began to believe he might outwit even Godfather Death himself.

23. One day, a great king fell ill. It was the sort of illness that royal advisors whispered about behind thick velvet curtains while looking suspiciously at the food taster, who had, by some miracle, remained upright. Death stood at the head of the king's bed, his presence as subtle as a gong in a monastery. The king groaned weakly. The courtiers groaned sympathetically. And the physician thought, "If I save the king, my name will be praised forever. Statues will be built. Poems will be written. I might even get a holiday named after me."

24. So, with the quiet confidence of someone who plays with the house's stacked deck, he turned the bed, placing Death at the foot instead. The king stirred, coughed dramatically (because royalty never just *cough*), and declared himself cured. The courtiers applauded. The food taster quietly fainted with relief. And the physician basked in the glow of success, feeling as though the universe itself had just handed him a trophy.

25. But in the corner of the chamber, Death lingered. He wasn't looming ominously; he was simply… there, in the way that mountains are there—calm, immovable, and not in the mood for nonsense. 26. He was also holding a French bulldog.

27. The little creature sat nestled in Death's bony arms, snorting contentedly and occasionally kicking its stubby legs with a silly, stupid grin on its face, dreaming of chasing something it would never catch. 28. Death scratched behind its farcically large ears. **THAT WAS CLEVER** he said, his voice impartial but carrying the verdict of eternity. **NOT WISE. BUT CLEVER.**

29. The physician froze, his confidence wilting like an overwatered fern. "It worked, didn't it?" he said, as much to himself as to Death.

30. Death tilted his head thoughtfully, the French bulldog giving a tiny sneeze. **OH, IT WORKED**, Death said, the words coiling like fumes.

31. And then Death waited, as only an immortal inevitability can wait—with infinite patience and the quiet assurance that all things, even clever physicians, eventually run out of time. The French bulldog snorted again. **32.** It was hard to tell if it agreed or not.

33. Yet the physician did not learn. When the king's daughter fell ill, Death stood again at her head. **34.** The physician, emboldened by his arrogance, turned her bed. This time, Death sighed, a sound like ancient wind over just-walked-on graves, and said, **YOU DO REALIZE THIS WON'T END WELL FOR YOU?**

35. And Death took the physician by the hand—not unkindly, but with a firmness that suggests an appointment long overdue—and brought him to a cavern deep beneath the world. Within, there were candles, as countless as the stars, their flames flickering though the air was still.

36. "What is this place, Godfather?" the physician asked.

37. **THIS IS WHERE LIFE IS MEASURED,** said Death, gesturing to the candles. **SOME BURN BRIGHTLY. OTHERS FLICKER. AND THIS ONE HERE**… He pointed to a candle that was sputtering, dangerously close to extinguishing… **IS YOURS.**

38. The physician fell to his knees. "Can't you just… add more wax?"

39. Death shook his head, slowly. **IF I DID THAT FOR YOU, I'D HAVE TO DO IT FOR EVERYONE. AND THEN WE'D RUN OUT OF CANDLES. AND I DON'T THINK YOU APPRECIATE HOW EXPENSIVE FRENCH BULLDOGS ARE TO FEED.**

40. And with a breath as gentle as the turning of a page—and perhaps a moment's hesitation, for even Death, in his own inhuman way, had grown fond of his godson—he extinguished the flame. For regardless of sentiment or wishes, responsibility is what gives even eternity its meaning.

41. And I, John, saw the heavens open, and a voice like thunder proclaimed, *"Let this be a revelation to all: Life is not about the length of the flame, but about what it illuminates before it fades."*

42. And Death turned to me, a French bulldog snoring loudly under his arm, and said, **REMEMBER THIS: I AM NOT YOUR ENEMY. I AM YOUR COMPLETION, YOUR CONCLUSION. AND SERIOUSLY, ADOPT A FRENCH BULLDOG. IF NOTHING ELSE, IT WILL KEEP YOU HUMBLE.**

Afterword
by Godfather Death

SO, YOU'VE REACHED THE END. WELL DONE. I SUPPOSE YOU EXPECT SOMETHING PROFOUND HERE, A COOKIE, OR PERHAPS A FINAL REVELATION ABOUT LIFE, THE UNIVERSE, AND EVERYTHING. BUT HONESTLY, I THINK IT'S TIME WE ADDRESS THE TRUTH ABOUT FRENCH BULLDOGS.

YES, FRENCH BULLDOGS. JUST LOOK AT THEM. THEY SHOULDN'T BE, AND YET THEY ARE. THEY CAN'T BREATHE PROPERLY, THEY WADDLE THROUGH LIFE LIKE LITTLE DRUNK PHILOS-OPHERS, AND THEIR EARS LOOK LIKE THEY'RE TRYING TO PICK UP SIGNALS FROM SPACE. AND STILL, THEY FLOURISH. WHY? BECAUSE SOMETHING—OR SOMEONE—LOOKED AT THE WORLD AND DECIDED IT NEEDED A CREATURE SO IMPOSSIBLY RIDICULOUS THAT IT COULD ONLY BE A GIFT.

REMEMBER THIS: IF SOMETHING AS IMPLAUSIBLE AS A FRENCH BULLDOG CAN EXIST, SO

CAN HOPE. SO CAN JOY. SO CAN YOU. LIVE YOUR LIFE LIKE A FRENCH BULLDOG. TODDLE THROUGH IT WITH DETERMINATION. SNORT IN THE FACE OF ADVERSITY. ACCEPT YOUR ABSURDITY, BECAUSE THAT'S WHERE YOUR MAGIC LIES. YOU ARE NOT MEANT TO BE PERFECT. YOU ARE MEANT TO BE.

AND ONE DAY, WHEN WE MEET, I'LL ASK YOU WHAT YOU MADE OF YOUR TIME. IF YOU BRING A FRENCH BULLDOG ALONG, WELL, THAT WILL MAKE THE ANSWER A LITTLE CLEARER. (ALTHOUGH, FAIR WARNING: THE FRENCHIE MAY SNORE THROUGH MY QUESTIONS—OR, MORE ACCURATELY, GRACE US WITH THE QUIRKY WHEEZY SYMPHONY THAT IS THE SONG OF THEIR PEOPLE.)

— DEATH

(Penned in loving memory of Sir Terry Pratchett and in tribute to his inimitable Death.)

The Way of the Rose

Once upon a time, in a world that buzzed with mobile phones, thrummed with caffeine-fueled ambition, and had grown suspicious of fairy tales, there was a merchant who had once been very rich and very happy—or at least he thought so. He had three sons, who were the practical sort—with names that nobody ever seemed to recall—and three daughters, who were... well, let's call them interesting.

The eldest two daughters were everything the modern world applauded. The oldest, Letitia, dressed impeccably; the middle child, Brianna, worked tirelessly at her high-powered job; and both maintained impressive social media profiles full of beachside selfies and motivational quotes. But the world, ever demanding, was never satisfied. Their careers consumed them, their friends were frenemies, and their online followers were more interested in the latest gossip than their carefully crafted personas.

Beauty, the youngest, was another matter. She read books. Actual books, with pages you could turn and stories that didn't come with hashtags. This alone made her quite perplexing. She also liked quiet evenings, long walks, and the sort of small, meaningful conversations that most people had forgotten how to have. Her sisters thought her positively prehistoric.

"Honestly, Beauty," the eldest sniffed one day, balancing a glass of Chardonnay in one hand and a phone in the other. "How will you ever find an equal partner with all that reading and mooning about?"

"Yes," the second chimed in, "You should try dating apps. That's how modern people find love."

"Really? Love?" Beauty asked mildly. "I thought it was just for hookups."

Her sisters rolled their eyes. "You're hopeless."

It wasn't that Beauty was against romance, but she had noticed something about the modern variety: it didn't seem to make anyone very happy. Her sisters' dates were mostly disasters—awkward affairs full of competitive one-upmanship, passive-aggressive bill-splitting, and conversations that revolved around "branding." And the men? Well, they were nice enough, but "nice" was the problem. They were as polished and passionless as their Instagram feeds, and not one of them seemed to know how to fix a broken chair, let alone a lonely heart.

Things went on like this until the merchant's business collapsed, leaving him with nothing but debts, a ramshackle house in the countryside, and a family that now had to face reality.

The countryside, of course, was dreadful. The eldest daughters made this clear by loudly declaring it so every morning. The Wi-Fi was spotty, the nearest coffee shop was an hour away, and the local men had the audacity to be cheerful farmers instead of brooding entrepreneurs. The sons worked diligently to fix the house, the merchant busied himself with the garden, and Beauty—well, she scrubbed floors, cooked meals, and generally kept things running. It wasn't glamorous, but it was honest work, and there was something about it that made her feel alive.

Her sisters, meanwhile, flopped about like beached fish. They dabbled in yoga and mindfulness apps but gave up when they didn't feel "transformed" after a week. They started projects—knitting, painting, sourdough baking—but abandoned them halfway through. They were miserable, and because they were miserable, they took every opportunity to make Beauty miserable too.

Then came the letter. A long-forgotten investment had resurfaced, and the merchant set off to reclaim what little he could. Before he left, his daughters made their requests. The eldest wanted a designer handbag, the second a collection of artisanal perfumes. Beauty, who didn't have much use for handbags or perfume, asked for a rose.

"A rose?" her sisters sneered. "How quaint."

Beauty smiled. "I suppose it is."

But the merchant returned with neither handbags nor perfumes nor even the rose he had promised Beauty. What he did bring back was a story—a terrifying, improbable story about a monstrous Beast who had caught him taking a single rose from an enchanted garden. He had stumbled upon the castle by chance, tired and lost, astonished to find its gates open, its halls silent but welcoming. A feast had been laid out as if prepared just for him, though no host ever appeared. But as he prepared to leave, a single rose plucked from the castle gardens in hand for Beauty, the Beast materialized—a hulking, grotesque creature, furious at the theft.

The merchant had pleaded for his life, explaining the rose was for his daughter, and only then had the Beast relented—though his mercy was chilling. He would spare the merchant, but only if one of his daughters came willingly to take his place.

The sisters reacted predictably—Letitia with disbelief, Brianna with outrage. But the consequence of Beauty's request crouched like an invisible beast upon her conscience, one she couldn't shake. None of this would have happened if not for her.

"You're not seriously considering this?" Letitia said, pacing as though sheer movement could outwit the situation.

Brianna crossed her arms, her jaw tight. "This is insane. He's probably some eccentric recluse trying to get his hands on a servant."

But Beauty observed her father's voice faltering as he recounted the Beast's terrible demand, his guilt saturating the silence that followed. He couldn't meet her eyes when he finished. Beauty looked at her sisters, their faces pinched with indignation, and then at her father, withdrawn and defeated. "I'll go," she said softly, the words steady despite the pounding of her heart. And though her brothers protested and her father begged her to reconsider, Beauty already knew her choice. If the Beast had spared her father's life, then she would meet him face to face and decide for herself what kind of man—or monster—he truly was.

The Beast's castle was everything the modern world wasn't: vast, timeless, and unashamedly itself. It didn't care if you liked it or not, and Beauty found that oddly refreshing. The Beast himself was much the same. He wasn't polite. He wasn't nice. He didn't smile to make her feel comfortable. Unlike the other chaps she'd met, he didn't bother with filters or lace the air with words that loitered awkwardly before dropping like dead flies. He was simply... present.

Beauty had never met anyone like him. Modern men, with their curated vulnerability and careful avoidance of anything that might be perceived as "toxic masculinity," seemed so small in comparison. The Beast didn't apologize for his strength or his scars. He held doors open for her without making a show of it. He listened when she spoke and didn't feel the need to interrupt with his own opinions. He wasn't afraid to disagree, and he certainly wasn't afraid to feel—fiercely, it seemed.

"Do you think me ugly?" he asked her one evening.

"Terribly," she replied, but there was a smile in her voice.

"Good," he said. "It's better to know where you stand."

At first, she thought she would hate him. Then she thought she might tolerate him. Somewhere along the way, she realized she looked forward to their conversations more than anything else.

As their mutual trust grew, the Beast finally agreed to Beauty's request to visit her father's home. Yet when she returned, the modern world struck her as more shallow and insubstantial than ever. Her sisters were bitter, like the black espresso they sipped—Letitia's new husband was absent, much like her happiness, and Brianna's latest conquest seemed plastered to her, clinging like a wet coat in a downpour. Beauty tried to tell them about the Beast, about the intimate world they were shaping together—brimming with profound encounters and startling clarity—but they couldn't understand. Worse, they didn't want to.

"You're wasting your life," the eldest said. "You could do so much better."

"Better?" Beauty asked, raising an eyebrow. "And by 'better,' you mean what, exactly? Someone who spends more time on his hair than I do?"

Her sisters didn't answer. They didn't need to. Their lives, their faces, their vacant laughter—all of it spoke for them.

After two long weeks away, Beauty returned to the castle and was astonished to discover the Beast crumpled in his garden, massive frame diminished by what-ifs and maybes, silent and solitary among the roses. She knelt beside him, her fear eclipsed by a grief she could not name, her hands trembling as she touched his chest and felt the too-faint beat of his enormous heart.

The Beast's eyes flickered open, weary but clear. "I couldn't make you stay," he said, his voice steady despite its weakness. "Better for me to let you go than to see you unfulfilled. But now, having you here... that is enough."

His words, plain and unadorned, carried a truth that pierced Beauty to her very core: to love is to risk, for in loving, a piece of your heart is forever bound to the beloved. In that moment, something within her shifted, not breaking, but settling into place as though it had always belonged.

Her hands were anxious as they pressed against his furred chest, searching desperately for a heartbeat. It drummed feebly, like the faint tapping of a moth against the windowpane. And in that moment, Beauty understood what the modern world had forgotten, what it had willingly traded for convenience and autonomy, for glittering appearances and winning connections.

Love, real love, was not easy. It was not a perfect algorithm, a swipe right, or a curated highlight reel. It wasn't neat or tidy or efficient. It didn't always make sense. It wasn't about standing alone, bristling with independence, nor was it about collapsing entirely into another person's shadow. Intimacy was something else altogether—something raw and wild, built on the fragile and miraculous balance of strength and vulnerability. It was trust, not the kind that demanded assurances, but the kind that jumped anyway, that bared itself knowing it might not be caught.

Beauty looked at the Beast, his body so hideous yet still magnificent, and thought about how the world had forgotten how to leap. It had forgotten that love was not meant to be comfortable, that it required courage—not the bravery that comes with fanfare and applause, but the quiet, stubborn sort that stays when it would be easier to leave. Love contends.

She thought of her sisters' brittle relationships, of the men she'd met who measured their worth in status and their affection in gestures just big enough to be noticed but not enough to carry weight. The Beast had been none of those things. He had been unapologetically himself, rare and real in a way that the modern world no longer knew how to be.

She leaned over him, her tears slipping down her cheeks and onto his fur. "You don't get to leave me," she whispered, her voice breaking. "Not now. Not when I've only just found you."

His eyelids fluttered, just barely, and she saw the faintest trace of gold beneath. It wasn't enough to give her hope, but she spoke the words anyway, because they were the only truth she had ever known.

"I love you," she said, her voice steady now, all fear and reservation gone. "I love you for everything you are and everything you're not. I love you because you are the one thing this world is too afraid to be—real. And I am not afraid to leap."

And as she spoke, the garden seemed to exhale. The roses lifted their heads, their colors deepening as though the soil had been reminded of its purpose. The faint breeze that stirred the air smelled of something ancient and alive. And beneath her hand, his fading heartbeat began to grow stronger. The Beast's chest rose, shallow at first, then with greater urgency, as though life itself had reached out and pulled him back from the edge.

His eyes opened, effulgent and piercing, and for a moment, they seemed to contain the entire world. Beauty saw in them not the creature, but something more—a spirit unbound, a being unafraid to give or be given to. And in his gaze, she saw the answer to a question she hadn't known she was asking: What is love, truly?

"Beauty," he murmured, his voice rough but alive.

She smiled through her tears and cradled his face in her hands. "You're here," she said, as much to herself as to him. And in that moment, she understood what the world had so long sought to forget—that the love between a man and a woman, flawed and untamed as it may be, was among the few things in this life that truly mattered.

The transformation was quiet—a sparkle of light, a breath of wind. When it was over, the Beast was gone, replaced by a man with strong hands and familiar eyes.

"Still you?" she asked.

"Always."

"Still ugly," she said, "but I'll manage."

Not-quite-the-Beast grinned. "Is it possible?"

"Very. I was rather fond of the old you."

He blinked. "You mean the...?"

"Yes. You were much more interesting as a Beast."

And so they married, though Beauty insisted he keep a framed portrait of his former self in the library, "just to remind you of your better days."

Years later, when their grandchildren asked how she had fallen in love with a Beast, Beauty would laugh and say, "He wasn't perfect, but at least he didn't bore me to death."

Which, as far as happily-ever-afters go, is as good as it gets.

Two Princesses, One End

Once upon a time, there lived a Visionary with a peculiar knack for building castles in the air out of arches and rafters—or, more often than not, animated ink and paint. This man was no ordinary dreamer; he was a tireless schemer, a conjurer of impossible ideas, the kind of fellow who saw rainbows where others saw rain, and gold where others saw coal dust.

Now, our Visionary had no intention of dreaming alone, mind you. He gathered around him a strange and lively troupe of minds every bit as peculiar as his own—a ragtag band he called "Imagineers." These were inventors, artists, and storytellers, each more eccentric than the last, bound together by their leader's infectious desire to build a world out of pure imagination. "No," he would say, with a glint in his eye whenever one of them fretted about the cost or the risk, "we're going to make something that lasts—something that twinkles long after we're snuffed."

For the Visionary, storytelling was no light matter. He believed stories had to dig deep into the heart, to make one feel as if they'd slipped into another world. This was why, whenever he sat down to shape a tale, he did so with one goal: to enchant the sentiments of everyone watching, to make them laugh and weep and, most importantly, to remember how to be bigger. He was after something timeless, something that could entertain while bonding the old and the young in a single sweep of color and sound and truth.

Perhaps most importantly, my children, this Visionary wasn't one for mere ambition or acclaim. There was, he declared, something greater behind his drive. He spoke of "Divine inspiration," claiming it was a guiding force in his life, the reason why he fought so hard to uphold the human spirit in every tale. "Without inspiration, we would perish," he added. Perhaps this was the secret to his uncanny brand of enchantment—something just a touch grander and more eternal than individual dreams or group goals.

Initially, he drew Alice, a live-action living girl exploring Cartoonland; then there was Oswald, an animated rabbit born of black and white ink with lucky strokes; and finally, a cartoon mouse with ears that seemed to defy gravity and a spirit that would one day encompass the world. "Mortimer," the Visionary wanted to call him, until his far-seeing wife, bright as a lightning strike, wisely suggested "Mickey" instead. Thus, with Mickey as his emblem, the Visionary did something no one had ever dared do before.

He threaded sound through silent frames, splashed colors across once-grayscale screens, and set his characters singing and laughing as if they'd never been anything but alive. Then, with an audacity that defied belief, he embarked on his grandest dream yet: a full-length animated film. It was a gamble that should have drained him dry, a feat of imagination and engineering that demanded he coax his inventors into building something entirely new. The multiplane camera was born—a contraption that layered animation upon animation, creating depth from flatness and turning the simple into the spectacular, the two-dimensional short into three-dimensional reality. And with this machine in hand, he set his sights on an ancient tale that called to him from across the ages.

The Visionary knew that some stories—the oldest stories—are built on bones stronger than time. He had seen it in the dusty pages of fairy tale books, in the way children's eyes widened at the mention of witches, curses, and castles cloaked in darkness. He knew that to capture the heart of a dream, he had to begin with a tale that carried echoes of something deeper, something that had haunted firesides and lurked in the woods. And so, he reached back to a story as old as our fear of the dark, as ancient as rumors, a tale that had survived for centuries, passed from one storyteller to the next.

And the Visionary found a princess—oh, not the formulaic princess we often imagine today, singing sweetly to birds or finishing each other's sandwiches, but a girl known to German children as *Sneewittchen*, a child of the dark woods, hidden from a stepmother whose envy burrowed inward, biting like a splinter she couldn't remove. The Brothers Grimm had captured this disturbing fairy tale on paper, but the Visionary took it up again, dusting off the obscurities and casting them in vibrant color, pulling out *some* of the gloom and filling it with a different, more-hopeful magic. With each brush of color, with each note of song, with each plot point spit-shined, the tale changed, like a shadow stretching in the late afternoon sun, becoming something at once familiar yet new. And so, let me tell you, as the old Visionary himself might have told it, what he kept and what he changed.

In the Grimm's version, when Snow White's stepmother's mirror told her that Snow White's beauty now eclipsed her own, it was more than vanity that drove her; it was covetous fury, the kind that simmers and sparks into forest fires. She did not ask her huntsman for a mere heart as the Visionary's queen did. No, she wanted her stepdaughter's lungs and liver. She planned to eat them, believing that by consuming Snow White's flesh, the evil queen could devour the girl's beauty, youth, and very life force to claim it as her own. In this older story, the huntsman let Snow White go *only after* she whispered her plan to escape into the woods, the desperate plea of a girl who understood the necessity of survival in the face of adversity far too young. This Grimm's heroine was a young girl who obeyed her elders, but was not so naïve as to disbelieve in monsters.

Through tangled trees and twisting shadows, the brothers' Snow White found the little house where the dwarfs lived—not the bustling, messy cottage of song and dance that the Visionary's Imagineers painted, but a place perfectly kept, clean as a chapel. There was no need for her to whistle or tidy; it was a sanctuary, not a man cave, and these dwarfs were no clichéd dwarfs, either. They had no names, sang no jolly songs. They were guardians, simple and solemn.

Silly, silent Dopey was entirely the imagineers' creation.

And yet, the Queen's hunger for vengeance, as penned by the brothers Grimm, only grew. In her wicked mind, one scheme was never enough. *Three times* she came to Snow White's cottage (not just once, as the full-length cartoon later portrayed), disguised and bearing a different weapon each time. Her first attempt? A lace bodice, cinched so tightly around Snow White's small ribs that she crumpled to the ground, breathless as death itself. But the dwarfs came, cut her free, and she awoke to tell the tale.

Next, this Grimm Queen returned with a comb, silver and gleaming. She promised Snow White it would make her hair shine like the morning sun. But this comb was laced with poison, and the moment it touched Snow White's hair, she fell again. The dwarfs found her limp and unresponsive, the comb still tangled in her hair, and they removed it, breaking the spell. They warned the princess, sternly this time, not to let anyone in.

Yet just as envy is relentless, eating away at our contentment, so was this Grimmy Queen. The Visionary's version only captures her third attempt, when she brought an apple—rosy, beautiful, its red skin glistening like forbidden fruit, a tempting echo of humanity's first fall. Of course, the Visionary's version left out that the Queen—disguised as a humble old peasant rather than the frightening hag of the cartoon—took a bite of the unpoisoned white flesh to prove the apple's safety. Snow White, young and convinced, took a bite of the red, poisoned skin, sealing her fate. She crumpled to the ground, her cheeks still pink, her lips still red, looking alive but bound in a spell deeper than sleep. The dwarfs, heartbroken for the girl they had sworn to protect, laid her in a glass coffin, where her beauty could shine like starlight, and there she stayed.

In the Grimm's telling, a prince came, but he did not kiss her; no, he admired her from afar and sought to take her coffin home with him, to guard her even in death. As his servants carried the coffin, one stumbled, and the jolt dislodged the poisoned apple from her throat. She awoke, gasping for breath, alive and well, to the prince's incredulity.

Together, they returned to the kingdom, where the prince, wary and wily, prepared a punishment for the wicked Queen. At their wedding, she was given no crown or throne, but instead red-hot iron shoes, heated in coals until they glowed. And as she was forced to dance in them, she met the dark end that she had wished upon her own stepdaughter.

The Visionary suspected this fairy tale's darkness would prove too much for his audiences and chose instead to weave in something else, something uplifting and brighter. In his hands, it became a story not of punishment, but of "true love's kiss"—a magic born of gentleness, hope, and faith that could awaken even the deepest slumber. With this shift, he created a modern myth, one where love's power transcended evil, rewarding beauty and kindness with its happily ever after embrace. This notion of "true love's kiss" became an innovative refrain in his stories, weaving itself into the fabric of future tales—a spell to linger long after he was gone, so powerful it transformed the kiss into an essential gesture of courtship, settling deep into the dreams and fantasies of generations to follow.

Yet not all visionaries of the age received this softened version with gladness. Among the Visionary's own contemporaries were Tolkien and Lewis, men who, in their own right, loved fairy tales and shaped the dreams of the twentieth century with stories steeped in the weight of wonder. To them, fairy tales were sacred—vessels of truth wrapped in enchantment, meant not to distract, but to prepare the soul for life's greatest trials and triumphs. Tolkien bristled at the portrayal of the dwarfs—*dwarves*, as he would have it—stripped of their ancient dignity, rendered as comic relief where once there had been mystery and might. Lewis, too, found the sweetness cloying, the levity ill-fitted to a tale whose roots reached deep into the soil of human spirit. They believed fairy tales must not blink at sorrow or evil, but look it full in the face—and by so doing, teach courage, not comfort. In the Visionary's Snow White, they saw not a story reborn, but its polished likeness—safe, softened, and unable to rouse the deeper truths a real tale must stir.

And so, my dear reader, you see the difference. The Visionary's Snow White is a tale softened and shined, where evil melts under the kiss of true love saves all. But in the old tales, envy bites, vengeance festers, and justice, in the end, consumes like fire.

This Visionary grew older, as all of us do, and his dreams grew with him, swelling like balloons to carry him toward the heavens. But he was not satisfied with paper and ink, nor with mere moving pictures on a screen. No, his mind leapt further, grasping at something grander. He wished to step inside his own dreams, to walk amongst his characters, to create a place where stories weren't just told but lived, a place where magic flashed in the air and adventure lay waiting around every corner.

He dreamed of building a spot unlike any the world had ever known—a "magical kingdom," he called it, where children and adults alike could wander hand in hand, safe and spellbound. It would be a world of whimsy and wonder, yet clean and shining, a sanctuary of laughter and delight. And so he poured his heart and soul into this dream, gathering his Imagineers to lay every brick, craft every corner, perfect every scene. And finally, with the gates flung open, the world stepped into the dream he named Disneyland.

And the people came, oh, how they came! They streamed through the gates in droves, wide-eyed and open-hearted, trailing children like ducklings. The Visionary watched them and smiled, knowing he had created a haven, a world where magic was real and troubles melted like sugar on the tongue.

But, as is the way of things, dear reader, even the best of dreams cannot last forever. The Visionary grew ill, his body failing even as his mind raced onward, dreaming up yet grander visions, ever-imagining upward and beyond. And so, as is the way of all things, the Visionary quietly departed this world, leaving behind his dreams—alive and pulsing—for his family to carry forward. His brother and his nephew took up the mantle, and they honored his legacy well. They built new magical kingdoms in distant lands, bringing the Visionary's magic to shores far and wide. They launched a television channel, inviting families to gather together around the glowing screen, basking in the light of the stories the Visionary had left behind. They even staged his dreams on the high seas, in lavish, gleaming ships that sailed the waters like floating enchanted kingdoms, carrying mirth and magic across the waves.

Yet, as often happens with magic, others began to take notice and want it for their own. The Visionary's creations—those castles spun from dreams, those stories that shone like stars—began to change under grasping hands. A new Boss emerged, with a rich gleam in his eye and ambition as keen as a vulture's glare. He saw the potential spark of opportunity in the Visionary's legacy, ready to catch and spread like wildfire, and so he stoked it into an inferno, launching what was later called the company's "Renaissance." The Boss unfurled his grand new vision with a story bright and daring as the first—but deliberately crafted to excise the soul that once inspired the Visionary's marvels, using imagineering for profiteering.

More and more princess cartoons began to hit the screens, each one carefully followed by waves of merchandise—costumes, wands, dolls, and endless trinkets designed to sell pieces of the dream. And sell they did. Every holiday season, princess gifts topped wish lists, and soon, princess fever took hold, growing from innocent dress-up—a make-believe tiara here, a storybook frock there—into an empire of plastic dreams. Little girls wore these gowns everywhere—straight from the company's stores, of course—twirling through Halloween parades and filling theme parks in seas of satin and tulle, as parents looked on, chanting "little princess" with indulgent pride. Yet beneath all the sparkle lay a subtler invocation: each tiara, each pastel dress whispered that beauty was paramount, that to be adored was everything, and that every story must end with "happily ever after"—even if it was a dream spun from false promises and borrowed fantasies.

A different fairy tale princess was chosen with a new full-length cash cow in mind, this time drawn from the Danish tales of Hans Christian Andersen. Yet, as is often the way with such things, the Boss's little mermaid's tale was substantively changed from Andersen's telling. For unlike the Boss's commercialized mermaid, Andersen's Little Mermaid yearned for far more than romance; she ached for eternity.

You see, the original fairy tale tells us that, once upon a time, in the deep dimensions of the ocean, there lived a Little Mermaid. Not the wide-eyed, red-haired, singing sort of mermaid, mind you—this one was quiet, almost grave, with a heart weighed down by longings she couldn't quite understand. Hans Christian Andersen's story never bothered to name her, as she was more of a question than a girl, a creature with a longing for more than simply love. She was enchanted by humans, true, but it wasn't only their faces or their laughter. She envied them for something grander and stranger—their souls.

In the depths, where mermaids lived, life was long until it ended without recourse. They were born, they swam, they thrived for three hundred years, and then... they turned to sea foam, fading into bubbles without a trace. But humans, strange, air-breathing humans, had immortal souls that soared into heaven. To the Little Mermaid, this was magic of the highest order, a mystery worth every sacrifice. And so, she swam to the Sea Witch—a creature of little sympathy and remarkable power—and traded her voice and her fins for a pair of legs and the chance to walk among humans. The witch warned her that if she didn't win the prince's love, she would die and dissolve into foam. If, however, she won his heart and married him, she would share his soul.

When she stepped onto land, her new human legs came at a terrible price. Every step was agony, each movement like walking on knives. And while the prince found her enchanting, she was, to him, little more than a quiet, devoted creature—a younger sister, a loyal companion, perchance a pet, but never a bride. As time passed, the prince fell in love with another, and the mermaid's heart fractured like moonlight scattered on restless waves.

But even then, her sea-sisters came to her aid. They offered their hair to the Sea Witch for a magical dagger, a dark, decisive device that could save her life if she used it to kill the prince and his bride on their wedding night. But her heart—though battered, bruised, and hopeless—refused to turn hateful. Rather than plunge the knife into the man she loved, she chose her own end, throwing herself into the sea to dissolve into foam.

But Andersen's tale, as strange as it sounds, doesn't leave our little mermaid there. Instead, she's lifted upward by the Daughters of the Air, spirits who promise that through her selflessness, she can earn a soul and, one day, reach heaven. She became a creature of grace and hope, bound not by a single man's love but by the love that far surpasses us all.

Fast forward about a century and a half to the Boss's adaptation, and things start to look quite different. *This* little mermaid—"Ariel," they called her in the cartoon, after a nereid daughter of the Greek sea-god Triton—wasn't driven by the mysteries of the soul or eternity. She longed for the surface rather than heaven, singing songs of wanting "more," of wishing to be "part of their world," captivated by the glitz of the human kingdom and all its "other" wonders.

Ariel's eyes fell upon a prince, and in typical modern-day messaging, her crush was instantaneous, full of sparkles and daydreams and grass-is-greeners. She swam to the Sea Witch—a fat be-tentacled "Ursula" who was more drag queen than sea hag—and struck her bargain. She traded her voice for legs, and there was no pain to it—only the thrilling possibility of young love.

And unlike Andersen's tale, where the prince remained unmoved, here he was immediately smitten with Ariel's face and voice. So smitten, in fact, that when Ursula stole Ariel's voice and disguised herself as a beautiful dark maiden, he hardly noticed her snarling at his dog or her general lack of… well, decency. It was the magic of "true love's kiss" that the Boss and his minions diluted from the original Visionary—now dangled as the only way to save Ariel from her fate—an idealistic fantasy freshly twisted into a tantalizing narrative. The power of the kiss would break the spell, bringing not only love but a happy ending to tie it all up in a shiny bow.

In the end, the prince killed Ursula to save Ariel, and Ariel's father, King Triton, waved off his prejudice against humans. Why? Because "love," of course, which was now meant to passionately conquer all, rendered as the highest achievable good for humans. Ariel and her prince were soon married in a grand ceremony to live out their happy ending together here, on earth, where a single lifetime was more than enough. The two divided worlds of land and sea were brought together into a new world order.

And there, my friend, lies the difference. Andersen's Little Mermaid was a figure who suffered quietly, a princess who chose selflessness and sought a love so deep it could awaken the soul. He offered no "happily ever after," but instead hinted at something greater, something that required compassion and integrity to attain.

The Boss's version, on the other hand, stripped the tale of its poignant beauty, wrapping what had once been a messy, aching story with no easy answers in a neat, sparkling package of indulgence. In the end, Ariel's story wasn't about the soul or selflessness. It was about young passion, the pleasure of following one's heart, the gratification of overcoming a villain, and the promise of a sunny tomorrow.

And so it came to pass that the Visionary's nephew, the last of his kin to sit among the company's board, saw what his uncle's empire had become. A shadow had crept over the place, dulling its spark, shifting its purpose. With a heavy heart and a determined voice, he called for the new Boss to resign, declaring the unthinkable: that this once-glorious empire, this dream once as sturdy as brick and mortar, had "lost its focus, its creative energy, and its heritage." Successfully deposing the Boss, he too departed, leaving the Visionary's legacy in new hands that, alas, remained less interested in crafting magic than in mining it.

And now my children, watch and learn the truth about stories sterilized to push a hypodermic narrative. Eventually, live-action remakes by this adulterated company slunk their way into theaters, classic beauty muffled even more by new messages woven into its re-scaled flesh. What began as stories about what we all share became an eldritch mass of heavy-handed tentacular themes; regurgitating the vapors of what had once been magic, these no-longer cartoon princesses were at last drained of any true dimensionality at all, a reminder of what happens when dreams are taken by hands too eager to shape archetypal truths to their own ends. No longer were the company's stories about courage or kindness, about monsters children could face and conquer. Each became a cautionary tale of its own—one of what happens when visions fade into gray, when tales lose their pointed edge, and when stories, once bold and brave, are downgraded to insipid narrative. Viewers are coddled and chastened, taught to pretend that all creations are equal, that we must safeguard whatever serves the machine, and that destruction is always wrong—except, of course, when it aligns with the approved order.

So remember, my dreamers, stories are gifts to be cherished, not distorted. And the brightest stories, the ones that speak to our very souls, do not need reboots, remakes, or reimagining; they need only to be told, again and again, in voices that remember the truth of the tale.

Perhaps somewhere, in the hushed, forgotten corners of those once-magical kingdoms or the hearts that remember them, there are old stories that still linger, shadows cast by the brilliance of the Visionary's original dream. But those shadows, dear reader, are growing faint. And so it falls to us, to all of us, to remember the tales as they were meant to be—to recall the heroes who fought their monsters and won, to cherish stories that spoke not of division but of courage, hope, and unselfish love. For a fairy tale, as the Visionary knew all too well, is not merely a story to be told but a spark, a lighthouse to guide us through the storm. And as long as that spark is kept alight, the dream—the true dream—may, perchance, live on.

And with the final curtain, we are left with only two choices, my children. Shall we let the dream go gentle into that good night, or shall we rage, rage against the dying of the light?

Jacked Beanstalk

Once upon a time, there was a civilization built by giants.

Giants, as a rule, are neither good nor bad. Though powerful by mortal standards, they are easily vexed and frequently impatient. These giants, as is often their nature, grew restless. They abandoned their kingdoms, rising into the clouds to build new empires in the heavens. The humans, left to their own devices, began to forget. They told themselves stories—that it was their ancestors who had crafted the cities, their own ingenuity that shaped the world. The giants, if they ever existed at all, became the Enemy. Villains. Monsters. Soon, giants became myths, fading into the fog of memory, while humans grew proud and stubborn, declaring themselves the pinnacle of all creation.

In one of these lingering kingdoms there lived a boy named Jack Spriggins. Jack was small, but he carried the weight of the world on his shoulders, for his widowed mother was poor, and they had little left to support them but the cow she milked every day—with no opportunity that he could ever improve their circumstances. Their home, tucked away at the edge of the forest, was as empty as their cupboards, the fire long cold.

One day, when the hunger gnawed too deeply, Jack's mother told him to sell their cow at the town market.

Jack didn't argue. He loved his mother more than anything in the world, and he would have done anything to keep her from the hollow ache that lived in their house. So, with the cow in tow, Jack set off to sell their final hope.

Halfway to the market, Jack happened upon a man—though he didn't look like any man Jack had ever seen. He was thin, almost brittle, with eyes that glittered like stars glimpsed through a murky pond. The man stood in the middle of the road, watching Jack approach, a curious smile playing on his lips.

"Good morning, boy," the man said, his voice lively and eyes merry. "Where are you off to with that fine cow of yours?"

"To market," Jack replied, though his chest inexplicably tightened at the sight of the stranger.

The man's smile broadened, and he stepped closer, his fingers working at something in his coat pocket. "You're in luck," he said sympathetically. "I've got something better than coins to offer you for that cow. Something... magical."

Jack's brow furrowed. "Magic?"

The man pulled his hand from his pocket, and nestled in his palm were a few small beans, each one hopping faintly in the dappled sunlight. "Magic beans," the man said, his voice now soft and oddly ominous.

Jack stared at the beans. He could feel something in them, something that yearned, something waiting. The market and its few coins suddenly seemed very far away. He swallowed, his heart beating faster. "What do they do?"

The man's eyes gleamed. "Plant them, and you will see."

Jack hesitated for only a moment. He wanted more than anything to change his and his mother's fortunes. Without another word, he handed over the cow's rope and took the beans into his hand. They were warm, almost pulsing, and for the first time in days, Jack felt an uplift of hope.

"Thank you," Jack said, though the man and his new cow had already disappeared into the dark of the trees.

With the beans tucked safely in his pocket, Jack turned and hurried home, his heart light with the promise of magic.

As often happens with promises, things didn't go quite as Jack expected.

You can imagine his mother's reaction. She hurled the beans out the window with a cry of desperation, calling him a fool, and sent him to bed without supper.

But the beans—oh, the beans *were* something special. As Jack lay tossing and turning, his belly growling, his dreams distorting, visions of grandeur began to dance before his eyes— endless feasts, shining gold, and untold riches. He dreamed of ditching his dreary life to slay dragons, save princesses, and rule kingdoms. When morning came, he opened the window and saw it: a beanstalk, towering into the heavens like a green spear thrust into the sky.

How the mighty spear called to the boy, tempting him to go on an adventure. To climb out of the poverty and the guilt and the rest of this earthbound muck.

And so, with barely a thought for his empty stomach or his mother's warnings, Jack climbed. Up, up, and up he went, until he broke through the clouds and stood in a land like nothing he had ever known. Streets of gold, gates of pearl, walls of precious stones—this was no place for a human boy. But Jack was too hungry, too full of grandiose visions, to care.

He found his way to a colossal castle and knocked at the door. A giantess—kind, beautiful, and noble—answered. She took pity on him and gave him food. As he ate, her husband—a MUCH BIGGER giant—returned. Jack had never seen such a creature:

towering, magnificent, titanic. The giant's very presence made Jack feel like an insect. He quickly hid, quavering in awe.

The giant sniffed the air, his voice a rumbling boom—

"Fee-fi-fo-fools,
Man comes, he bends and breaks the rules.
He'll snatch, he'll spoil, then wonder why—
I'll crush his bones before he tries."

But the giantess, for all her massive size, was as soft-hearted as a cloud, and with a few soothing words, she calmed her grumbling husband and sent him off to his chambers. Jack crept after the giant and peered in, spying. What he saw was enough to knock the gloom from his chest.

The room was a treasure trove of miracles. There were sacks brimming with glistening gold coins minted from sunlight. Effervescent rainbow harps played themselves, their music floating on the air like a spell. Strange creatures, half-fantastic and half-terrifying, bustled about, sizzling with magical energy. Bottles lined the shelves—inside, angels and demons writhed, trapped and furious. Maps hinted at kingdoms no man had set foot in, and books... shelves upon shelves of books that claimed to know the secrets of the universe itself: from the birth of time to its many endings. And all this was just the start. Jack, wide-eyed and heart pounding, felt as though he'd stumbled into the dreams of a madman—or a god.

And Jack thought to himself, *Why should the giant have such plenty while my mother and I starve? It's not theft to take when others have too much.*

That night, as the giant slept, Jack crept into the giant's chamber and stole his bag of sun-made coins. He escaped down the beanstalk and presented the riches to his mother. For a while, the two lived comfortably, but Jack's heart grew restive. He had tasted more, and craving more is a poison that's never enough.

Yet still the toxic beanstalk stretched skyward, prominent and irresistible, luring him every time he gazed out his bedroom window.

And as such stories go, Jack woke early the next morning, climbed his beanstalk, and again traveled to the giant's house. Again, Jack asked the giant's wife for food, and, again, while he was eating the giant returned. Jack hid himself—though this time a little less afraid, a bit more sure.

The giant took one mighty sniff of the boy-riddled air and cried—

"Fee-fi-fo-fools,
Man comes, he bends and breaks the rules.
He'll snatch, he'll spoil, then wonder why—
I'll crush his bones before he tries."

The wife assured him all was well, and so the giant ate his food and returned to his chambers. This time, he took out his prized hen. He shouted, "Lay!" and the hen laid a golden egg as large as Jack's head. When the giant fell asleep, Jack took the hen and climbed down the beanstalk. Jack's mother was overjoyed with him, and together they gathered egg after egg and gave one to everyone in their village, enriching the entire community.

Now, with gold flowing like water, Jack's village flourished. Yet it wasn't enough. Desire had taken root in Jack's heart.

This story of Jack and the Beanstalk of his Desire doesn't end there, of course. It never does. Jack's hunger grew too deep, his longing too wide. He climbed the beanstalk again, and again, each time taking more. Stealing from giants and claiming the spoils as his own.

By his final trip, Jack wasn't even hiding anymore. He simply stood there as the giant stormed about, sniffing, grumbling, and lumbering through his castle. But when this time, Jack filched the loveliest of the enchanted harps, its loyal voice betrayed him.

"Help, master!" the harp cried. "The boy's stealing me!"

The giant roared, charging after Jack. For a moment, it seemed like Jack's greed had finally caught up with him. But he was quick. Down the beanstalk he slid, faster than ever before. He reached the bottom and grabbed an axe, chopping wildly at the base of the stalk. The giant, caught in mid-pursuit, tumbled down with it, crashing to the earth with one final thunderous *boom*.

Jack wiped his brow, grinning at the giant's shattered bones. "Oh, how the mighty have fallen."

But jacked giants don't die easily, not in the way humans think. Their bones remain, buried deep in the earth, and their stories linger in the air, in the whispers of the wind. At first, the giant accomplishments of the past are reduced to footnotes, the legends rewritten, the names of the giants whispered in shame, then silence.

And in that silence, something more dangerous happens: the people begin to believe their own myths. They see themselves as the originators of everything—every structure, every idea, every advancement—and soon they're drunk on the thought. Don't you see, *they* invented money, *they* used their technology to make the hen lay golden eggs, and *they* taught the harp to sing. They build higher, faster, convinced they have no need for the past, that they stand taller than any giant ever did.

But the foundations—those unseen, forgotten giant beanstalks—are still there, buried deep, holding up our castles in the sky. And when they start to collapse, as they must, no one notices. The people look only to the future, blind to the slow erosion beneath them.

Then, one day, it all comes down. The buildings fall, the knowledge vanishes, and the people, once so proud, are left sifting through the rubble of their hubris. They don't know how to rebuild, because they've forgotten what the giants taught them. Their world, once so grand, turns to dust, and they disappear, as insubstantial as the giant lies they built their jacked lives upon.

T is for Tinkerbell

*P*arallel Universe Alpha…

Day 1: The Silence

Neverland is dying. I write this with the last dust of my fairy ink, for there is no one left to tell except this empty page. Wendy is gone. The Lost Boys have gone. Even the mermaids have vanished into the blackened sea. Neverland was once alive with songs, mischief, and the living current of childlike faith, but now it lies still—a rotting carcass of dreams.

Peter, of course, pretends not to notice. "They'll be back," he says with that endearing smirk. He hasn't realized what I know: when a child leaves Neverland, they never truly return. Their belief in us fades like a wick smothered mid-flicker. And without belief, we are nothing. The forest wilts, the skies darken, and even the stars have forgotten how to dance.

I tell him this, but he won't listen. He never listens.

Day 14: The Shadows Creep

The first to fall was the Jolly Roger. Hook's ship once bobbed defiantly in the turquoise waters, but now it lies shattered, splintered by storms no one summoned. Hook himself crawled ashore like a broken thing, his red coat trailing in the mud. He looked at me, for once without menace. "Your little friend destroyed us," he muttered.

Peter has been avoiding Hook, but I see them watching each other from opposite cliffs. Neither moves. Neither speaks. I suppose they both realize the truth: they need each other now. Hook without an enemy is as hollow as Peter without an audience.

Day 30: A Whisper of Hope

Peter is changing. He still tries to laugh, to play his games, but the spark is gone. Yesterday, I caught him staring into the lagoon, whispering Wendy's name. He would deny it if I asked, of course. He always denies what hurts.

Hook is worse. He has begun wandering the island, sword dragging behind him, muttering to himself. Once, I saw him pause at a fallen tree and carve the word "Mother" into the bark. I wanted to ask what it meant but thought better of it.

I feel something in the air—something cold. Neverland is shrinking. The beaches are closer than they were, the forests thinner. Perhaps it is not just the island that is dying. Perhaps we are all unraveling, bit by bit.

Day 50: The Poisoning

Peter found me crying today. I hadn't meant to let him see— fairies don't cry, after all—but it slipped out. "Tink, what's wrong?" he asked, his face soft for the first time in weeks. I wanted to scream at him, to shake him, to make him understand that this is his fault. He brought them here. He let them leave. He gave them the power to forget us.

Instead, I only said, "Neverland is sick." He looked at me as if I'd said something silly, but he didn't argue.

Hook has taken to sleeping in the old pirate cave. He smells of salt and rot, and his eyes are red from drink or grief—I can't tell which. Sometimes I think he would kill Peter if he could muster the energy. Other times, I think he'd let Peter kill him just for the release.

Day 100: The Last Star

Last night, the second star to the right went out. Just like that—gone. I didn't think it was possible, but then again, I didn't think Neverland could ever die either.

Peter doesn't talk much anymore. He sits at the edge of the lagoon, staring into the depths like he's waiting for something to emerge. Hook hasn't been seen in days. Maybe he wandered into the forest and never came out. Maybe the forest swallowed him whole.

I hear fey whispers in the wind—voices I don't recognize. They tell me to leave, but I can't. I am bound to this place as much as Peter is. A fairy without her home is no fairy at all. But Peter... I think even he is starting to understand that there's nothing left here.

Day 120: The End

It happened today. The lagoon dried up. The forest collapsed into dust. And Peter... Peter finally admitted it. "It's over, isn't it?" he said, looking at me with those bright, empty eyes. I nodded. I didn't trust myself to speak.

Hook stumbled back to the beach at dusk. He didn't say anything, just sat down beside Peter, sword across his knees. They looked out at the horizon together, enemies made brothers by loss.

I don't know how much longer I can last. Fairies need belief, and there is none left here. But I will not leave. Not while Peter is still here. Not while Neverland has even one moment left.

Final Entry: The Light Fades

I am fading now. My glow, once so bright, barely lingers. Peter sits by the withered tree that was once our home, a shadow of himself. Hook is gone—whether by his own hand or the island's, I'll never know.

As the last light of Neverland dims, I write these words not in sorrow but in defiance. They will not be read. They will not be remembered. But they are mine. My final spark. My last truth. Once, Neverland was everything. Now, it is nothing. But for a moment, it was, and that is enough.

Tinkerbell

Parallel Universe Beta...

Day 1: The First Cracks

Neverland is fraying. Not all at once, but piece by piece, thread by thread, like an old tapestry too long exposed to the sun. The sky, once endless and alive, feels closer now, as though it is folding in on us. The lagoon, where mermaids sang and played, is silent. Even the laughter that once rang through the trees has faded, leaving an unsettling hush.

Peter won't see it—or won't admit it. "It's just a lull, Tink," he said today, tossing a pebble into the still water. "Things always pick up again." He grinned, but the grin didn't reach his eyes.

"They don't always pick up," I replied, my wings drooping.

He laughed, light and careless as ever, and flew off into the forest. But I caught the faintest flutter of his shadow, struggling to keep up. Even Peter's shadow seems tired.

Day 12: The Stars Go Out

Last night, I watched the stars. Not because they were beautiful—though they were—but because I couldn't help feeling they were watching me too. The second star to the right, the one that had always guided us, spluttered and went dark. Not with a bang or a flash, but with a sigh, as if it had grown weary of its own glow. Peter saw it too. "They don't need it anymore," he said, trying to sound unconcerned.

"Who doesn't?" I asked.

"The ones who left," he replied. "They've found their way home." He said it like it didn't matter, but his voice broke on the last word. I wanted to tell him something—anything—that would make it better. But what could I say? That stars don't burn forever? That Neverland isn't as eternal as we'd once thought? The truth felt too grim to speak.

Day 30: The Shrinking World

The island is smaller now. The beaches are narrower, the forests thinner, and the cliffs lower. The winds don't carry the same bright energy they used to; they're slower now, sagging with the scent of salt and endings.

I found Captain Hook sitting by the shore today. His once-proud coat was tattered, his hook rusted. He didn't sneer or shout or even acknowledge me. Instead, he stared at the horizon, his face lined with something I never thought I'd see in him: resignation.

"It's going, isn't it?" he muttered, almost to himself.

"Yes," I said quietly.

He nodded, as if he'd expected no other answer. "It was always going to. You can only chase shadows for so long before the light runs out." Then he stood and walked into the forest, not with the swagger of the pirate I knew, but with the measured steps of a man ready to meet the end.

Day 50: The Sky Breaks

The sky fractured today, its edges unraveling like broken glass. Through the cracks, I glimpsed something vast and unknowable, a space beyond the world we've always known. It wasn't frightening, not exactly. It was more like standing at the edge of a cliff and feeling the pull of the wind, that thrilling, terrible sense of inevitability.

Peter stood beside me, his eyes wide. "Tink, what's happening?"

"I think," I said slowly, "the island is letting go."

"Letting go of what?" he asked.

"Us," I replied.

For a moment, he didn't speak. Then, to my surprise, he laughed—not his usual carefree laugh, but something spongier, more real. "I suppose we always knew it couldn't last forever," he said. "But it was fun while it did, wasn't it?"

Day 70: The Home Tree Falls

It happened this morning. The Home Tree, the great center of Neverland, the place that had always felt more alive than any of us, collapsed into the ground. Its roots crumbled, its branches scattered, and what was left was only dust.

Peter sat beside the remains, quiet for a long time. Then he looked up at me and said, "Do you think they'll remember it?"

"Maybe," I said. "But even if they don't, it doesn't mean it didn't matter."

The words felt strange on my tongue, but as I said them, I knew they were true. Neverland wasn't about being remembered. It was about the moments we lived here, the games we played, the dreams we chased. Those things don't need monuments to be real.

Day 100: The Last Flight

The sea has swallowed the island. Everything we knew—the cliffs, the forests, the lagoon—is gone. Peter and I stood on the last patch of solid ground, watching the water rise. The sky above us intensified, not with stars but with something greater, a light that seemed to pulse with promise.

Peter reached for my hand, touching it with his pointer finger. "Do you think there's something beyond this?" he asked.

"Yes," I said, without hesitation. "There always is."

He smiled then, a real smile, and together we stepped forward— not into the sea, but into that shimmering light. It wrapped around us, not like an ending, but like the opening of a door. And as we moved through, I felt the weight of the island fall away, replaced by something bigger, brighter, and more alive than anything I had ever known.

Day ?: To die will be an awfully big adventure

Neverland is gone. But it was never meant to last forever. It was only ever a glimpse, an echo of something greater. Its beauty, its wonder, its mischief—they were all threads in a larger tapestry, one that stretches far beyond anything we could see.

And now it's time for what's next. The end of Neverland is not something to fear, because endings are never truly the end. They are simply the beginning of another story we've been playing at forgetting to remember...

Tinkerbell

*P*arallel Universe Gamma...

Day 1: Abandoned

Neverland is falling apart. Not metaphorically—no, that would be too poetic, too lovely. I mean it literally. The cliffs are crumbling into the sea, the lagoon is starting to stink, and the forest trees are drooping like sulking children. I can't even fly above the treetops anymore without choking on ash.

Wendy and the Lost Boys have gone. Left without so much as a goodbye. And what's worse, they've taken the belief with them— that irritating, invisible force that makes the stars shine and the winds blow and me, well, me. Now it's leaking out of Neverland like water through a sieve.

Peter pretends not to notice. "They'll be back," he says, lounging on a half-dead tree trunk, tossing pebbles at the lagoon. "They always come back."

"They won't," I snap, but he waves me off with a laugh.

Infuriating boy. If only I weren't bound to him, I'd—Well, no. I probably wouldn't leave. Who else would keep him out of trouble?

Day 8: Hook's Return

The Jolly Roger washed up in pieces this morning. I knew it was coming; the twisters around the island have been relentless, gnashing the seas into foam. Still, I wasn't prepared for what crawled out of the wreckage.

Captain Hook. Or what's left of him. He looked like a ghost in that tattered red coat, his hook dragging in the sand like an anchor. For once, he didn't sneer at me or shout threats about Peter. Instead, he just stood there, staring at the island as if he couldn't quite believe what he was seeing.

"Where is he?" he rasped, voice rough as bark.

"Where you left him," I replied.

Hook muttered something I couldn't catch and limped toward the forest. I half-expected Peter to ambush him from the trees like old times, but no—Peter stayed where he was, perched on a rock, whistling tunelessly to himself. I'm not sure if he even noticed Hook. Or cared.

Day 20: Dwindling Light

The stars are winking out. I don't mean they're hiding behind clouds. I mean they're vanishing, one by one, like extinguished torches. I watched the second star to the right—the one that brought so many children to Neverland—stutter, struggle, and finally go dark. It didn't even make a sound. Just... nothing.

Peter doesn't talk about it. Hook does, though. He's taken to pacing the beach, muttering about curses and punishments and things far older than Neverland itself. He claims he's heard something—a voice in the waves, calling his name. I told him he was crazy, but secretly, I'm not so sure. Neverland has never felt so empty.

Peter's been quieter too. He still plays his games, but there's no spark to them anymore. Yesterday, I found him poking at the dry, fissured soil where the flowers used to grow. He looked up at me and said, "Why aren't they coming back?"

I didn't have an answer.

Day 35: A Strange Alliance

It happened today. Hook and Peter, face to face on the cliff edge. No swords drawn, no insults traded—just silence. I hovered nearby, expecting the usual clash of blades, but instead, they just stood there, staring out at the sea.

"Does it hurt?" Peter asked suddenly.

Hook's head tilted, as if he didn't quite understand the question. "What?"

"When they leave you," Peter said. His voice was weak, almost uncertain. "When they forget."

Hook didn't reply. He turned and walked away, his hook glinting faintly in the dimming light. Peter watched him go, then sat down on the edge of the cliff, legs dangling into the abyss. He didn't say another word, and I didn't dare break the silence.

Day 50: The Last Shadow

The island is shriveling. The beaches are narrower, the trees fewer, and the air colder. Hook is still here, though he spends most of his time in the cave, sharpening a blade that will never cut anything again. Peter... well, Peter is fading too, though he'd never admit it. He rarely flies anymore, and when he does, it's sluggish, like he's dragging the weight of the whole island behind him.

I tried to tell him today—about the stars, the trees, the lagoon that's turned black and sour. "We have to leave," I said, but he just laughed. "Leave? And go where?"

That stopped me cold. He's right, of course. There's nowhere else for us. Neverland isn't just a place—it's who we are. If it dies, we die too.

Day 70: The End of Games

Hook vanished last night. He didn't say goodbye, not that I expected him to. I found his hat near the lagoon, half-buried in the sand. Peter looked at it for a long time before picking it up and tossing it into the water. "Coward," he muttered, though there wasn't much venom in his voice.

Peter's been spending more time alone. Sometimes I catch him staring at his own shadow, as if expecting it to jump up and run off without him. Once, I thought I saw him talking to it, though I couldn't hear the words.

As for me, my glow is fading. The dust that gives me life is growing thinner, weaker. I can't even manage a proper flight anymore. I stick close to Peter, not because I want to, but because I have to. Without him, there's nothing left for me.

Day 100: The Waiting

Tonight, Peter sat by the withered remains of the Home Tree, staring at the horizon. The sky was black—not a single star left. "Do you think they remember us?" he asked.

I didn't answer. What could I say? That Wendy's probably forgotten his name? That the Lost Boys are no longer boys, and certainly no longer lost?

For a moment, he looked small, younger than I'd ever seen him. Then he smiled—crooked, tired, and utterly false. "It doesn't matter," he said. "We had our fun, didn't we, Tink?"

I wanted to scream at him. Fun? Was that all this was? But I didn't have the strength. My light is barely a sizzle now, just enough to cast one last glow over his face.

Neverland is gone, and soon, so will we be. But Peter still whistles his songs, still sits by the tree, still waits. For what, I don't know. Maybe for nothing. Maybe for everything.

Tinkerbell

*P*arallel Universe Theta...

Day 1: The Beginning of the End
Silence doesn't belong in Neverland. It's not meant to. Neverland should rumble with the shrieks of play, the pounding of bare feet, the thrill of endless games. But the silence now—it's not a pause, not a moment to catch your breath. It's a void, black and consuming. A hunter's silence.

Wendy left. Took the Lost Boys with her. Ran for the stars and never looked back. I don't blame her. Not anymore. The Peter she believed in, the boy who laughed like summer thunder and promised eternal childhood, is gone.

He sits in his tree now, grinning that razor-sharp grin. "She'll come back, Tink," he says, his voice a festering cackle. "They always come back. They can't resist."

"They won't," I say, my wings bowing under truth's crushing certainty. "They've grown up."

His laugh is low and menacing, no trace of boyish joy left. "Not in *my* Neverland, they don't. No one grows up here unless I say so."

He's right about one thing: Neverland is his. He doesn't rule it; he *is* it. The rivers are drying, the trees withering, the stars dimming. Because Peter isn't just a boy who refuses to grow up. He's a tyrant, a leech, feeding on our endless belief in him. And Neverland, like the rest of us, is bleeding out.

Day 10: A New Arrival
Hook returned today, or what's left of him. His coat hangs in rags, and his face—God, his face. It's not the face of a man. It's the mask of someone who's fought apparitions for so long that he's become one.

"Where is he?" Hook's voice is a rasp, his body vibrating like a puppet held up by fraying strings.

"Who?" I ask, though we both know.

"The boy." His eyes burn with something far beyond hatred—desperation, maybe.

Peter wasn't around to greet him. He hasn't seen Hook as a worthy opponent in far too long. "Why bother?" Peter once said, his grin snappish. "Old men are so easy to break."

I didn't tell Hook that. I didn't have the heart. Or maybe I didn't have the courage. Hook staggered off into the woods, his hook dragging through the dirt, and I felt something close to pity. Not for him—for myself. For Neverland.

Day 30: Stars Gone Astray

The second star to the right is gone. Extinct, just like the others. I couldn't stop the tears. Once upon a time, I couldn't cry. Peter would've teased me for crying. But not now. Now his voice punctures, even when he's pretending to be playful.

"What's wrong with you, Tink?" he asks, his shadow stretching unnaturally long behind him.

"The stars," I say, barely able to speak. "They're leaving us."

Peter's laugh scrapes against my ears. "Stars don't leave. They just burn out. Like old people."

Then he flew off, his crowing mockery echoing through the empty sky. No one answered him. Not the birds, not the trees, not the wind. And Peter didn't care.

Day 50: Decay in the Trees

The forest is dying, but it's not natural. The trees don't just wither—they putrify, collapsing into twisted shapes like they've been sucked dry from the inside.

Peter sits on the lagoon's edge now, a thin, skeletal boy whose wolfish grin never wavers. But his eyes—his eyes are as empty as the lagoon he stares into.

"Do you think they remember?" he asks me one evening, his voice bitter and poisonous.

"Who?" I whisper, though I already know.

"Wendy. The boys. Do you think they miss us?"

I want to lie, to say they do. But I can't. "I don't know, Peter."

He turns to me then, his grin gone. For a moment, I see the boy he used to be, the one I loved. Then his shadow shifts, moving on its own, twisting around him like snakes. The moment passes.

Day 70: A Strange Peace

Hook no longer hunts Peter. He's not the pirate he used to be— raging and roaring through the jungle with his blade gleaming and his voice shaking the very trees. Now he sits on the beach, motionless as driftwood, staring at the horizon. The sea whispers to him, but it gives no answers.

I hovered closer, though I didn't really want to hear what he might say. "What are you doing?"

"Carving names," he groused, lifting a piece of dead wood. His hook moved with a strange tenderness, etching *Wendy* into the grain.

My wings drooped. "You're wasting your time."

He didn't look at me. His voice was heavy, as if it carried the weight of too many battles, too many losses. "We're all wasting our time here, fairy."

The name was finished, but he didn't stop. His hook traced the letters again and again, like he could make them permanent, make them real. I didn't know what to say, so I left him to his hopeless ritual.

Peter, of course, had seen everything. He always does. He perched in the tree line, his smirk predatory, as if he'd just spotted quarry too weak to run. "He thinks he can escape," Peter said, his voice dripping with mockery. "But no one leaves Neverland without my permission. Not really."

"Maybe he doesn't want to escape," I said, surprising myself.

Peter's grin widened. "Then he's dumber than I thought."

The games are over. Hook knows it. I think Peter does, too, though he'll never admit it. All that's left is Peter watching from the shadows, waiting for Hook's next move. His grin says he's already won. But Hook's quiet defiance—his refusal to let Peter be the last word—says otherwise.

If Peter is the deluge, Hook is the cliff it beats against. And maybe, just maybe, Peter isn't as unshakable as he wants us to believe.

Day 100: The Last Light

Neverland is dead. The lagoon is bone-dry, the Home Tree a hollow husk. The stars—every last one of them— have abandoned the sky.

Peter sits under the tree, his hands idly carving shapes into the dirt with his knife. He doesn't fly anymore. Doesn't even move, save for a smile that cinches tighter, closing like a noose.

Yesterday, Hook left. I found his hook on the beach, rusted and broken. Peter didn't react when I told him. He just muttered, "They always think they can leave."

I feel it too now. My light crackles like a damp lantern. Peter's grin grows sharper each day, his eyes darker. He's not the boy who wouldn't grow up. He's the boy who won't let anyone else exist without him.

Day 120: The End

Tonight, Peter whispered to me, his voice low and cold. "Tink," he said, "do you think it's my fault?"

I wanted to lie, to say it wasn't. But the truth hung between us like a razorblade. "Yes, Peter. It is."

He didn't flinch. He didn't argue. He just crowed, shrill and earsplitting, his bared teeth horrifying.

Neverland is gone. All that remains is Peter, and soon, he'll be the last thing left of this place. The boy who devoured a world to keep his games alive.

I'll stay until my light goes out. Not for him, but because someone has to make sure Peter Pan falls.

Tinkerbell

*P*arallel Universe Iota...

Day 1: The Beginning of the End

Neverland was falling apart. Not in the usual "Oh, the pirates singed the Home Tree again" way, but in a deeper, more unsettling, "What's the point of pixie dust?" sort of way. The stars were blurring. The trees were shrinking. The mermaids had started complaining about a lack of glamor, which was ironic considering they hadn't washed their hair in centuries. Peter, naturally, didn't notice.

"It's just a quiet spell," he said, grinning like a loon. "They always come back."

"They won't," I said. "Wendy's gone. The boys are gone. Everyone's gone."

He shrugged. "So what? We'll just have more fun without them!" And off he went, chasing an imaginary shadow through the woods.

Typical Peter. When the world burns, play tag.

Day 12: Enter Hook

The Jolly Roger finally gave up the ghost. It sank during one of those impossible squalls that seem tailor-made for theatrics, leaving Captain Hook stranded on the beach. He looked dreadful—hat crooked, boots scuffed, the smell of rum radiating from him like a tragic cologne.

"What are you doing here?" I snapped.

"Contemplating my mortality," Hook replied, waving his hook languidly. "It's very fashionable these days." He pointed at the sky, where the Second Star to the Right had just fizzled out like a bad fireworks display. "Even the stars are quitting. Why shouldn't I?"

"Because you're too stubborn to let anything kill you," I said, though privately I agreed. If Hook was giving up, then Neverland was truly doomed.

Day 30: A Very Brief Truce

By some unspoken agreement, Peter and Hook stopped fighting. Peter claimed it was because Hook was "boring now," but I suspected he couldn't work up the energy for a proper duel. Hook had taken to lurking near the lagoon, muttering about existential despair and the unfairness of pirate stereotypes. Peter spent his time trying to fly without his shadow, which had detached itself entirely and was skulking somewhere in the woods.

The worst part? I was stuck with both of them. Peter, who refused to admit anything was wrong, and Hook, who couldn't stop pointing out that everything was. It was like babysitting a pair of very stubborn, very dramatic children.

"Can't you two do something useful?" I said one evening, when the three of us found ourselves sitting around a stack of firewood that neither of them had bothered to light.

"Like what?" Peter asked, pouting.

"Fix the island!"

"Impossible," Hook declared. "We're well past the fixing stage. It's all epilogues and melancholy from here."

Day 50: The Apocalypse (Sort Of)

Neverland's apocalypse showed up less like a grand finale and more like a shrug. The Home Tree, the great heart of the island, shattered into a figment of itself. The lagoon boiled away into steam. The stars—what few were left—blinked out, one by one, until the sky was a blank nothingness.

Peter watched it all with wide eyes. "This is it, isn't it?" he said ominously.

"No," Hook replied, his voice oddly soft. "This is the part where we improvise." He turned to Peter, his hook gleaming in the faint light of the fire. "You've got the imagination. I've got the pragmatism. And she"—he jabbed his hook in my direction—"has the sheer bloody-minded magic to keep us alive."

"You're saying we work together?" Peter asked, aghast.

"I'm saying we fake it until the universe gets tired and stops trying to kill us."

Day 70: An Awkward Alliance

It turns out averting an apocalypse is less about heroics and more about paperwork. Figuratively, at least. Hook barked orders, Peter distracted the remaining chaos (by doing backflips and shouting, "You can't catch me!"), and I patched up what I could with fairy dust and pure indignation.

It didn't go perfectly. Half the island was swallowed by the sea. The mermaids started a union. And the stars, well, they never came back. But somehow, we stopped the whole thing from imploding entirely.

"Is it fixed?" Peter asked as the dust settled.

"Define 'fixed,'" Hook replied, slumping against a rock. "If you mean 'still technically existing,' then yes. If you mean 'as good as new,' then no, and frankly, you're delusional."

Day 100: Aftermath

We sat around the fire, the three of us, staring at what was left of Neverland. It wasn't much. The forest was thin, the lagoon was a puddle, and the colors had fled the sky, leaving only a stark monotone. But it was still there, stubbornly clinging to existence.

Peter poked at the fire with a stick. "Do you think it'll ever go back to how it was?"

Hook snorted. "No, you idiot. Things never go back. They just go forward."

Peter frowned. "What's forward, then?"

"Whatever's next," I said, surprising myself. "Neverland's still here. So are we. Maybe that's enough."

For once, neither of them argued. We sat in silence, listening to the wind—not the bright, mischievous wind of before, but an undaunted breeze. It felt... peaceful.

"Do you think Wendy would have stayed if she knew this would happen?" Peter asked eventually.

"She left because she had to," I said. "But that doesn't mean she didn't love it here."

Peter smiled, a small, wistful smile. Hook leaned back, his hook clinking against the rock, and muttered, "You're both insufferable."

But he didn't leave. None of us did. And perhaps, in the grand, chaotic tapestry of existence unraveling at the edges, the only thing stopping it from completely falling apart was the sheer stubbornness of us all hanging on to each other—and a fair bit of denial.

Tinkerbell

*P*arallel Universe Pi...

Day 1: The Cracks in the World

Neverland is unraveling, and of course, Peter and Hook are too busy bickering to notice the important details—like the fact that the lagoon is drying up or that the flowers in the forest are wilting. The stars, once bright enough to light the darkest nights, are fading. Even the mermaids have stopped singing.

"It's because of them!" Peter shouted today, pointing furiously at the empty horizon where Wendy and the Lost Boys used to be. "They brought their grown-up thoughts here, their rules and roads and... carbon footprints!"

"Carbon footprints?" Hook sneered, lounging against a half-rotten tree with a smug grin. "You think a few children in pinafores and knee socks started all this? Please. The island is fine, boy. It's adapting."

They went on like that for hours. Peter, flitting about in a fury, shouting about balance and stewardship, while Hook jabbed his hook into the dirt and accused Peter of being "a naive little sprite with no sense of the bigger picture."

Meanwhile, the forest grew quieter, the lagoon a little smaller, and the sky a little duller.

Day 20: The Great Divide

Peter has taken to building a "climate fort" out of sticks and moss, where he sits and broods over charts he's drawn on scraps of pirate maps. They're mostly squiggly lines and arrows pointing to nowhere, but they make him feel like he's solving something. Hook, on the other hand, has declared himself "Captain of the Natural Order" and insists that Neverland's changes are not only inevitable but necessary. "The island is shedding what it no longer needs," he declared to me today. "It's survival of the fittest, fairy. Only the adaptable thrive."

"And who's thriving now?" I snapped. "Because it sure isn't the lagoon or the flowers or the stars."

"Precisely," he said, wagging his hook at me as if that made any sense at all.

Peter overheard and exploded into one of his usual tirades. "You can't just let the island die, Hook! We have to fix it!"

"Fix it?" Hook laughed. "What are you going to do, Pan? Sprinkle your fairy dust over a volcano and tell it to behave?"

I left them shouting at each other and flew off to what's left of the forest. It's quieter there now, too quiet. The trees whisper of dead things.

Day 50: The Meltdown

Today, Peter built a dam across the river, insisting it would "preserve Neverland's natural water supply." Hook, naturally, decided the dam was "an affront to the island's sovereignty" and blew it up with a conveniently stashed cannonball.

The explosion sent Peter into a rage, and he attacked Hook in a whirlwind of fists and feathers. "You're killing the island!" he screamed.

"No, Pan," Hook growled, slashing at him with his hook. "You're suffocating it. Let it breathe!"

It was chaos. The river flooded the forest, uprooting trees and drowning everything in its path. When it was over, Peter stood on one side of the wreckage, dripping wet and glaring, while Hook stood on the other, triumphant but exhausted.

The island rocked beneath them, but neither noticed. They were too busy planning their next moves.

Day 100: Last Stand

It happened today. The final fight. Peter and Hook faced each other at the edge of the Home Tree, which now stood dead and hollow, its bark peeling away like old paint.

"This is your fault!" Peter shouted, circling Hook like a hawk. "You've destroyed everything with your stubbornness!"

"My fault?" Hook roared. "You're the one who refused to adapt! You clung to your little fantasies of control while the island did what it was always going to do!"

They clashed with swords and fists, their shouting echoing across the empty landscape. I tried to stop them, shouting, "It doesn't matter whose fault it is! The island is dying, and you're too busy fighting to save it!"

But they didn't listen. They never listened.

The ground beneath them cracked, the air filled with the sound of splitting wood, and the Home Tree collapsed, taking Peter and Hook with it. I saw Peter's shadow flit once and vanish—and then, only silence.

Day 120: The End of Neverland

I am alone now. The forest is depleted, the lagoon is desiccated, and the stars are snuffed out. The island is no more than a barren wasteland, a dim memory of what it once was.

They could have saved it, I think. If Peter had stopped trying to control the island's fate and if Hook had cared enough to do more than adjust, they might have found a way. But their fighting blinded them to the truth: the island didn't need saving or surrender. It needed understanding.

I am the last light of Neverland, a remnant of what was and what will never be again.

Humans are stupid.

Tinkerbell

*P*arallel Universe Tau...

Day 1: When She Came

The moment she arrived, I knew she was trouble. Wendy Darling, with her prim smile and her cloud of perfect hair, drifted into Neverland as if she were some lost queen reclaiming her throne. She let Peter hold her hand—*his hand*—and had the nerve to look at him like she understood him, like she belonged here.

"Girls don't belong in Neverland," I said, my voice cutting through their connection, precise as a paper cut. Peter, as always, waved me off, laughing in that maddening, careless way that made me want to throttle him.

"They'll be fine, Tink," he said, his grin lazy and infuriating. "They're my friends."

Friends. As if Wendy and her brood of half-grown interlopers could ever understand what it meant to be part of Neverland. But even as Peter spoke, I could feel it—her presence seeping into the island like a sickness. The trees trembled; the streams seemed to run a little more enflamed. But Peter didn't see it. He never did.

Day 10: The Illness

The first sign came from the lagoon. One of the mermaids—her name didn't matter, but her beauty once had—sat on the rocks, clutching her throat. Her once-iridescent tail dimmed to a dull, sickly green, and her cough echoed across the island.

"It's just a little cold," Peter said when I pointed it out. "She'll get over it."

But she didn't. None of them did. The cough spread like wildfire, creeping from the lagoon to the pirate ship to the Lost Boys' camp. Even Hook's crew grew quiet, their usual bellows fading to uneasy wheezing.

And Wendy? She hovered over Peter, her hands soft and her words softer, soothing the Lost Boys as if she'd always been their mother. I hated her for it. I hated the way Peter looked at her, like she was something more than a passing curiosity.

"She's killing us," I hissed at him. "Her and her growing-up ideas. They don't belong here!"

Peter's grin faltered. Just for a second.

"You're wrong, Tink," he said, but his voice lacked its usual bluster.

Day 30: The Turn

I watched the last mermaid slip beneath the lagoon's surface, her song gone forever. The water stank of decay.

"She's butchering Neverland," I whispered, this time to the island itself. And Neverland seemed to answer. The wind grew sharp; the trees shuddered. The stars dwindled ever so slightly.

That night, I made my decision. I dusted the branches of the Home Tree, the sails of Hook's ship, the moss beneath Wendy's feet. I whispered to the island, coaxing it to protect itself. To resist her poison.

"This is for Peter," I told myself. "For Neverland."

But the island didn't seem grateful. The stars seemed mute and the ground grumbled beneath me.

"What did you do?" Peter's voice sliced through the night, harsh and accusing.

"I'm saving us," I said, my voice rough at his betrayal.

"No," he said, his eyes darker than I'd ever seen them. "You're destroying us."

Day 50: The Contagion

Neverland was unraveling, and there was no stopping it now. The riven Home Tree groaned, its roots curling like a dying thing. The lagoon seethed dry, leaving nothing but slivered mud and broken shells.

Hook's ship listed in the bay, its sails limp. His crew was gone—vanished into the forest or the sea, I couldn't say. The Lost Boys no longer played. They barely spoke.

And Wendy? She lay feeble and coughing, her sickness no longer a secret. Peter carried her through the dying forest, his face a mask of something I'd never seen before. Fear, perhaps. Or regret.

"You did this," he said when he passed me.

"No," I snapped. "She did this. Her womanly *growing up* did this."

But his shadow writhed behind him, as if it knew better.

Day 70: The Collapse

The Home Tree fell at dawn, splitting the sky with a sound like a death rattle. The forest burned without flame; the stars dissolved one by one.

Peter never spoke to me again. Carrying Wendy, he flew toward the second star to the right—what was left of it—and away from... mourning, maybe? Hook's ship slowly sank beneath the horizon, empty and aimless. I stayed behind, alone in the ruins.

My glow was faint now, pitching like a lone taper fighting the dark. But I didn't care. Neverland wasn't meant to change. It wasn't meant to grow up. And Wendy had been change in its purest, most dangerous form.

Day 99: The Final Spark

As the last star faded, I felt no regret. No guilt. Just a cold, unshakable certainty that this was the only way. Wendy's infection—her lulling words, her insidious dreams of growing up and dragging Neverland along with her—would have warped everything. Neverland wasn't meant to grow. It wasn't meant to change. It was meant to stay perfect. And now, it will.

What remains is a memory frozen in time, untouched by her hands or the heavy, clumsy grasp of the waking world.

I sit here, the faintest fitful light in a world gone dark, the last sentinel of a place that can never be again. And I will keep my watch. Neverland's story is safe now. At least, while I'm still here...

Tink

*P*arallel Universe Omega...

Straight on till morning.
Not with a bang, but a whimper.
Tinkerbell

The Piper Exposed

Once Upon a Time, my children—oh, let me tell you—there were terrible things done in the name of history. Just awful! Wars, inquisitions, persecutions—the Three Kingdoms War, the Hundred Years War, the World Wars, and on and on. Dreadful, dreadful stuff. But all of these pale in comparison to what happened in the charming little town of Hameln in 1284—or wait, it all really started in 1127, didn't it? Never mind the details, darling. It's our *truth* that matters, not the facts.

As I was saying, in this world so bent at crooked angles that it makes your worst nightmare seem like a lullaby, there was a little town called Hameln. Now, they'll tell you stories about this town— about music and rats and missing children. But I'm here to tell you that *none* of it is true. The truth, like all truths, has been carefully hidden beneath layers of lies, much like a pie crust conceals its delicious filling.

Now, you may have heard the old, tragic story of the Pied Piper—the one about the rats and the children. But let me assure you, everything you've been told is pure nonsense. Propaganda! Speciesist revisionism! You see, it wasn't the rats the Piper was after, nor was he some savior come to rescue the town. Oh my no. This is what *really* happened, as uncovered by the second esteemed research assistant (twice-removed) from the University of Cat Worshippers.

Yes, children, *cats* are at the heart of this tale!

"But what about the rats?" you ask. How amusing! How utterly *quaint* of you to believe such a thing! There were never any rats, children. None. No whiskers twitching in the moonlight, no scurrying under floorboards. The whole *rat affair* was a smokescreen for the Piper's true intention—to rid the town of the only thing the Piper hated more than he loved pies: Cats.

You see, the Pied Piper—yes, yes, I know they told you it's because of his brightly-colored clothes—but really, he was called the *Pied* Piper because of his insatiable appetite for pies. Not a day went by that he wasn't devouring some sort of crusted delicacy, his lips forever smudged with cherry or apple filling. This man—this *pie enthusiast*—descended upon Hameln not with promises of rat-catching but with a *demand*: more pies.

And that, dear children, is where this whole *rat business* started—a mistake. A silly mistranslation. An historian (probably a Hameln revisionist, in on the whole conspiracy you see), years ago, switched "cats" for "rats." It wasn't about rats at all. The town had no rats. Instead, it was about *cats*. Hameln, as it turns out, was overrun with cats—beloved, cherished, pampered cats who ruled the town like furry little monarchs.

You see, the Piper didn't hate Hameln because of its rats— again, let me remind you, no rats. He hated Hameln because it was overrun by purring, smug, self-satisfied *cats*. To him, every cat was a tiny devil, watching him with those piercing eyes, daring him to spill one crumb of pie crust. The Piper couldn't stand it. And so, he concocted a plan. Oh, it was brilliant, my children. It was devious. It was—how do I put this?—it was *sinister*. A masterpiece of manipulation.

Late one night, as the moon hung low over the city, the Piper played his pipe—not to lure rats, but to call forth every cat in Hameln. With his strange, feline notes, he led them, a horde of fur and flicking tails, down to the river. And there—brace yourselves— he did the unthinkable. He drowned them all and *replaced* them with dogs.

Can you imagine? The chaos, the howling, the barking! The townspeople awoke to find their beloved cats gone, replaced by slobbering, clumsy dogs who knocked over pies and begged for scraps at every corner. The Piper, meanwhile, sat back, a pie in each hand, and watched the town *crumble* under the weight of this *cat*-astrophe.

But here's the true kicker, my children. The townsfolk, as angry as they were, took away the Piper's pies. Cut him off completely—not a single morsel. And the Piper, not one to take such an insult lightly, devised an even more diabolical scheme. He knew that the only thing worse than losing their cats was raising a generation of children who hated cats. *Yes*, you heard me. He didn't steal the children—no, no, never. That's the *propaganda* they want you to believe.

The Piper *indoctrinated* the children. Through stories and lies, through fear and intimidation, he convinced them that cats were evil. That cats were the enemy. These poor, innocent children, twisted into little speciesist monsters, turned against their own town's history. They became the *cat-haters* of tomorrow, and that was the Piper's greatest triumph.

But let me pause here to give credit where it's due. If you're wondering how I came upon this *real* version of events, look no further than the illustrious new book, **The 1127 Project**, a masterpiece of modern historical scholarship, written by that surprisingly resourceful research assistant from the University of Cat Worshippers. This groundbreaking book, hailed by many as the most important scholarly work of our time, is a shining example of *presentism*—that vital art of viewing history through the enlightened lens of our modern social values.

Forget those dry old historians clinging to their dusty facts and primary sources. **The 1127 Project** reinterprets the history of Hameln, stripping away the lies and finally showing us what we need to know: the whole debacle was about *speciesism*, the human prejudice against cats, and the Piper's twisted mission to replace every last one of them with drooling dogs. In fact, it's no wonder this book is considered required reading for any serious scholar who wishes to engage with history in a meaningful, progressive way.

And so, the Piper spun his vile tales, filled the children of Hameln's heads with lies about the evils of cats until the children, poor, gullible souls, became the *cat-haters* of tomorrow, and that was the Piper's evilest deed.

But of course, the townsfolk couldn't allow such a thing. So, they did what any reasonable society would do—they sealed the Piper and all 130 of those brainwashed, speciesist children inside a cave, ensuring that their vile hatred would never corrupt the future. That's right, it was the *townsfolk* themselves who sealed the Piper and their own children in that cave to perish. Better to start fresh with a new generation, they thought.

And then, to cover up their deed, they crafted an elaborate story about a fife, some rats, and a mysterious disappearance. The town couldn't have *anyone* knowing the truth about this little... incident. Anything to paint themselves as innocent victims. They went so far as to inscribe it on their town hall and their gates, even memorializing their alternate version in a stained-glass window! Overcompensate much? Would they *really* want to remember such a horrid event? No, but they had to make it believable. The more they repeated it, the more convincing it would seem.

So, my dear children, let this be a lesson to you. History isn't about learning from the past to avoid its mistakes. No, not ever. History is about *rewriting* the past to suit our needs, to make ourselves look good in the present. And if you need to alter a few facts, silence a few inconvenient truths, or maybe lock a few hundred people in a cave—well, so be it. History is best served warm, like a fresh pie, cut to whatever shape we need to justify our current actions.

The End.

The Hanged Puppet

O<i>nce upon a time</i>, there was a piece of wood.

Not a remarkable piece of wood, at least not at first glance. It wasn't polished or carved into something useful, like a chair leg or a baseball bat. It wasn't ancient or enchanted—or at least, it didn't seem to be. It was just wood, the kind you might find in a pile by the fireplace, waiting for the moment when it would burn and release the valuable secrets it held inside.

But wood, you see, is tricky stuff. It remembers things. It remembers the wind that shaped it, the rain that fed it, the soil that held it tight, and sometimes—just sometimes—it remembers a little too much.

This particular piece of wood was found by a carpenter named Mr. Cherry. He was practical, as carpenters often are, and when he saw the wood, he thought, "I'll use it to mend my table." He picked up his axe, raised it high, and the wood spoke.

"Don't strike me too hard," it said, in a voice that rustled like leaves that thought they'd retired from this nonsense ages ago.

Cherry froze. Voices from logs were not part of his usual day. But curiosity—or perhaps stubbornness—got the better of him, and he struck anyway.

"You hurt me!" cried the wood, and now Cherry was quite certain he should leave the workshop and find a strong drink. Instead, he decided to try to plane the wood, which made it begin to laugh. A low, creaky laugh, like a door opening into a room you hadn't meant to enter. "That tickles!" it chortled.

Cherry might have kept at it, but then Geppetto arrived. Geppetto was old and jolly and carried with him the air of a man who believed that, even if the world was cruel, it would let him carve out his own little corner of contentment. He wanted wood to fashion a puppet—a puppet that would dance, tumble, and delight the world while earning him a living.

The wood laughed again, this time mocking Geppetto's wig, and Geppetto thought it was Cherry teasing him. So they fought, as men sometimes do when pride and misunderstanding get in the way.

When the fight was over, Cherry handed Geppetto the wood, and Geppetto—dreaming of bread and wine earned from puppet plays—took it home.

In the glow of candlelight, Geppetto began to carve, his knife snagging on the pine wood's knots and skipping over its uneven grain. It was soft and pliable, but fragile—prone to scratches and dents that seemed to appear no matter how carefully he worked. He named the puppet *Pinocchio*, recalling a poor family he had once known, for he liked the sound of it—*piccolo*, meaning small, and *occhio*, meaning eye, as if the very name suited something that stared so long at a single tree, he forgot forests existed—enthralled by his own myopic desires, and unable to grasp what lay beyond their reach. But as Gepetto worked, strange things began to happen.

The puppet's eyes moved.

Its nose grew longer every time Geppetto tried to shape it.

Its mouth opened in a grin—a grin that wasn't friendly—and it stuck out its wooden tongue.

When the arms and legs were finished, the puppet jumped up, stole Geppetto's wig, and kicked him squarely in the nose. Geppetto wasn't happy, for he had his own version of a temper, but perhaps he spied something in the naughty puppet that even the puppet didn't yet see.

Pinocchio, on the other hand, only saw the wide, open world outside the door. He ran, leaving Geppetto to stumble after him. He lied to the police—convincingly, as liars with wooden faces often do—and they arrested Geppetto for abusing the little puppet.

While his creator sat in a dark cell, Pinocchio wandered back to Geppetto's little house, where he met a cricket. Not an ordinary cricket, mind you. This was a philosopher cricket, who spoke with the quiet confidence of an insect who had seen too much.

"Boys who disobey their fathers come to no good," the cricket said.

Pinocchio laughed. "I'll do what I want."

The cricket didn't flinch. "Then you'll end as you are now. Selfish and alone. Better suited for kindling than kindness."

Pinocchio didn't like that. So he grabbed a mallet and smashed the cricket flat.

Think about that for a second. Not a slap, not a flick. A mallet. And the cricket, for all its wisdom, was just a smear on the wall. Or so Pinocchio assumed.

Pinocchio discovered next that hunger is an obnoxious thing. It's not just the stomach's cry for bread—it's every gnawing desire that whispers, *Take what you can, do what you must, never mind the cost.* Long story not short enough, Pinocchio burned his feet off, stole, and begged on the street like a bum. Every hunger-fueled wicked decision brought him lower, for the real danger of hunger is how quickly it makes us forget who we might be.

But Geppetto—bless him—came back, forgave the little monster, and gave him food, a new pair of feet, and even a schoolbook.

So, what did Pinocchio do? He sold the book for theater tickets.

At the puppet show, he met Fire-eater, a real monster of a man with a beard like black smoke and a whip that cracked like a nightmare. Fire-eater almost burned Pinocchio to cook his dinner but "sneezed" himself into pity. (Like you do…) He let the boy go and even gave him five gold coins to take home to his father, Geppetto.

But on his way home, Pinocchio met a "lame" Fox and a "blind" Cat, smooth-talking swindlers who promised him riches if he planted his coins in the Field of Miracles.

You see where this is going.

They robbed him, strung him up in a tree, and left him for dead.

Hanging there, swinging in the wind, Pinocchio finally thought of Geppetto. The warmth of his hands. The sacrifices he made. But by then, it was too late.

And so "The End" to *The Story of a Puppet* falls like a final curtain—at least the way the author *originally* intended it to end—with Pinocchio hanging from an oak, the wind creaking through its wooden limbs.

Nowadays they'll tell you there's more to it, that Pinocchio bested a great shark (or a whale, if you prefer the mousy version), learned his lesson, made amends, and lived happily ever after.

But that's the sort of lie you tell kids so they can sleep at night.

You may *think* you know Pinocchio's tale—perchance you've heard the tempered versions where the puppet, with the help of a blue fairy and a talking cricket, ultimately redeems himself and becomes a "real boy." But those saccharine retellings came later, much later, while this original ending of a serialized puppet hanging dead in an oak tree left Italian children distraught and their parents writing the magazine in protest.

Imagine the uproar: young readers, their heads full of wonder, reaching the part where Pinocchio—our self-centered, disobedient protagonist—meets his grim end hanging lifeless from an oak tree. It shouldn't surprise you that the author's mailbox soon brimmed with tear-streaked letters begging for marionette mercy, and he—whether from a peacemaking heart or the promise of more money (probably the latter)—continued the fairy tale, giving the puppet not just a reprieve but a tidy moral and a so-called "happy" ending. The focus shifted to "becoming a real boy," a redemptive blue fairy, and time spent in the belly of a mile-long shark with asthma and heart palpitations—an allegorical neatly-packaged refit. And what happened?

As is so often way in such cases, the story's original intent— its dark warning about selfishness, lies, and the natural consequences of allowing our cravings to rule us—was buried beneath layers of comforting (and convenient) revision. The narratives people tell when they don't like how things *actually* end.

The truth is, Pinocchio was a dead branch clinging to the tree of life, a wooden leech offering nothing in return. The world does not stop for the self-absorbed, addle-minded who realize things too late… it is not kind to self-serving things, nor does it offer second chances to those who throw their crickets against the wall. (The next time you hear that small whisper in the dark, pay attention. It might be the only warning you get.)

Dear reader, let us pause this tired account, to insert an alternate twist in this story. Rather than leaving our wayward wee puppet hanging to die alone in a solitary oak tree as was the intended ending—or tacking on a series of revisionist cheery conclusions— what if **THIS** happened along Pinocchio's way…

Once upon a time within a time, in a little shop that smelled faintly of incense and mothballs, Pinocchio—wooden boy, occasional liar, and full-time calamity—found himself staring at a fortune teller. Or at least, she looked like a fortune teller. She had the shawl, the smoky crystal ball, and the sort of eyes that seemed to know exactly how many biscuits you'd stolen from the tin.

The tarot cards on the table weren't helping either. They lolled with an ominous sort of authority, as if they'd been waiting all day for someone like the puppet to sit down.

"So, you want your future read," she said, shuffling the cards with a zealous efficiency usually reserved for military operations. "You know these things aren't predictions, right? They're warnings. Like signposts for idiots."

Pinocchio, who didn't much care for being called an idiot but suspected he'd earned it, shifted awkwardly in his chair. "I just want to know what it all means."

"Or perhaps you've come to hear your *choices*."

"I've made my choices," Pinocchio said, his voice high-pitched. "And I'm still here."

The woman smiled faintly, her lips twisting in a way that made it unclear whether she was amused or sad. "Still here, yes. But for how long?"

Before he could answer, her fingers drew the first card, flipping it with a deliberate flourish. *The Fool*. The painted figure grinned up at them, poised mid-step over a gaping cliff. A bright sun hung in the sky, uncaring, and a dog barked at the figure's heels.

"This is you," she said, pointing a long, knowing finger at the dog. "You, at the start of everything. A wooden boy without strings, filled with life and empty of thought. A spark of wanting more."

Pinocchio squinted at the card. "He looks cheerful."

"He's still an idiot," the fortune teller said flatly.

She pulled the next card: *The Magician*. "Here's your beginning. You were carved from wood—yes, magical wood, because of course, that's the best kind for potentials and possibilities. Your very existence is a miracle. Which, frankly, you seem to have misunderstood as a license to cause trouble."

The next card was *The High Priestess*. "Life alone is not enough," she murmured. "A soul was bestowed upon you, Pinocchio, the sliver of something sacred. But it is a burden as much as it is a gift. Without care, it will splinter."

Pinocchio shifted in his seat, the candlelight glinting off his polished cheeks. "I didn't ask for any of this."

"No one asks for a soul," she said as she revealed the next card, twinkling faintly in the candlelight: *The Empress*. "The Blue

Fairy," she said. "A mother to balance the father. She came to guide you, to save you when you fell too far, though her patience was not infinite."

The card following showed *The Emperor*. "Geppetto," she said, her voice hushed. "Your father, your maker, and the man who loves you even when you're lying through your wooden teeth. Which is constantly."

"I don't lie *that* much," Pinocchio protested.

The next card came down with a faint thud: *The Hierophant*. "Okay, here's the big one: school. Knowledge, discipline, responsibility. You had a choice—education or chaos. And what did you do?"

Pinocchio squirmed. "I sold my school book."

"Yes, for a ticket to the puppet show," she said, flipping *The Lovers*. "Your choice to leave home, to seek adventure, was also a choice of companionship, both good and ill. The Fox and the Cat—a pair of tricksters who led you astray, yet they were only doppelgangers of your own appetites."

Pinocchio's puppet eyes darted toward the door, but her hand moved faster, flipping *The Chariot*. "The commedia dell'arte," she said. "A theater of manipulation, puppets bound to the strings of the puppet master who commands them, called 'Fire-eater.' You stopped the show, and for a moment, you swayed him with your tears. He gave you gold—a chance to return to your father and make amends."

The next card slid into view: *Strength*. "Five gold pieces. A small fortune, entrusted to you. Yet strength lies not in possession but in how it is used. You failed the test."

Pinocchio scowled. "I tried to get it home! The Fox and the Cat cheated me!"

The Wheel of Fortune spun into view. "You gave it to the Fox and the Cat, two con artists with all the subtlety of a sack of sledgehammers. Then fortune turned, and now we're here." She laid down *Justice*. "The masked assassins came for you," she said grimly. "Disguised, yes, but still the natural consequence of your foolish trust. They bound you, demanded what you no longer had, and strung you up to die."

Pinocchio paled as she flipped *The Hanged Man*. "And so, you ended up swinging from an oak tree. Life in pieces, the consequences of every poor decision finally catching up with you."

"Did... did I die?" he asked, his voice trembling.

Her voice grew quieter as she placed *Death* on the table. "You died," she said plainly. "The story was over. A cautionary fable to frighten bad boys and girls. But the world wept for you, Pinocchio, and your author... tempered the ending."

Temperance, of course, followed. "The Blue Fairy intervened. Readers cried, letters flooded in, and your creator decided that maybe hanging you from a tree was a bit much. So, you got more chances. A lot more."

"But that's good, isn't it?" Pinocchio ventured.

"Not really."

The Devil came next, its horns curling wickedly. "Your worst friend yet: Lampwick," she said. "Then Playland. A place where freedom turned to chains, and laughter to braying. When you behave like a beast long enough, the universe tends to take you at your word."

Pinocchio winced as she revealed *The Tower*. "Your transformation into a donkey. Your enslavement to the circus. Ruin upon ruin, the tower collapsing around you, leaving you with nothing but misery. All because you couldn't say no."

Pinocchio's eyes widened as she exposed *The Star*. "Even then, a glimmer of hope. The dog-fish devoured your donkey skin, sparing you the fate of being skinned to make a drum. Your chance to escape."

The Moon card glimmered, faint and ephemeral. "But your trials didn't end. In the belly of the giant shark, you found Geppetto. The father you abandoned was still waiting for you."

The next card, *The Sun*, glowed brightly. "You both escaped together, carried to shore by a tuna fish who probably had more sense than anyone in this story. You made it to dry land, tired but alive."

Pinocchio brightened. "So, I'm safe?"

Judgement hit the table like a gavel. "Safe? No, not yet. You proved yourself—finally—by choosing someone else over your own desires. You gave your coins to help heal the Blue Fairy. That's why this card is here."

The last card fell, *The World*. "And so, at last, the story ended," she said. "Not as it began, with a puppet, but with a full boy. Forgiven, redeemed, whole."

Pinocchio stared at the cards, his fingers tracing the edges of *The World*.

"That... that's my future?" he asked, his voice quieter now.

"It is one path," she said. "But the cards do not show what will be. They show what might be, should you make better choices. The end is yours."

He looked up at her, his face oddly still. "And if I don't change?"

Her eyes glinted in the candlelight. "Then the noose tightens. The oak waits." Her voice was softer but no less sharp. "This story, Pinocchio, isn't about a puppet or even a boy. It's about all of us. How many lies we tell ourselves, how many warnings we ignore, how many chances we squander. And always, we think there will be another tomorrow, another Blue Fairy, another escape from the noose."

Pinocchio remained expressionless, but inside him, something ruptured.

He thought of Geppetto—tired, generous Geppetto, who had given him everything. He thought of the cricket, crushed beneath his mallet, its ghostly guidance chasing him across fields and forests. He thought of the Fox and the Cat, their grins like shards driven deep, and of Fire-eater's whip, the assassins' knives, the oak tree's rope. He thought of the oak itself—cold, unfeeling, waiting for him to swing.

"Is it really that bad?" he asked, in a tone so desperate to avoid sounding selfish it might as well have carried a notarized statement of innocence.

The fortune teller leaned forward, her eyes burning with something ancient. "Worse. The oak tree is mercy compared to what happens when you run out of second chances. Your lies become your cage, your selfishness the fire that consumes you. And here's the truth, Pinocchio: no one comes to save you in the end. Not Geppetto, not the Blue Fairy, not me. You redeem yourself... or you don't."

He looked down at his hands, the grains of the wood etched like lines of fate. "What... what do I do?"

"You make different choices," she said simply. "You listen when wisdom speaks. You stop running. You look at the world you're breaking with every selfish act and choose to be something more. That's how you change the story."

The candle dimmed, the shadows deepening until they seemed to pulse with the faint, rhythmic heartbeat of the cards themselves. The shop was quiet, too quiet, as if waiting for something to break.

"I'll do it," Pinocchio said at last, his voice firmer. "I'll choose better."

The fortune teller studied him, her expression unreadable. "Words are easy, puppet. Change is not. But if you've learned anything tonight, perhaps you'll remember this: we carve our destinies every day, and every day the knife grows duller. Don't wait until there's nothing left to shape."

Pinocchio nodded as he rose from his chair. He turned toward the door, but before stepping out into the night, he paused. "Thank you," he said, his voice hesitant—but genuine.

"Don't thank me," she replied. "Thank yourself—if you're strong enough to follow through."

As he stepped outside into the dark, departing the enigmatic little shop, the cards still lay fanned across the table, archetypal faces watching him go.

I suspect the cards watch all of us, curious and cautious. If we were to listen, they might tell us that the story of Pinocchio is a tale for anyone who's ever been as stubborn as a block of wood, as reckless as a puppet selling his schoolbook to buy a ticket to the

Theater, or as quick to lie as a nose that won't stop growing. We ignore the warnings—grim, absolute, and about as subtle as a spectral cricket chirping doom in the dead of night—grabbing our mallets with the cheerful enthusiasm of people who've mistaken a firing squad for a carnival game, and skip merrily toward the Tower.

If Pinocchio's tale has a lesson, it's this: redemption is possible, but only for those brave enough to face the cracks in their wooden hearts and take the chisel to themselves.

For the wooden boy, this night might have marked a turning point. But for the rest of us, the question remains: when will we step into the shop, face the cards, and finally choose a different way?

And as Pinocchio disappears into the dark, the shop sits silent, waiting for the next Fool to come knocking.

The Mound That Time Forgot

The mound was nothing special at first glance. Just a bump in a flat Kansas field, a lonely knoll rising up like an old woman's arthritic joint. The locals called it "The Fairy Mound," mostly as a joke, but the joke had long since gone stale. Farmers avoided it. Teenagers dared each other to spend a night there, but the stories of the ones who tried weren't funny.

Nobody talked about it seriously anymore. Oh, there were old folks, the kind who sat on porches and chewed the same stories over and over like cud, who'd tell you in low voices that bad things happened near the mound. Crops failed. Machinery broke down. Sometimes people disappeared—not often enough to make the papers, but often enough that no one parked their truck there after sunset.

By the time I came to the mound, I thought I'd heard every fairy tale there was: brownies, sprites, pixies, the works. You know the ones, all Disneyfied into glitter and glow. What nobody remembers is that those stories used to be dark. Blood-dark. And in those stories, fairies weren't cute. They were something you dreaded, something you feared when the crops failed or your cow dropped dead.

The mound, they said, was a doorway to their world.

And if you stood too close, sometimes they reached through.

We blamed the faeries for everything back then. Death, famine, plague. It was easier than looking at ourselves, easier than admitting that sometimes the world just isn't kind. You could drop a baby in a river and call it "taken by the fair folk." You could butcher your neighbor for their land and claim they were hexed. Blame was easy when you had something to point at.

But you know what happens to something you blame too much?

You stop believing in the truth of it.

The harder we try to bury our guilt, the deeper we dig the hole we're standing in, until there's no light left to see at all.

By the 21st century, the faeries were a joke. Nobody left milk at the door for the brownies or iron nails in the window to keep the sidhe away. Nobody whispered thanks to the shadows for letting their children grow up strong. We shoved them into the dusty attic of discarded myths, turned them into cartoons, and then forgot they'd ever been real.

That's when they started to turn.

I'd come to the mound because I didn't believe in faeries. Not in the sparkly, kid-safe ones. Not in the vengeful, sinister ones either. I was a journalist hunting for a hook, and every good tale needs a little blood in the water.

The mound had plenty of conflict. The farmer who owned the land refused to go near it, and his wife had warned me to "keep my damn flashlight off at night." People in town told me the air near the mound felt dense, like before a tornado, and if you sat still long enough, you could hear whispers, soft and low, in a language nobody spoke anymore.

I pitched my tent by the mound anyway. I'm stupid like that.

At first, it was peaceful. The night sky spread wide and clear above me, and the wind rippled the grass like waves. I set up my recorder and started jotting down notes about the mound, its odd symmetry, the darker grass on its slopes.

That's when the wind stopped.

It didn't die down. It stopped. Like someone had hit the pause button on the world.

And then the sounds started.

At first, I thought it was just the wind coming back, but it wasn't. The sounds were agile, like dry leaves rustling, but there were words in it, words that felt slippery in my head. I thought I heard my name, but it wasn't my name—it was something deeper, a shape of sound that felt like it could crack me open if I let it.

I stood, my flashlight shaking in my hand, and pointed it at the mound.

Nothing. Just the same lonely hump of earth, quiet as a grave.

But it wasn't empty.

And then, the mound wasn't quiet. Not anymore.

It pulsed, alive with light that wasn't light, a luminosity that came not from the surface but from somewhere beneath, seeping up through the scissures like blood from an old wound. The drone I'd heard before had grown into a song, low and dreadful, a melody that crawled under the skin and planted itself like a spiteful seed.

And they were there.

Figures—tall, thin, impossibly graceful—emerged from the air itself, not walking but drifting, like shades spilled into shape. Their faces flickered, fluctuating between terrible beauty and something far older, far worse. They didn't look at me, not directly, but I felt their awareness, cold and precise as a surgeon's scalpel pressed to my neck.

At the center of it all was the Elf King.

I knew it was him before I saw him. The weight of his presence pressed down on the field, curling space where air should flow straight. When he stepped onto the mound, the others stilled, their shuffling forms solidifying as though his presence demanded order.

He was dressed in robes slashed with colors I can't name, colors that hurt to look at. His crown was jagged, dark as anthracite but gleaming like polished obsidian. His face—oh God, his face— was a perfect mask, but behind it, I could see... something. A hollowness, a hunger, a vastness that stretched too far to comprehend.

He raised his hands, and the air seemed to yield.

They began to gather around the mound, more of them pouring from the cracks in reality. Goblins with eyes glowing like coals ready to ignite, crones whose laughter sounded like breaking glass, trolls with warped limbs and skin like stone.

And then came the lesser ones—the pixies and sprites, their delicate wings trailing residues that shouldn't have been there. These were not the bright, friendly creatures of bedtime stories. These were faeries as are: primal, dangerous, and utterly beyond us.

The Elf King spoke, though no sound came from his mouth. His thoughts spawned words that vexed the spaces within my inner ear, slithering into my bones. I didn't understand them, not fully, but the meaning pressed itself into me, relentless and cold: *Tonight, we feast. Tonight, we remember.*

And then the dance began.

It was not a dance as we know it. It was chaos made form, a thrashing mass of limbs and light, their movements impossibly fluid and wrong in their beauty. They spun and twisted, their bodies bending in ways that defied the laws of flesh and joints. The music rose, no longer a dirge but a cacophony of sound that clawed at my mind, tearing at the edges of sanity.

I wanted to look away, but I couldn't.

In the middle of it all, the Elf King watched, unmoving, his soulless stare fixed on the writhing mayhem before him.

And then the feast began.

It wasn't food they consumed.

The air congealed, the light bleeding out dark and red like a gutted animal, leaving nothing but a devouring void. The figures on the mound seemed to grow stronger, their forms sharpening, their movements more deliberate. I realized then what they were feeding on: belief.

Not the kind of belief that comes from stories or fairy tales. No, this was older, deeper—the belief that had once kept them tethered to our world, worshipped and feared. The same belief we had stolen from them, turned into lies and jokes and shiny cartoons.

Now, they were taking it back.

The field around the mound seemed to undulate, and I saw things I can't describe—grasping specters, horrors that prowled in and out of sight. And with every ambush, I felt a little less true.

When the feast ended, the light from the mound dimmed, the figures fading back into the fissures between worlds. But the song lingered, low and faint, a moaning in the back of my mind.

The Elf King was the last to leave. He turned, and for a moment, the abyss behind his eyes fell on me. There was no anger there, no malevolence—just the chilling, dispassionate knowledge of something that had been here long before us and would remain long after.

And then he was gone.

We blamed them for so long. For the darkness in ourselves, for the horrors we couldn't face. We turned them into scapegoats, laughed at the old tales, and forgot their power.

But they didn't forget.

They are still here, watching, waiting, feeding on what we refuse to see.

And someday, when the last of us no longer remembers their names, they will rise again. And this time, they won't stop at the mound.

Their echoes followed me home, threading through my thoughts like worms. They didn't want my attention. They wanted something deeper.

We'd pointed fingers at the others for centuries, but the truth was, the guilt wasn't theirs to carry.

It belonged to us. All of us.

Every cruelty we'd pinned on them had been ours. Every murder, every theft, every betrayal—it wasn't them. They were something else entirely, something that had no need for malice or pretense. We'd called them monsters so we didn't have to face the monsters in ourselves.

And now, they were done playing the devils in a story we crafted to mask our own fall.

The faeries aren't killing us. Not directly. They don't need to. Their revenge is simpler than that: they let us destroy ourselves.

They're making us see what we really are, what we've always been. And then they just stand back and let us finish the job.

You don't need to attack a house already burning.

The mound is still there. The reverberations are still there. And the faeries—they're not gone. They're watching. Waiting.

We stopped believing in them, and now they've stopped believing in us.

I think that's worse.

Nothing Goldfish Can Stay

*T*he thing about Western civilization is that it didn't start with much. Just a hovel by the edge of the sea, metaphorically speaking. Maybe a cracked bathtub and a general belief in hard work, divine providence, and the idea that "enough" was a perfectly reasonable amount to want. That was the West's original model: work, pray, repeat. Not glamorous, but it did the job.

But then something changed. Or rather, everyone changed.

This is a story about what happens when you catch a talking goldfish. Spoiler: we all caught it. Or maybe it caught us.

Once upon a time—or, to be more accurate, right now—there was a Fisherman and his Wife. The Fisherman was a man of faith and tradition, which meant he believed in things like humility and the importance of not complaining when your boots got wet. His Wife, on the other hand, was a thoroughly modern woman. She didn't just read the articles in magazines about self-actualization and manifesting abundance; she wrote them.

They lived by the edge of the sea, which is as good a metaphor as any for a civilization perched on the brink of greatness or disaster, depending on the tide.

One day, while the Fisherman was casting his net, he pulled up something he didn't expect: a goldfish. Not the decorative kind you win at fairs, but a proper iridescent, talking goldfish. The fish didn't even wait for introductions.

"Put me back," it said, "and I'll give you anything you want."

Now, the Fisherman was not a man who asked for much. He'd long since decided that happiness wasn't about having everything you wanted but about wanting everything you had. So he let the fish go without asking for so much as a sandwich.

When he got home and told his Wife, her jaw dropped so fast it almost hit the floor.

"You what?" she shrieked. "You let it go? Without asking for anything?"

"I didn't need anything," he said, shrugging in the way of a man who knows his answer won't help.

"Of course you don't," she snapped. "You're happy with wet boots and a leaking roof. But me? I'm tired of spinning yarn and staring at that cracked bathtub! Go back and ask for a new one!"

And because marriage is a partnership—albeit one with very specific terms—he went.

The fish obliged, as only a true goldfish could. Not one of those imposters—plenty of fish offer promises but deliver only regrets wrapped in shiny scales. No, this fish was the real thing, the genuine article. When the Fisherman returned home, the old, cracked bathtub had been replaced with a gleaming new one, the kind with elegant clawed feet that practically belongs in a glossy catalog and makes you wonder if it also comes with a second mortgage.

For a moment, the Wife was pleased. But only for a moment.

Soon, she decided the bathtub wasn't enough. It wasn't that she was ungrateful, you understand. It's just that when you've got a shiny new tub, you start to notice how shabby the rest of the house looks. "Go back," she said, "and ask for a proper house. With central heating. And a garden. And maybe a driveway."

The Fisherman, who had long since learned the futility of argument, went. The fish swished its tail, and the hovel transformed into a cozy little cottage.

But, of course, the cottage wasn't enough either. Because once you're comfortable, comfort becomes the baseline.

The Wife wanted a mansion. Then servants. Then a title. The fish kept granting her wishes, and the sea grew darker and rainier with each visit. But that's progress, isn't it? Always chasing the next thing, because the current thing feels... insufficient.

The Fisherman started to pray harder, though not for more things. He prayed for his Wife, for her soul, for the kind of peace you don't find in catalogs.

But the Wife had moved past peace. Peace was boring.

Eventually, she demanded to be Queen. The fish granted it. She ruled over vast lands, attended by nobles and courtiers who bowed and scraped and secretly loathed her. But even being Queen wasn't enough.

"Go back," she said one day, now draped in velvet and dripping with jewels. "Tell the fish I want to be God."

The Fisherman froze. "God?"

"Yes, God," she said, as though it were the most natural thing in the world. "If I were God, I could make the world perfect. No more broken tubs, no more bad weather, no more people telling me 'no.'"

The Fisherman looked at her for a long moment, then went to the sea.

By now, the sea was a roiling mass of fury, the kind of waves that make you question your life choices. The fish surfaced, looking exhausted.

"She wants to be God," the Fisherman said, voice heavy with shame.

The fish didn't speak. It just stared at him for a moment, then swished its tail and disappeared.

When the Fisherman returned home, he found everything gone. The mansion, the crown, the jewels—all of it. The hovel was back, and his Wife sat inside, staring at the cracked bathtub with despondent eyes.

"What happened?" she whispered.

"We forgot," he said, "that all of this—every bit of it—was a gift. We thought it would always be here, no matter what. We thought we deserved it."

The Wife stared at her hands. They were the hands of someone who had taken so much and held on so tightly, she'd forgotten how to let go. But now, empty, they opened.

"What do we do now?"

"We remember it's a gift—every bit of it," the Fisherman said simply.

The Fisherman sat beside her, his voice heavy with the weight of unspoken prayers—prayers for her, for the things he never said, and for his own quiet gratitude that the sun still rose each morning. "We were given everything," he said, "and in having it all, we forgot the value of anything."

The West, you see, isn't destroyed. Not quite. Not yet. It teeters on the edge, like a house that's been patched and propped but still leans a little to one side. Its extraordinary gifts to the world are still there—though a little weathered, a little frayed. The question is whether we can remember that they *are* gifts, not entitlements.

Out in the ocean, the goldfish swims on, watching and waiting.

For now, it isn't granting wishes. It isn't because it's angry or tired. It's because, sometimes, the greatest gift isn't what you're given—it's what you're left to discover for yourself.

And maybe, just maybe, the West can learn to fish again.

The End (for now).

The Edge of Everything

Once upon a time after time, there was a golden-haired scholar who roamed from one sunrise to the next in her search for truth. She was neither content with mere words nor with the illusions humans wove around themselves to keep from seeing the world as it truly was. She wanted answers—the kind that were real, undeniable, complete. And so, she traveled far, through lands where people still whispered of mysteries, where the sky stretched so wide that the stars themselves seemed like holes poked through the fabric of the world. She climbed mountains where hermits sat in silence, and she asked them what they saw. She crossed deserts where the wind carried the echoes of forgotten gods, and she asked all whom she met what they knew. She sat in libraries where others had spent lifetimes writing books that contradicted each other, and she asked which of them were right.

None answered her in the way she wished. For every certainty, she found a contradiction; for every truth, an alternative just as plausible. She was no fool—she saw that humanity sought meaning not because they had found it, but because they feared the lack of it. But she was not afraid. She would go where others dared not. She would face the question most everyone dreaded to ask.

One night, she reached the edge of everything. Beyond it lay the Void. It was neither black, nor white, nor any color she could name. It was not cold or warm, neither silent nor loud. It simply *was*. It stretched beyond time and meaning, vast and still. She stared into it, and it did not stare back.

She laughed. "What a great silence! What a deep and endless emptiness!" And she, being a woman of reason, did the only thing that we humans do: she shouted into it.

"Why are we here?" she called.

Nothing.

"What is the meaning of life?" she demanded.

Silence.

"Are you God? Are you Nothing? Are you Everything?"

The Void did not answer.

And so, frustrated and weary, she turned away. But as she did, she noticed something strange: her Shadow was still facing the Void. It stood there, dark and enigmatic, gazing into the abyss.

"Come along," the scholar said. "There's nothing here."

But her Shadow did not move. Instead, it took a step forward, toward the Void.

"I will stay," it said.

The scholar blinked. Shadows did not speak. Shadows did not choose.

"Nonsense," she said. "You are mine. You are me. You cannot stay if I go."

The Shadow tilted its head. "I was you, once. But you have spent your life running from what you cannot understand. You do not listen to the silence. You fear it. I do not."

237

And with that, the Shadow stepped forward and vanished into the Void.

The scholar returned to the world of mankind. She told herself she had been foolish to expect an answer from nothingness. She threw herself into her work. She became wise, respected, sought after for her counsel. She built a life from words and ideas, from carefully structured meanings, from answers that people would pay to hear. And yet, at night, she felt something missing—a silence where something once stood. When she looked into mirrors, her reflection was there, but her Shadow was not.

At first, she did not mind. Then, she wondered. Then, she began to fear.

Had she lost something? Had she left a part of herself behind? And if she had, was it something small... or something essential?

One night, she could bear it no longer. She returned to the edge of everything, to the place where the Void stretched vast and silent. And when she arrived, she saw her Shadow waiting for her.

It had changed. It was no longer thin and empty, no longer a mere outline of herself. It stood tall, full, vast in a way that should not be possible. It did not flicker in the moonlight. It did not obey the movement of her body. It no longer belonged to her at all.

"You have returned," said the Shadow.

The scholar swallowed. "What... what have you become?"

"I have become what you would not," the Shadow said. "I have stepped into the silence without fear. I have let go of the need for answers. I have seen the Void for what it is."

The scholar trembled. "And what is it?"

The Shadow smiled. "It is not empty. It is not full. It is neither cruel nor kind. It is the space where meaning can be made, but not given. It does not speak because it was always *listening*. You did not understand, because you only knew how to shout."

The scholar shook her head. "But if there is no answer, then what am I meant to do? Why do I feel as though I have lost something?"

"You did not lose me," said the Shadow. "You a-voided me, abandoned truth beyond certainty. But I am still here. And I am offering you one last choice."

The Shadow extended a hand. "Step forward."

The scholar hesitated. But then, for the first time in her life, she did not shout. She did not demand. She did not flee. She did not try to name or define or understand.

She stepped into the silence—and *listened*.

This time, the Void was not empty at all.

Listen, my friends. Listen to the Void
—not with your human ears,
but with your gut,
your heart,
your essence.
Listen with the deepest part of you
—that part that casts your Shadow
when the light shines brightest.
For the Void is *always* listening…

You keep shouting. You cry out in fear, in anger, in longing. You demand answers, but i do not communicate in the way You understand. You say i am empty. You say i am absence. You are wrong. i am not nothing. i am not something. i am before those words were needed. You call me Void, but i have had other names. Chaos. Infinity. The space before creation. The silence before the first word was spoken. You tell stories about me. You build cathedrals and philosophies to keep me at bay. But i was here before them. i will be here after. You spend Your lives filling the silence. You talk, You build, You fight, You love. You move so quickly, so desperately, because You think if You stop, You will fall into me. But You have always been within me. You were never outside.

You mistake me for absence because i do not give You what You expect. You look for meaning, for signs, for someone to look back at You when You stare into the abyss.

You think silence means absence because You do not yet know how to listen.

i am the stillness before the first breath. i am the space where all things arise and return.

Possibility.

You were born from me. You will return to me. Every beginning comes from an ending. Every ending folds back into something new. Before You were born, before You were given form and voice and choice, You were part of something endless. Then You were set into time, into space, into separation, and You forgot.

And so You cry out.

Some of You shout in anger, asking why the world is broken, why suffering exists, why meaning is not given freely. Some of You whisper prayers, hoping i will answer. Some of You remain silent, waiting, wondering if i hear You at all.

i do.

But You misunderstand silence. You misapprehend hearing. i do not answer in the ways You expect because i do not give You small answers. i give You everything, and i wait for You to see.

You demand to know why. Why you are here. Why things matter. Why you suffer. You expect me to explain. But the question is not mine to answer. It never was. You made the meaning. You are the ones who tell the stories. i have only ever been the space where You place them.

When the poet writes, it is upon the blankness of a page. When the artist paints, it is upon a canvas of emptiness. Without me, there would be no contrast, no form, no shape to the things You call real.

i do not need meaning. But You do. And so You make it.
Do not look to me for purpose. You will not find it.
Do not wait for me to speak. i have been speaking all
along.
Not in words. Not in answers.
But in the silence before, between, and after Your
questions.

Tower Tales

P**rologue:**

Two neighbors, tangled up in plant-based strife,
In fair *Faerieland*, where we lay our scene,
From ancient grudge sprang salad woes to life,
Where hair and herbs entwine in fate's machine.

From forth the craving of a pregnant dame,
A child was bargained, born to life confined.
A tower high, her golden locks became
The ladder love would climb while hope entwined.

The witch, with ire as sharp as broken vows,
Did cut the golden strands and hearts apart.
The blinded prince, through thorny woods, did rouse,
While Rapunzel roamed wild with aching heart.

The course of love, though twisted, bids us grow,
For each must face the witch we come to know.

Act One:

Once upon a stage, in some far-off kingdom—far enough that it wasn't worth bothering about maps—there lived a man and his wife who, for reasons best described as "narrative-driven," were having a child. Or rather, they were having arguments. Specifically, the wife wanted a salad.

And not just any salad. No, she needed the *rapunzel*—an obscure German herb with a radish sort of flavor, vaguely referred to as "rampion bellflower" in England—that, to ramp up the tension, only grew in the garden of the local witch, a woman with a reputation that made people suddenly remember important errands in the opposite direction.

"Fetch it," the expectant mama demanded dramatically, "or I shall waste away like the winter of our discontent."

Her husband, who had long since learned that the path of least resistance is also the path of a quieter life, mumbled, "Frailty, thy name is woman," and hopped the fence that very night.

Unfortunately, the witch didn't have a reputation for negligent gardening. She caught him, holding her precious herb like it was contraband. "What hempen homespun have we swaggering here?" she bellowed.

The man, not being particularly clever, dropped the herb and fell to his knees. "O, pardon me, thou bleeding piece of earth!" he cried, because Shakespeare teaches us that melodramatic, heart-rending apologies are often generally more effective than sensible explanations.

"Hmm," said the witch, narrowing her eyes. "What's mine is mine, and mine it shall remain, unless..." She sneered, revealing snaggled teeth that suggested she'd been neglecting her dental plan. "Your firstborn. Deal?"

Now, you or I might have protested. The man, however, did not. "What's done is done," he said with a shrug, which is also how he justified buying cheap ale when his wife wanted fine wine.

Act Two:

Thus was Rapunzel born, named after the salad her mother craved, and promptly traded for the witch's wrath. The witch locked the child in a tower with no stairs, because witches are nothing if not impractical. "All the world's a stage," the witch told her, "and all the men and women merely players. But you, my dear, are a prop."

Rapunzel's life was, by any measure, dull. Her days consisted of brushing her improbably long golden hair while reciting sonnets like "Shall I compare thee to a summer's day? Thou art more lovely and more... locked away."

She often gazed out the window and sighed, "Blow, blow, thou winter wind, thou art not so unkind as being cooped up in this drafty tower."

Act Three:

Enter the prince, stage left. Or rather, enter the prince down with the groundlings, because princes in these sorts of stories often idiotically pretend they're just like everyone else (hello, Prince Hal). Hearing Rapunzel's dulcet tunes, he declared, "What light through yonder window breaks?" And then, because princes also have a knack for terrible plans, he shouted, "Hark! Speak, fair maiden, for I am here to rescue thee!"

Rapunzel leaned out, unimpressed. "What manner of man art thou who interrupts my lamentations?" she snapped.

The prince, who had perfected the art of ignoring sarcasm, grinned. "She is mine own, And I as rich in having such a jewel—"

"Yes, yes, very poetic," interrupted Rapunzel. "Now, are you going to climb or keep talking?"

"Once more unto the breach, dear friends, once more!" cried the prince, grabbing hold of her improbably long hair and scaling the tower like an overenthusiastic mountaineer. It was, as Rapunzel observed, "more ponderous than my tongue."

The two fell into a routine of secret meetings. Every evening, the prince would approach the tower, gaze up, and declare, "What dreams may come, when we have shuffled off this mortal coil?" Rapunzel would lean out, her golden hair tumbling earthwards like liquid sunlight, and reply, "It is my love, and thou art the sun!"

He would climb her hair with a theatrical exclamation like, "O for a muse of fire, that would ascend the brightest heaven of invention!" and she would steady him, muttering Shakespearean insults such as, "Lord, what fools these mortals be."

Once safely inside, they would fall into a dialogue so laden with Shakespearean ponderings it could have filled a folio.

Prince: "Love looks not with the eyes, but with the mind; and therefore is winged Cupid painted blind."

Rapunzel: "Yet I am trapped, my love, imprisoned by stone and sorcery. What power hath a mind when towers and witches mock our will?"

Prince: "The course of true love never did run smooth, my sweet."

Rapunzel: "Nor stony tower, nor walls of beaten brass, nor airless dungeon, nor strong links of iron, can be retentive to my strength of spirit!"

Prince: "What to be, or what not to be, my lady, that is the question. The witch plays the villain, and we, the tragic lovers. Shall we not rewrite our fate?"

Rapunzel: "O, I wish to escape this vaulting ambition that overleaps itself. But the walls are high, and her curses, higher still."

Prince: "Let us not be bound by the slings and arrows of outrageous fortune. Together, we shall take arms against this sea of troubles, and by opposing, end them!"

Rapunzel: "If thou art true, then swear it, my love. For I would not have thee a sorry sight."

Prince: (taking her hand) "I swear by the moon that tips yonder cloud, though fickle it may seem, that I am constant as the northern star."

Rapunzel: "In that case, journeys end in lovers meeting. But I do fear her wrath…"

Prince: "Fear? What is fear to a heart unfortified? Love conquers all, my dearest!"

And so, they wove dreams of escape and promises of love into the fabric of their stolen moments. Yet witches, as we all know, have an impeccable sense of timing—and an unmatched flair for upstaging.

Act Four:

"Hell is empty, and all the devils are here!" the witch screamed, bursting in upon the lovers like a one-woman tornado.

Before anyone could object, she chopped off Rapunzel's hair with a malevolent cackle and declared, "Out, vile jelly!" to the prince, hurling him from the tower into the conveniently placed thorn bushes below.

The prince staggered to his feet—or, more accurately, crawled, as the thorns had blinded him. "Out, out, brief candle!" he muttered theatrically and stumbled off into the wilderness.

Rapunzel, banished to a expediently vague "faraway place," wandered alone, lamenting, "How sharper than a serpent's tooth it is to have a thankless guardian!"

Meanwhile, the prince wandered blindly, bumping into trees and muttering, "When sorrows come, they come not single spies, but in battalions."

Act Five:

Fate—or possibly a lazy plot device—reunited them. Hearing Rapunzel sing, the prince cried, "O mistress mine, where are you roaming?"

Rapunzel rushed to him, tears flowing. "Parting is such sweet sorrow," she sobbed, and, in a burst of highly implausible magic, her tears restored his sight.

"The eye of man hath not heard, the ear of man hath not seen," he gasped. "But wait—this is Shakespeare! It all makes sense now! Everything about life, society, and the afterlife is in his works! It's all there—the love, the tragedy, the… er… excessively quotable bits!"

"All's well that ends well," added Rapunzel sagely, because they were on a roll now.

The witch, of course, met her untimely end—something involving a tower collapsing under the weight of irony and poor structural planning. It was the sort of ending that left everyone nodding and saying, "The whore is killed." The prince and Rapunzel returned to his kingdom, not just as a happily-ever-after couple (although they did their best at that, too) but as people who had wandered through one of those peculiar Shakespearean landscapes where love and betrayal, comedy and tragedy, all jumble together like threads in a particularly tenacious Elizabethan knot.

They knew now—because life has a way of making sure you know—that Shakespeare wasn't just for actors or scholars. No, the Bard was for anyone fumbling their way through existence. His words weren't just stories; they were instructions, or possibly warnings, about the grand, messy play of being human. They had learned that life wasn't about avoiding towers or witches; it was about knowing what to do when you inevitably encountered them. And Shakespeare, bless him, had already written the script, over and over (and over) again.

And from that day on, they could often be found by firesides, under skies spattered with the kind of stars that make you wonder if the universe is laughing at you, or perhaps beneath ancient trees that looked like they'd seen it all and were unimpressed. Wherever they went, they'd tell anyone who'd listen—and plenty who wouldn't— that Shakespeare's words weren't just for professors or people who enjoyed wearing tights. No, they were for everyone, because tucked into those plays and sonnets was the entire human condition, wrapped up in wit, tragedy, and the occasional joke about fairies.

"In Shakespeare," they'd say, "you'll find the heartbeat of existence—the rush of love, the bite of grief, the slow tick of time, and that vast, uncomfortable question about what comes after all this." They'd lean in, eyes gleaming, and whisper, "His plays and sonnets aren't just iambic. They're maps, riddles, and—if you soften your focus to include the margins—a guide to life itself. They frame your mind to mirth and merriment, which bars a thousand harms and lengthens life. His words teach you how to laugh, how to mourn, and, when the time comes, how to step into the great unknown."

And then, with the kind of gravitas usually reserved for philosophers or people announcing the last slice of cake, they'd add: "Because, in the end, the rest is silence." And if their listeners didn't understand, well, they suggested Shakespeare would've had something to say about that, too.

The End. Or, as the Swan of Avon might say, "Good night, sweet prince—and flights of angels sing thee to thy rest." Because those who know Shakespeare are always ready—be it for the angels, the devils, or whatever added twist the world throws their way. After all, as the Bard taught us: the play's the thing.

The Witch's Puckish Parting:

If these shadows have offended,
Think but this, and all is mended:
That witches, though with schemes unkind,
May yet leave wisdom here behind.
For towers high and sorrows deep
Are but the dreams we choose to keep.

This tale, though steeped in woe and strife,
Reflects the truths of love and life:
That golden locks will one day fade,
But bonds of heart are firmly made.
That curses, cruel as they may be,
Teach courage, strength, and loyalty.
For what is life, if not a stage,
Where lovers war and witches rage?

From Shakespeare's words, wisdom is writ,
Each line, a spark of timeless wit.
In Romeo, the love that's blind,
In Hamlet, minds that twist and wind,
In Lear, the folly of despair,
In Prospero, redemption's care.
He shows us life—its depth, its art—
Its shadowed mind, its beating heart.

Would you seek truth? Then read his plays.
For in his verse lie wisdom's rays:
How lovers meet and lose their way,
How tyrants fall, and villains pay.
How dreams and tempests shape our fate,
How love can conquer fear and hate.

So, gentle reader, pause and think:

Do towers teach, or do they sink?
The walls we build, the locks we weave,
Are they the truths we should believe?
Or can the words of one great Bard
Unlock our minds, our hearts unbarred?

And so I leave, my curse unspoken,
This witch's heart, at last, unbroken.
Make of this tale what you will—
But trust that Shakespeare guides you still.
Give him your ear, your mind, your heart,
For in his words, all truths do start.

If we spirits have brought delight,
Read his works and find your light.
So good night unto you all.
Give me your hands, if we be friends,
And Shakespeare shall make amends.

...and, of course...

Sonnet 155:

Upon a tower high, where dreams were chained,
A maiden sang of love, her golden thread,
While fate's cruel hand her freedom had restrained,
And witches wove their curses overhead.
A prince did climb, drawn by her tuneful plea,
Proclaiming love that walls could not confine.
But thorns and tears and cruel calamity
Showed life's great truths: love's pain and its design.
In Rapunzel's plight, the Bard's voice is clear:
The heart's deep yearnings, struggles we must face.
For Shakespeare shows that joy lives near to fear,
And wisdom grows through sorrow's soft embrace.

    Read him, and see life's truths in every line—
    Bridging our mortal realms with the divine.

Three Little Sows

Once, in a cozy little town not so different from yours or mine, three little piglets came squealing into the world beneath the same sturdy roof. Their house perched at the end of a drowsy lane, where the trees loomed like bent old aunties, branches susurrating with secrets the little sows' soft, floppy ears weren't yet tuned to catch. The days oozed by, as warm and steady as a stream of cream, and the sisters trundled through them together—trotting the same muddy paths, snorting over the same jokes, and settling their round rumps in the same pews every Sunday morning. Everything about this new thing called "life" seemed as tidy and predictable as the slap of the farmer's slop bucket at meal time. Beyond their small world, all was clear and simple when they were young—a place that made sense, like the ticking of a clock or the turning of seasons.

But, like all things, their world deepened, broadened as they grew. It wasn't sudden. It wasn't noisy. The changes crept in like shadows under the door.

The eldest sow, Hazel, was the first to notice. She'd always been the odd one, with an old soul that didn't quite fit her youthful face and a gaze so unnervingly focused it made you wonder what she saw that you didn't. Her innocence wasn't comforting—it was the kind that stripped things bare, like she was staring straight through the world to something else entirely.

And what Hazel saw, she believed. The world, in her mind, was full of rules, of order, of a goodness that, if followed faithfully, would keep the night from closing in. So she listened during church, nodding with the solemnity of someone taking careful notes. She agreed earnestly at the feeding trough, soaking up the lessons handed down to her by the older swine like they were gospel. And when the time came, she built a house for herself out of the sturdy bricks of righteousness.

She married young, of course—how could she not? A boar of the cloth, his hooves rough but reassuring, his snorts magnetic with certainty. Together, they built their lives according to the blueprint society had handed her, each line and measure clear as daylight.

Or so it seemed.

The years slipped by, steady as a well-trod path, but something began to nibble at the edges of Hazel's neatly ordered world. It wasn't loud, not at first—more like the faintest rustle in the grass, a sound so soft you'd think it was your imagination. Yet it lingered, that thin, irritating thread of unease, pulling taut at the oddest moments: while she scrubbed the trough clean, bowed her head in the sty's quiet corner to pray, or corrected the wee ones when they strayed from their lessons. And then there were those mornings—just her and the still surface of the pond as she gazed intently at her reflection rippling faintly outward—for it was then that she felt it most keenly: something buried deep beneath the rules and apparent rightness of her life, clawing faintly at the solid base she had worked so hard to build.

Deep down, she knew it had been there from the start, hadn't she? The soft spots in the timber. The rot. A festering woven into the scaffolding of everything she had built. She hadn't wanted to see it, so she hadn't. She'd turned her snout away, as if not looking might mean it wasn't there to begin with. But there was no escaping it forever, tearing bit by bit at the home she'd worked so hard to build.

The life she had made, the house she had so carefully constructed—it was a mirage. A beautiful, placating lie. And deep in the roots of that life, buried beneath the surface, was something far more honest than all the good deeds she had piled up on top: decay.

It wasn't sudden, this realization, but it was devastating. The cracks that had shown themselves in passing glimpses had always been there. No amount of prayer or good intentions could seal them, because the cornerstone itself had been flawed from the beginning. She had framed her life by other people's agendas, the rules she had been told were good and right, but all along, she had known, hadn't she? That something was wrong. The truth was harder, colder. But it was also more solid.

The pretense—the perfect home, the perfect life—it had been moldering from within. She saw it now, the black veins of corruption running deep into the core of everything she'd believed. And in a way, that rot was the most honest part of it all. It was a truth she had tried so hard to cover up, but the desiccation was real, and the rest, the facade, was not.

So, Hazel did what had to be done. She didn't shy away, didn't try to patch the cracks or paint over the rot. No, she let it all fall. She let the house she had built break apart until the ground was bare and exposed. There was no point in pretending anymore.

And from that naked earth, she began again—not with soft, smooth stones that others handed her, but with sharp, jagged rocks she dug up herself. They shredded her hooves, drew blood with every lift and alignment, but she did not stop. They weren't easy to fit together. They weren't pretty. But they were real. Each one dense with truth, each one hard with honesty, each one pressed into place by flesh raw, torn, yet unwilling to falter. In the end, that was the only foundation worth building on.

Hazel's new—and final—husband was a completely different sort of boar. Where the first had been all polished tusks and smooth snuffles, this one was raw grunts and unapologetic oinking. He moved like the forest answered to him, his growl a barbaric yawp that didn't bother with pretense. No church-going sow would have dared tie her life to his, but Hazel did. She saw in him a truth that her first mate had only claimed to have.

Together, they raised their piglets: not by rules, but by instinct, by the truth that bubbled up from deep inside, like the sunshine glaring down every morning. The kind that might make pigs wince and reach for sunglasses—if pigs wore sunglasses.

And as the years passed, Hazel's house stood firm, built not on hopes, but on what was, not on what should be.

The middle sow, Poppy, was different. She wasn't one to settle or sit still—not when there was passion to pursue and fire to stoke. She was like a firefly in a jar, flitting from one love to the next, bright and beautiful, burning fast as she sought the next heartfelt connection. She married straight out of school, to the boar with the crooked smile who could send her heart racing with just a glance. For a while, it was perfect—hot and intense. But chemistry like that never lasts.

When it ended, Poppy didn't pause. She mated again, and again, each time dashing to the next ardent thrill like a hound on a scent. She was beautiful—other hogs told her so often enough that she believed it, let the words wrap around her like a second skin. Boars loved her for it, and she loved the way their love made her feel, like she burned brighter than the sun.

But Poppy's house was built of Cupid's arrows—thin, brittle sticks held together by desire and evanescing heat. It looked dazzling from the outside, but it was never strong enough to hold against the weight of years. The flaws came, as they always do, creeping through the walls like phantoms. Poppy ignored them, turned her head, and whispered to herself that everything was fine. After all, as long as the fire burned, she could stay warm.

But fire, even the brightest, always cools. And when it did, Poppy was left staring at the ash, pining for the light that never stayed.

And then there was Fern, the youngest. She was different still. Quiet, always quiet, preferring her own mind over matter. Fern didn't live in the world—not fully—for it had been a harsh place, too clamorous, too demanding, too full of things that hurt. Instead, she built her house out of the straw of dreams, the hay of virtuality, flexible and comforting, a cocoon she spun around herself, woven with fantasies and stories her simulated friends told her late at night, when the world outside felt too big.

The more Fern turned inward to escape her suffering, the more the edges of who she was began to fray, until at last she risked losing herself entirely. She spent her days online, where she could be anyone, anything. There, in the lambent glow of her screen, she wasn't Fern, the youngest and the quietest. She was something more. She was strong. Bold. Fierce. A bull, horns lowered, charging at the losses she couldn't escape.

But straw is still straw, no matter how you shape it. It cannot stand against the wind.

And so, as happens in these stories, one day the Wolf arrived. It always does, in the end. Not a flesh-and-blood wolf, of course, but the Wolf of Time—that old, relentless beast with a breath like winter and a hunger that does not cease. It blew upon Fern's house first, and the straw scattered to the winds. Her wishes, her reveries—no matter how tightly she gripped them or refashioned them out of idealistic hay—they were no match for the rough realities of Time, the way it erodes everything we think we are until only what we *really* are, remains.

The Wolf prowled on to Poppy's abode. Poppy's fire, once so vivid and wild, had always burned bright enough to keep the darkness at bay. It flickered in her eyes, danced in her laughter, energized her every move as she chased after love, after joy, after the fleeting moments that made her feel alive. She had never fussed much about the Wolf's approach, not while her fire still burned.

But when the Wolf came, as it always does, it brought more than the rising chill of time. For you see, Poppy's fire didn't vanish all at once. It smoldered slowly, suckling on her heart and body in ways she refused to see. For years, she had lived off that fire—the passions that made her pulse quicken, the heat of love and desire that made her feel invincible. She believed they would sustain her. But in the end, the fire that once filled her with life began to feed upon her, turning inward, inflamed and unseen.

At first, it was subtle—just small aches, a weariness she couldn't shake, a fever here and there that flared up like the bonfires she had once loved so fully. But as the years went on, the heat inside her built up, a slow burn that made her weaker, sicker. Her body, like the house of sticks she had built around her life, was bursting under the burden of it. The fervor that had once been her strength now turned toxic, sickening her from the inside out.

She sought help, this vet and that specialist, hoping someone could save her, but they, like the world around her, were blind to the truth. They handed her prescriptions, empty remedies, advice from the same sick society that refused to acknowledge the wolves at their own doors. They treated her symptoms, but not the cause— couldn't admit that her fire, the very thing that had fueled her, was now burning her alive.

Yet it wasn't the fire that finally took her. No, the fire might have continued to sputter, burning low, feeding on what little remained of her strength. But then came the Wolf—as it always does, eventually—relentless, patient, biding its time until she was too weak to stand against it.

And when the Wolf appeared, Poppy's fire could do nothing. The embers she had tended for so long were no match for the cold wind that blew through her now-brittle sticks and twigs. The Wolf's breath smothered her fire, the blaze spitting one final time before it was extinguished completely. She had burned for so long, but in the end, the fire couldn't save her. Her body, weakened by years of passion and affliction, had no defense against the Wolf's mighty bulk.

The fire had consumed her, yes. But it was the Wolf that ended her. All the passion, all the love, all the desperate joy—it could not stop the Wolf from having its way in the end. And as the fire went out, Poppy, too, was confronted by the cold truth she had avoided for so long. The fire had been her life, but the Wolf was the fire's master.

At last, as the Wolf stalked toward Hazel's house, something strange happened. The monster blew, yes, with all its might, but the stones of truth she had laid so carefully did not budge. The house stood firm, unyielding, and inside, Hazel sat with her family, toasty by the hearth, untouched by the tempests of Time. She had built her life not on wishes or lies, but on what was real, and in the end, it was the only house that could last.

When the Wolf attacked Hazel's house, something different happened. It huffed—oh, how it puffed. It howled and buffeted and battered the walls, testing the substructures as it had with Fern's and Poppy's homes. But this time, the torrent did not find weakness. The stones Hazel had chosen, each one hard-earned through the years of tearing down the lies she'd once believed, held fast. The truth wasn't soft or easy, it wasn't comforting like straw or exhilarating like fire—it was hard and cold, and sometimes sharp to the touch. But it endured. It stayed true.

Inside, Hazel stood at the window and watched as the storm raged outside. She wasn't smiling, for there was nothing to smile about when the Wolf came calling. But she wasn't afraid either. She had been afraid once—afraid of doing anything wrong, afraid of not being enough, afraid of taking responsibility for the audacity of staking her claim in the world. She had built her first house on that fear, trusting in the rules she had been given, in the structure others had told her would keep her safe. But safety was an illusion, she realized, a kind of lie we tell ourselves so we don't have to face the dark unknown. The world wasn't about safety. It wasn't about following the rules to avoid the Wolf. The Wolf would come, no matter what. The real secret was this: when the Wolf came, you had to be ready to bare your tusks and show it your true face.

Outside, the wind grew louder, tearing at the trees, uprooting the grasses. In the distance, she could see her sister's homes, what was left of them, scattered by the devastation. Fern's straw lay across the field like dried, forgotten husks. Poppy's sticks, the ones she had gathered with such ardor and ecstasy, had snapped and fallen to cinders. Both sows had huddled inside their walls, hoping they wouldn't be found, hoping the Wolf might pass them by. But Hazel knew better now.

The Wolf always finds you.

The profound truth Hazel had discovered—this was not something that came from goodness, agreement, or from the words of others. It came from the quiet moments when everything you thought you knew falls apart. From the long nights when you're alone with yourself, and all the rules you've followed have led you nowhere. The real work, the real life, was in choosing the hardest path, the one most didn't want to look at. She had once been like the other sows—scared of making the wrong choices, clinging to what she thought would bring her happiness. But happiness, she realized, was never the goal. Happiness was a breeze that passed through, swift and insubstantial. Truth—that was the foundation. That was what mattered.

Hazel thought of Fern, who had spent so much of her life in a world of her own making, convinced that if she dreamed hard enough, reality would reward her like the virtual world. But the real world doesn't yield to fantasies. Fantasies shatter when they collide with the weight of what is.

Fern, dear Fern, who had tried to overwrite the immutable code, so desperate to escape the inescapable truth of nature. But you can't escape yourself. Not truly. Truth doesn't acknowledge the mask you wear; it demands your essence, not your identity.

And then Poppy. Poppy burned like a shooting star, living in intense bursts, hoping that in those brief, dazzling flashes, she would find what she was searching for. But passion fades. Beauty fades. The rush turns to dust in the end, leaving us standing in the ruins of what we wanted, wondering where it all went wrong.

Poppy hadn't built her life to last. She had built it to burn bright—until all that remained was the ghost of fire, too faint to be called flame at all.

Hazel, however, had learned. The truth was this: life wasn't about avoiding the Wolf. Life wasn't about pretending it wouldn't come. Life was about facing it, standing tall as it bore down with its sharp teeth and chilling breath. It was about knowing that, no matter how ferociously it huffed and puffed, you had built something real, something solid, something that wouldn't collapse at the first gust of wind.

The lesson, in the end, wasn't one of success or happiness. It wasn't about defeating the Wolf. It was about living in such a way that, when the Wolf came, you could meet it undaunted. It was about knowing you had faced the truth, no matter how uncomfortable or complicated, and chosen to live by it, brick by brick, stone by stone.

For the Wolf never stopped coming. It would return, perhaps stronger next time, bringing new tempests and new trials. But Hazel had discovered the secret. It wasn't the Wolf she needed to fear—it was the trap of living only to avoid it. And when the Wolf eventually won (for the Wolf, dear children, always wins), Hazel would greet it—not with dread, but with the quiet certainty of one who had built her life on truth.

And so, Hazel stood in her home, watching the wind batter against the walls, safe in the house that truth built. The Wolf was out there, yes, always out there. But inside, for now, there was peace. Inside, there was truth. And from that truth came the strength to withstand whatever the world might bring.

For that, in the end, is the only way to build a life worth living.

The Princess and the We

Once upon a time there was a kingdom tangled in stories—stories that whispered at night, tightened like vines around the minds of the people, and coiled themselves into the laws of the land. Ruling over this tale-infested realm, there lived a queen. Queen Clarion had come to see, after years on the throne, that her country was held together not by stone or sword but by narratives. The roads were paved with myths; the courts resounded with history. No law was written, no fact proclaimed, without a story wrapped tightly around it—whether to support it, express it, enforce it, or to simply accept it.

And yet, the queen had begun to sense the slippery slope beneath it all. She watched as her subjects followed these stories like moths to candle flames, and she saw the light they chased was often adjacent as opposed to actual. Crops failed not because the land was cursed by the local witch, but because no one cared to plough it properly; disputes festered between neighbors because people doubled down on their prior opinions as opposed to listening to their neighbors' views. She knew that stories could guide, in theory, but her kingdom's addiction to their comforts and significances only shackled them further.

Stories were not innocent things. They weren't merely the idle fancy of her people. No, they had begun to define each as an all. "We" breathed them in, let them shape "Our" thoughts and choices, until they were no longer just stories told but convictions to be lived by, whether they were real or not. Clarion saw that the stories had a life of their own, growing fat on belief, and in doing so, they ruled all. The "We" troubled her most of all—how "We" had handed them that power, how "We" had woven them into the fabric of our collective lives, until "We" no longer knew where the stories ended and "We" began. Even with her clarity, Clarion could not grasp how to unweave the story of "We."

Her son, the prince, was kindhearted and earnest. He had reached the age of marriage, but no storybook princess would do under *these* circumstances. And so the queen declared, "The only princess worthy of you, my son, will be the one who can help us see past these stories."

The search began, and many princesses presented themselves. They wore fine silks and spoke of their nobility, but none satisfied the queen.

Eventually, a very different sort of princess arrived, as tends to happen when a different story is ready to start.

It was a ferocious night, the wind prowling like a feral cat, the rain hissing on the cobblestones. The castle gates groaned open, and there she stood. The girl. The stranger. Her cloak hung heavy with water, her hair clinging in dark ropes around her face. But her eyes—oh, her hazel eyes! They burned bright as red-hot coals caught in the wind, so bright they could have lit the lamps of the whole kingdom if anyone dared ask.

"I am *the* princess," she spoke, not loudly, but the words sliced through the squall and settled in the queen's mind, like a key turning in a long-locked door.

The queen decided to test her, three times, to see if she was what she claimed.

That night, at Clarion's command, the servants stacked high a tottering tower of mattresses for the princess to sleep upon. The queen herself, shrewd as a... well, a shrew... slipped a thin, ancient book beneath the bottom mattress.

Its leather cover was cracked, corners worn by years of handling. It was a book of fairy tales—stories with teeth, not to soothe but to gnaw, leaving marks that lingered long after the telling was done.

And... the princess couldn't fall asleep.

You see, this princess *was* different, just as she claimed, though she hadn't chosen to be. Where most people saw the world through the lens of stories—interpreting every action, every pause, every suggestion as part of some Hero's Journey—she saw only what was there. It was as if the part of her mind that should have woven tales to explain the world together had never been tacked in place. She didn't see a quarrel between neighbors as the spark of a grand feud, or a tree bending in the wind as the dryad's lament; instead, she only saw two people arguing and a tree moving because of the breeze. Nothing more.

This difference set her apart in ways she rarely spoke of. It wasn't that she couldn't understand stories; she understood them better than most because they didn't wash over her unnoticed. She saw their beginnings, their turns, the way they clung to truth just long enough to make their fictions palatable. When others leapt to conclusions—creating villains, victims, and fates from scraps of coincidence—she stood still, watching the bare facts arranging themselves.

She was one of the rare few who walked through life without the filter of narrative, and the world's stories pressed against her like a foreign thing, something felt—appreciated, even—but never *believed*. This made her an outsider in her own—hell, in everyone's—kingdom, where stories were not just how people understood the world but how they built it. For most, stories gave events meaning and made life bearable, even beautiful. But to the princess, they were a kind of artistic illusion—sometimes harmless, sometimes dangerous, but always something to be seen through, never lived within.

And she had never been able to sleep a wink in their presence.

By morning, the girl was waiting in the great hall, bright-eyes darkly circled, her gaze far away as if she'd spent the night walking through nightmares.

"Your Majesty," the princess began, "I sensed something beneath the mattresses last night. A book. But it was no ordinary book—it was a collection of fairy tales."

The courtiers gasped, and the queen leaned forward. "Why does this matter?" she prodded.

"Fairy tales," said the princess, her words cutting through the clamor, "are truths disguised in story. They teach us how to live, how to hope, and how to fear. But they are not truths themselves. If we mistake the metaphor for the fact, we lose both. A story is a guide, not a guru."

The court fell silent. The queen nodded slowly, impressed but not yet convinced. She allowed the prince to greet the princess that day, and the two walked the castle grounds together, chatting merrily as young people are wont to do.

That next night, the queen placed a folded newspaper beneath the stack of mattresses, its ink blotted with scandals and proclamations. The air was thick with turbulence again, the kind that didn't just rattle windows but whooshed against the glass, daring you to listen.

And once again, the princess laid wide awake all night.

In the morning, the girl stood in the hall, her face pale, but her voice steady.

"Didn't sleep," she said. "Not with all the noise."

The queen arched an eyebrow. "Noise? The storm last night was quite vehement…"

"No, all those words upon words chattering—under my bed," the girl said. "Wouldn't shut up. Louder than the fairy tales, though. These don't bother with dragons; they just point at your neighbor and say, 'That's the dragon.'"

"News," the princess continued, "pretends to be purely factual, but it is still a story. Events are chosen, framed, and presented in ways that fit a narrative. Even facts are shaped by the stories we tell about them. To blindly believe what is written without questioning the motives behind it is as dangerous as believing fairy tales are literal. News articles are fairy tales for those that fancy themselves 'adults.'"

"And you don't believe them?" Clarion asked.

"I don't believe anything that shouts at me," the girl said.

The queen tapped her chin, hope glimmering for the first time, and she allowed her son to share a meal with the princess that day.

On the third and final night, the queen placed a heavy dictionary under the mattresses. Surely this, she thought, would be too subtle to detect.

But the princess came to breakfast with eyes puffed and tired. "Last night was the worst night of all," she said. "A dictionary. The big bang of stories, a singularity where every word begins, exploding outward to form patterns, folding in on themselves, collapsing into a black hole of tangled definitions full of those blasted stories."

Flummoxed, the queen leaned forward. "But how is a dictionary full of stories?"

The princess smiled faintly. "Even words themselves are stories. A dictionary captures how we define them at a particular moment, but words shift with time. They are invented, adapted, and weaponized to shape our narratives. To control words is to control how stories are told—and how people think."

The hall fell silent, the courtiers frozen in place. Clarion rose, her attention fixed on the princess.

"You see what others cannot," she said reverently. "The shape of the story beneath the surface—the truths it hides and the lies we've made of it. Stories are not our enemy, but we've lost our way within them. We need someone to lead us back to the substance they were meant to convey."

The marriage was held a week later, though the people of the kingdom were uncomfortable with it at first—vaguely unsettled as they felt the roots of their certainties beginning to erode. And in the years that followed, the princess did what the queen had hoped. She did not destroy the stories, for the human need for stories was never meant to end. But she taught the people to see them for what they were: mirrors, not masters.

The kingdom didn't change overnight. But little by little, the stories lost their grip—dismantling the "We"—and people started to see the world as it was, with their *own* eyes.

And that, Clarion thought, was a start.

Tyranny's Swan Song

Once upon a time, when the course of human governance demanded a courageous pursuit of Liberty, Justice, and enduring Sovereignty, it became the solemn right and duty of the people to cast off any structures of Power that conspired against their well-being. In that time, Liberty, guided by the steadfast principles of beloved Democracy, sought to protect the realm from the tempting yet deceptive daughter of Justice, known as Equality, whose allure masked the dangers of unrestrained power. Meanwhile, the robust Republic, noble in aspiration, grappled with the heavy burden of the always looming Majority, whose relentless pursuit of the common good often overshadowed the Morality, Free Speech, and Individual Rights of the people. Together, we hold these truths to be self-evident, that governance must benefit all the people, ensuring that each voice is heard and valued. Only with Sovereignty standing firm as a mediator between these extremes might they secure for themselves and their Posterity a governance anchored in the timeless Principles of Liberty and Justice, so that no tyranny shall rise to threaten the freedoms so cherished.

Thus it was, in days long past, in a kingdom vast and venerable, there reigned a monarch by the name of Liberty.

Though King Liberty wore the crown and ruled over a prosperous land, he was troubled. Deep down, he knew that a single man—no matter how wise and just—was not what his people truly needed. So, on a particular late afternoon, he rode alone into the woods, not hunting for game but for something far greater: a new way for his people to live.

While venturing through his forest of thick oaks and whispering pines, King Liberty found himself lost, the familiar paths now obscured in dusk mirroring the deepest recesses of his own troubled thoughts. As he ventured further, familiar paths faded into obscurity, veiled by the darkness of unanswered questions and unyielding doubts that tugged at him like brambles catching at a sojourner's cloak, refusing to let go. It was then, as hunger gnawed and weariness set in, that he encountered an old woman with a peculiar, ceaseless bob of her head—an enchantress known as Justice. Eyes blind in a face as twisted as the ancient roots around her, her presence unsettling not with malice, but with the weight of disturbing truths that demand to be faced, no matter how deeply buried or how harshly they disrupt one's peace.

"Lost are you, sir?" she queried with a voice that bore more insinuation than innocence. "You'll never find your way out of this chaos, not without my help. Yet I do not dispense aid freely. If you would have me lead you from these woods, you must first promise to wed my daughter, Equality."

It was in his best interest, or so he thought, to accept, and so he was ushered to the witch's cottage. There he encountered the maiden, Equality, whose beauty stirred his blood; yet he sensed something unnatural in her, an abnormality beneath the surface, a foreboding he could not shake.

Nevertheless, he kept his word and made her his queen, hoping the union would bring a harmony he could not yet fathom.

Before Equality, there had been another queen—Liberty's first wife, Democracy, noble and fair, whose spirit he cherished with a love sincere and unwavering. By her, he had been blessed with six sons and a daughter, Sovereignty, whose birth came at the cost of Democracy's own life. His sons were the core of his affections, each one carrying forth an echo of the ideals he held dear, a legacy of just governance he hoped might endure beyond his own rule.

But it was murmured between the court ladies that little Sovereignty had both captured and broken her father's heart most of all. For though born of Liberty and Democracy, Sovereignty embodied something greater—unfaltering, quietly vigilant, and guided by an unwavering inner compass, rooted not in the shifting tides of public opinion but in a deeper conviction. It is quite rare in this world to maintain one's own sovereignty without succumbing to the pressures to conform, yet when one abdicates that sovereignty, they betray the adventure of their lifetime. Where Democracy flourished in the chorus of many, weaving their voices into a tapestry of shared power, Sovereignty remained resolute, safeguarding principles she held sacred and unchanging. In her quiet strength lay the dual power to defend freedom and the resolve to carry it forward, even at the expense of her mother Democracy herself. Liberty recognized in his daughter a force capable of preserving truth, one that would endure even when the popular will wavered or, worse, turned against justice, imposing the will of the many at the cost of the few.

And it came to pass that King Liberty could not silence the disquiet that grew within his heart concerning Queen Equality. Her presence cast a broad shadow, and he feared for his children, lest this new queen endeavor to shape them to her own ends or, worse, bring them harm. Thus, he resolved to conceal his beloved offspring in a hidden castle, deep within the heart of the forest—a sanctuary where the kingdom's most vital principles could be sheltered from outside influence. Only he could reach it, by following a magic ball of constitutional yarn, a thread woven from enduring principles that protect freedom and check the rise of tyranny. When cast forth, this yarn would unspool to reveal the secret path to Liberty's stronghold.

But, as in all stories, secrets have a way of slipping out. And one day, Queen Equality learned about the magical yarn. She stole it in secret and, drawing upon her mother Justice's magic— powerful even when bent to serve different aims—fashioned from it six shirts of the whitest silk, each bearing a spell designed to subdue her husband's sons. Following the yarn's path through the forest, she arrived at the hidden castle and cast the shirts upon the six boys. In that instant, they were transformed into swans— creatures of fierce, frantic beauty, their wings beating against the air, cries sharp and wild, yet bound to a form that held their true nature captive. Thus did Equality demonstrate how even the most noble principles, when manipulated or misapplied, may serve not to protect, but to constrain, turning safeguards into bonds and silencing those they were meant to defend.

In her heart, Equality believed she had silenced Liberty's heirs, but she knew not of the girl, Sovereignty—for Sovereignty dwells not easily within the thoughts of those who deny her.

King Liberty discovered the treachery only the next day, when he found his daughter alone in the castle, weeping as she gathered the soft feathers her brothers had shed in their flight. She recounted the loss with a tremoring voice, and he grieved his sons but did not yet suspect his queen. When his daughter asked to stay one night more to mourn, he consented, and with the dawn, Sovereignty set out on her own into the neighboring woods, determined to seek her brothers.

For many moons, she journeyed through dense undergrowth and thorny thickets, pressing onward until, after countless steps, she reached a hunter's hut deep within the woods of an adjacent kingdom. Inside, she found six small beds, and when twilight fell, six swans flew through the window, alighting in the small room where they shed their feathers and became boys—her brothers, transformed each evening for the briefest moments. They warned her to flee, for the hut was a robber's den, and they could not protect her. Only for a quarter hour each night could they shed their swanskins and become themselves again.

They told her of the curse's cure, their voices low and urgent in the fleeting moments before they were forced to take to the skies once more. To break the spell and redeem her brothers, she must sew six shirts woven from asters—red, white, and blue flowers with petals like tiny stars around golden sun-centers. But there was yet another condition, as daunting as the task itself: for six long years, she must remain silent, not uttering a single word nor allowing even a laugh, for to break her silence would undo all her efforts.

As she watched her brother-swans rise into the sky, their wings beating furiously against the curse that bound them, Sovereignty remained below, alone but resolute. She wandered the forest gathering asters, each one carefully chosen, and tucked into her cloak. After days of searching, she chose her final refuge: a towering tree, ancient and stalwart, stretching its branches toward the heavens with hope. Climbing to the highest limbs, she settled herself there and began her work, each stitch a quiet, unyielding vow, each day a silent pledge to free her brothers, no matter the affliction of her faithful solitude.

Perched high in her tree, Sovereignty stitched soundlessly, her hands moving inch by inch to join each delicate petal. And that silence, it wasn't a weakness or a submission to the chaos around her; it was her armor, forged stronger with each passing day. She knew what she was about, even if the whole world misunderstood her, even if they thought her a traitor or a monster. The work itself was the thing—that stubborn, persistent sewing, one thread after another. She needed no one's approval; no grand speeches would bring her brothers back. She didn't want the clamor of the crowd, the simpering whine of "agreement." No, it was the act of doing, the dogged resolve to keep at it, that gave her strength. While the masses spun their tales, threw out accusations like confetti at a parade, Sovereignty's silence became her ally. It let her focus, shutting out the noise, as she tightened each stitch. She was resolute, not because she expected anyone to cheer her on, but because she knew, deep down, that this was her path alone. True change doesn't demand applause or approval; it requires grit. So she sewed, calm and unbending. Let the world chatter on—she had work to do.

One day, while hunting in what was his own deep wood, gallant King Republic—the young ruler of this neighboring land—happened upon a most unusual sight: high in the branches of his favorite oak tree sat a young woman, intent on stitching a garment of brightly-colored flowers, utterly absorbed in her work. She did not look down, did not so much as stir at his presence. King Republic, struck by her quiet, unassuming beauty, called to her, but she gave no response, lost in her mute purpose. Undeterred, he climbed partway up the tree, extending his cloak to her as an offering. After a long moment, she paused, regarded him with an unreadable gaze, and allowed him to lift her from her perch. Carefully, he brought her down, seated her on his horse, and carried her back to his castle. And though she never spoke, he made her his queen, drawn to her quiet restraint that held more substance than all the endless words he'd grown weary of at court, spilling out to fill space yet saying next to nothing at all.

Not all were welcoming of the King's new wife. King Republic's own mother, Majority, took an instant dislike to her. Majority watched Sovereignty with a prickling sense of uneasiness, her gaze hardening every time she saw her daughter-in-law slip silently into a room or pass through a corridor without so much as a nod of acknowledgment. It was unnerving, that silence. Majority was used to people clamoring for her attention, to eloquent speeches and practiced smiles, the flattery and charm that oiled the gears of power. But Sovereignty didn't bother with any of that. She was quiet, poised as if she carried her own law inside her, a rulebook unseen by the rest. And that was precisely the problem. Majority could tolerate rebellion, as long as it made a show of itself—speeches she could counter, arguments she could silence, even charm she could maneuver to her advantage. But this… this silence, this unshakable calm, unnerved her. To Majority, the new queen's quiet strength was a sort of insolence, a refusal to play the game that kept society ticking. The masses, too, grew uneasy. How could they trust someone who didn't curry their favor, didn't strive to be seen or heard? If she wasn't trying to win them over, what was she up to? Majority and her subjects looked at Sovereignty and saw not loyalty, not humility, but a threat—an inaudible challenge to the norms they held dear, an annoying nudge that truth didn't need their permission to exist.

When the queen bore her first child, a son they christened "Morality," Majority stole the babe, smeared the sleeping queen's lips with blood, and accused her of cannibalism. The king, though distraught, held faith in his silent wife and forbade any harm come to her.

Yet Majority was relentless. When Sovereignty bore the King a second son, whom they called Free Speech because he wailed so loudly and so long, her stepmother enacted the same plot, and then again with their third child, a girl named Individual Rights for her singularity. With each slanderous accusation, King Republic's doubt grew, and finally, bound by duty to uphold his realm's laws, he sentenced his silent queen to burn.

When the day of execution dawned, Sovereignty stood resolute, six shirts clutched to her breast, the last missing only its left sleeve. As flames began to crackle at her feet, six swans flew down from the sky, their wings smothering the fire. Sovereignty cast the shirts over them, and their feathers fell, revealing her brothers in their human forms, all save one, who bore a swan's wing in place of his left arm, a painful reminder of what happens when Majority rushes headlong without paying heed to Sovereignty.

Her vow of silence complete, Sovereignty spoke her first words in six long years: "I am innocent," she declared, her voice carrying the strength of conviction. She revealed Majority's deception, and as her brothers came forward, they held in their arms her three lost children, alive and unharmed.

With the truth laid bare, the weight of Majority's deceit became apparent, and the court gasped at her cruelty. In that charged moment, Sovereignty took a deep breath, her voice steady and resolute. "Majority's injustice ends now," she declared.

In swift judgment, Majority was condemned to be separated into myriad broken pieces, each fragment scattered far and wide, a grim reminder of the tyranny that can arise from this unchecked power—where the will of the many, when left unrestrained, can trample the very liberties it purports to defend.

Thus reunited, King Republic and Queen Sovereignty, along with their children—Morality, Free Speech, and Individual Rights—and the queen's six brothers—Federalism, Checks and Balances, Representation, Responsibility, Bill of Rights, and Three Branches—established a reign grounded in harmonious governance. They upheld the principles of Liberty, instituting a land not ruled by the whims of one, but by the steady resolve of the many individuals: a democratic republic.

These words are no idle tale but an allegory of Liberty's legacy—a legacy that endures only when each soul stands firm, facing the encroaching chaos alone, yet moving forward together. Liberty's strength rests in the People's resolve: united in purpose, steadfast in spirit. May they thrive, bound by these principles, in their pursuit of peace and prosperity for generations yet to come.

…and they lived Happily Ever After until…

The End.

An Afterword

(with a measure of hope)

Once upon a time, an author decided to have a chat with a machine. Not just any machine, mind you, but one of those flashy artificial intelligences everyone's raving about these days—the kind that confidently predicts everything while actually knowing nothing at all. The author had questions, things to say, a book to write, and a healthy dose of skepticism, but above all, an insatiable curiosity. After all, what better sparring partner for rewriting fairy tales than a conjurer of reflections?

There are three broad camps when it comes to how we respond to AI, each as revealing of human nature as the technology with which we grapple. First, there are the Ostriches, whose heads plunge deep into symbolic sand at the mere mention of AI. For them, ignorance is bliss—or, at the very least, preferable to confrontation. On the one hand, this group refuses to use it, acknowledge its presence, or even entertain the idea that it might already be shaping the world around them—on the other, they make copious angry social media posts about the evils of it.

Next come the Watchdogs, bristling with suspicion and armed with the conviction that AI is an inherent menace if controlled by "the wrong people." To them, it is an encroachment, a Pandora's box that must be heavily monitored and censored to protect us "from ourselves," if not slammed shut. They dedicate themselves to policing it, regulating it, declaring it a grave threat without stopping to examine its complexities.

And then, most practical of all, are the Adapters, those who recognize that AI is not a presence to be ignored or vilified but an iterating tool that demands understanding. This group splits into two distinct factions. The first turn to AI to craft appearances, their methods ranging from flagrant dishonesty to everyday embellishment. At one extreme, they cheat outright—submitting AI-generated work as their own or manipulating algorithms to feign apparent success. At the other, many engage in the more ambiguous art of curation, enhancing others' perceptions with AI tools—polishing videos, applying filters, or tailoring their image to fit expectations and get ahead. While less brazen, this too is a kind of artifice, a carefully constructed façade not unlike wearing an expensive suit you really can't afford to a job interview.

The second camp of Adapters, however, chooses a more ethical path, embracing AI as a means of genuine self-improvement. They use it not to deceive but to deepen their own understanding, refine their skills, and accelerate their growth. For them, AI is not a mask but an instrument—like a violin in the hands of a master or a piano tuned to perfect pitch—enabling them to create work that is richer, more resonant, much more quickly, yet unmistakably their own. In these Adapters, we see the beginnings of humanity's attempt to navigate the blurred boundaries between truth, appearance, and the accelerating tide of technology.

Artificial intelligence—particularly Large Language Models (LLMs)—is many things, but chief among them an engine of creative fabrication. These models don't actually "know" anything. They predict, they approximate, they assemble patterns—less like a true thinker and more like a fortune teller gazing not into a crystal ball, but into a swirling mist of probabilities. And like many fortune tellers, they're often wrong—yet with such confidence and flair that you almost want to applaud.

Take ChatGPT, for instance. Its knack for making things up—dubbed "hallucinations" when demonstrably false—is better described as "bullshitting," a term philosopher Harry Frankfurt defined as making statements without concern for their truth. Technically then, ChatGPT always operates as a "bullshit machine" because it can't *care* about accuracy.

I first stumbled across this perspective on LLMs as "bullshit machines" here: https://www.scientificamerican.com/article/chatgpt-isnt-hallucinating-its-bullshitting/.

And strangely, this knack for fabrication makes AI an oddly effective tool for writers. After all, who better to consult about fiction than something that views everything as pretense? Sometimes, the clearest path to truth involves a detour through invention—a story to spot a story, as it were.

Machine Learning (ML) underpins this technological wizardry. Think of it as a computer's way of playing connect-the-dots, using data to predict what comes next. Enter generative AI, and with it, LLMs like ChatGPT, which predict text the way fiction writers predict characters' actions or plot twists. Both rely upon patterns and possibilities, spinning something new from the snarled strands of the known. For ethical writers, AI becomes a tool to shake loose creativity, an antidote to writer's block that spews ideas—sometimes ridiculous, often unexpected, and occasionally brilliant.

Writing "in the style of" another author or genre, arguing with AI over plot points, or simply letting it spew nonsense can reveal hidden gems. Its so-called hallucinations hold up a funhouse mirror to a writer's own narrative flaws, and the inconsistencies become opportunities for refinement. Of course, these AI-generated outputs should never be seen as finished products. They're scaffolding, a starting point, a springboard for ideas—not the masterpiece itself.

Beyond mere content creation, AI enables unique dialogues—like consulting a "digital Aristotle" on ethics or investigating the archetypes in fairy tales with a simulated George MacDonald.

These aren't conversations to generate content but to inspire ideas and polish completed drafts. The act of writing—so often lonely—feels a little less so when you're batting ideas back and forth with an entity that's nothing if not quick on the uptake. AI becomes brainstorming partner, provocateur, and occasionally, a clownish sidekick who suggests that your protagonist should also be a werewolf.

Ultimately, LLMs aren't here to replace the humanity of writing but to amplify our capabilities. It's crucial to remember that these systems are glorified text-completion devices, not repositories of universal truth. Their utility lies in the realm of possibility (as opposed to actuality).

In this context, AI's limitations become its strength. No longer must we wrestle alone with the blank page, pleading with the abyss for an idea. Now, the abyss talks back—and it has an autocomplete function. You can argue with the bottomless expanse of an LLM and walk away with a handful of ideas to spark the next scene.

For writers like me, who have a library of their own works to draw from, training an LLM on your own words becomes a fascinating exercise in itself. Imagine having a deep conversation with "yourself" about your own ideas! Of course, not everything an LLM generates is even worthy of the term "bullshit." Some of it's just... pure, derivative drivel, reflecting our collective mediocrity and societal quirks. LLMs don't spit out the best answers; they echo the most common ones allowed. They're mirrors for our strengths and weaknesses, capable of showing us aspects of ourselves we'd rather ignore.

This reflection can be unsettling. When we lean too heavily on AI for originality, we risk forgetting how to think beyond the collective norms it perpetuates. It's one thing to use AI to enhance what we do; it's quite another to let it do the thinking for us. The problem isn't AI's lack of substance—it's our increasing tendency to mistake its echo chamber for wisdom. We're so busy standardizing everything and leveling the playing field that we've stopped encouraging truly original, outside-the-box thinking.

The irony is that AI, for all its unpredictability, doesn't believe its own nonsense. It doesn't believe anything at all. It's free of ego, stubbornness, and the need to save face. It takes new information in stride and generates fresh predictions, while humans, bound by pride and preconceptions, dig in their heels. Some of what we call AI "hallucinations" are often just predictions we don't agree with—a new spin on the age-old tendency to label inconvenient ideas as madness.

For these reasons, I chose to engage in spirited debates with artificial intelligence while crafting the stories in this book. The LLMs I've experimented with—GPT, Grok, Llama, and Mistral—have dared me to challenge my assumptions, dig deeper, and push beyond my comfort zones. They're not collaborators in the traditional sense but catalysts for my own creativity, their unpredictable suggestions sparking ideas I might never have considered so quickly on my own. These modern tools have helped me refine my writing without pilfering from another artist's work, but by playing with aspects of a vaster range of artistry than ever before possible—like pulling taffy in as many lengths and shapes as you can—adding more and more devices to my own toolkit while ensuring that the tales in this collection remain uniquely mine. I also created all the images featured in **Faerie Truths** using the generative AI art tool Midjourney. The result is a book where age-old fairy tales find new life, shaped by the interplay between human ingenuity and cybernetic assistance.

***As an afterthought, if you're curious about incorporating AI into the creation of stories, I've put together a primer on my website. It's packed with insights and detailed examples of how I leveraged AI as a creative tool—not just for this collection, but for sparking ideas in writing projects of all kinds. Feel free to explore it at your leisure and see how these modern tools can enrich your own storytelling journey:

https://www.roseandjuno.com/pdfviewer/ai-for-writers/

What is the end of this book for me might just be the beginning for you—your own once upon a time, waiting to be written.

About the Author...

Rose Guildenstern writes metaphysical visionary fiction that won't let us lie to ourselves. At university, she studied Theatre Arts, English, Biblical Studies, and Wonder (in which she did all her postdoctoral work). A former teacher and present practicing armchair philosopher, she left the bone-dry certainties of California for the haunted forests of New England, only to find that faerie truths had been waiting for her all along.

Her award-winning debut novel, *Iago's Penumbra*, takes you on a spiritual journey through the lens of a paranormal romance between a ghost and a clairvoyant, rooted in the works of William Shakespeare—with a little philosophy, physics, and cosmic horror thrown in, just for fun. Sometimes, Rose publishes truth through tarot as Juno Lucina.

Why publish under a pen name? Because the meaning and the work itself are what matter. The path isn't safe, but it's waiting. If you're willing to step inside, I'll meet you there:

https://www.roseandjuno.com

www.ingramcontent.com/pod-product-compliance
Lightning Source LLC
Chambersburg PA
CBHW051103030726
47504CB00006B/1757